TILL THERE WAS YOU

BUTLER, VERMONT SERIES, BOOK 4

BY: MARIE FORCE

Till There Was You
Butler, Vermont Series, Book 4
By: Marie Force

Published by HTJB, Inc.
Copyright 2019. HTJB, Inc.
Cover designer: Kristina Brinton
Interior Layout: Isabel Sullivan, E-book Formatting Fairies

ISBN: 978-1950654338

www.marieforce.com

CHAPTER 1

"Life isn't about finding yourself. Life is about creating yourself."
—George Bernard Shaw

It had taken exactly twenty-seven years for Lucas Abbott to wish he hadn't been born a twin. Most of the time, he embraced his status as one half of the younger set of Abbott twins, who spread good humor and cheerful dispositions everywhere they went in Vermont's Northeast Kingdom.

But right now? He was furious with the man who was his doppelgänger in every possible way. Not only were they so identical that their own siblings often confused them, but he and Landon shared almost all the same interests. They had the same friends, the same schedule, the same everything, including, Lucas had discovered to his dismay, the same taste in women.

Earlier today, he'd overheard Landon talking about his date the night before with Amanda Pressley, the woman Lucas had been out with two nights ago.

It had been the best first date of his life, but then he'd heard Landon say the same thing to their brother Will. Hearing that, the euphoria Lucas had walked around with since his evening with Amanda had fizzled like steam hitting cold air.

Tonight, he had to go make nice with Landon and the rest of their family, who were gathering at the barn where the ten Abbott siblings had been raised, to celebrate his and Landon's twenty-seventh birthday. Happy birthday to him and the last person on earth he wanted to hang out with right now. That, in and of itself, was a first. Lucas and Landon were known for being "thick as thieves," as their grandfather often said.

Lucas stepped out of the shower in his loft over the barn at the family-owned Christmas tree farm that Landon managed. He hadn't wanted to live on the property, so he'd given Lucas the apartment and found his own place on the outskirts of Butler, the town they called home. For a brief time, they'd entertained the idea of living together in the loft apartment.

Thank God they hadn't done that, because Lucas would be packing his stuff after today.

Studying his reflection in the mirror, he encountered the face of a changed man. Maybe it was his birthday, or perhaps it was meeting a woman who truly interested him. He wasn't sure what it was, but something was definitely different. He'd gone so far as to shave the beard he normally sported during the winter, because he'd thought she would prefer him clean-shaven. Now he was growing it back. Thankfully, his beard came in quickly. He didn't want anyone mistaking him for Landon.

The situation had him unsettled and pissed off as he dressed in his usual winter uniform of thermals, flannel, denim and insulated boots before stepping into the frozen tundra to head to his parents' house. He should've made up a fake illness to get out of the annual pizza and cake tradition, but like the rest of his siblings, Lucas was robustly healthy. They wouldn't believe him if he'd said he was sick.

Since the last thing he needed was an Abbott family inquisition, he got into his truck and headed for Hells Peak Road, taking the most direct route through town. On Elm Street, he drove past the family's Green Mountain Country Store on the right and his sister-in-law Megan's diner on the left. Technically, his grandfather, Elmer, owned the diner, but Megan was the one who made it happen.

As he approached the one-lane covered bridge that was located right before the turn onto Hells Peak, he stopped short, slamming on the brakes to avoid hitting Fred, the town moose, who stood in the middle of the road, seemingly without a care in the world.

Lucas laid on the horn.

Fred gave him a perturbed look, but he didn't move.

"Great." Lucas shifted the truck into Park, accepting that he was going to be late for his own party. He wished he could've headed to his woodshop and lost himself in the work that fed his soul, especially at times like this when his soul needed nourishment. Being at odds with anyone in his family was the worst. Being at odds with Landon had the power to break him.

In a family of ten kids, there'd been plenty of arguments and actual fights. But he had never once truly argued with Landon, who had been his ally and best friend for every day of their twenty-seven years.

Until Amanda came to town and they'd both asked her out. Not wanting to hurt any feelings, she'd accepted both invitations. No one ever took him or Landon seriously, so why should she? Especially after the way they'd behaved during the intimate line demonstration she'd overseen on behalf of her company at his family's store.

Lucas cringed thinking about the questions they'd asked and the comments they'd made. It was like they couldn't help themselves, although who could be expected to behave in a room full of family members and sex toys? Amanda had handled them with skill that indicated it wasn't her first rodeo when it came to dealing with buffoons. In her line of work, she probably met her fair share of guys like him and Landon, who'd found the whole thing hilarious.

She probably thought they were both jerks but had humored them by going on separate dates with them. Her company had landed a big account with their family's store, so she was just being nice—and professional.

That made him sad and mad at the same time. If Landon hadn't asked her out at the same time Lucas had, they wouldn't be in the unfortunate position of pursuing the same woman. It was ludicrous when he really thought it over—neither of them had ever had any problem attracting female attention. In fact, they usually had more attention than they could handle. So why, when it truly mattered to Lucas for the first time *ever*, did Landon have to set his sights on the *same* woman?

Being at odds with Landon made Lucas feel ill. It went against every natural impulse he had to go out of his way to avoid his twin the way he had all day today. They had been the best of friends their entire lives. Even when their other siblings had fought like tomcats, he and Landon had risen above it. Sure, they had fought with their *other* siblings, but never with each other. Hunter and Hannah, their older siblings, who were also twins, had been the same way—best friends.

He ached at the thought of losing that bond with Landon, especially since they were together more often than not. Between their shifts as firefighters and the time they spent doing other things, such as skiing, rock-climbing, hiking and other outdoor pursuits, they were constant companions.

And if it came to a choice—Landon or Amanda...

"Ugh." Of course he'd choose his brother over a woman he'd only just met, but what a bitch of a dilemma.

As if he could hear Lucas, Fred let out a loud moo.

Lucas laid on the horn again, hoping to convince Fred to move along, but Fred wasn't intimidated by a horn—or much of anything, for that matter, except Hannah. She had a way of dealing with the moose that made her husband, Nolan, crazy. He feared tiny Hannah would be smooshed by the moose that Hannah called a pussycat.

Lucas tried the siren that was built into his truck for times of emergency, but Fred shot him a look full of disdain, as if to say, *Is that all you got?*

Thinking about Fred was preferable to wondering what the hell he was supposed to do about his brother and Amanda.

Lucas's date with her had been close to perfect. The conversation had flowed, they'd laughed at the same things, had similar interests, and she absolutely loved their tiny town of Butler, Vermont, as well as the Green Mountain Country Store his family had run for four generations.

She'd had a million questions about the family business and how it worked and how the Abbotts managed to keep business and personal separate. Though Lucas didn't actually work in the store, it had always been part of his life, and he could answer her questions about the family dynamics as well as any of the others who worked in the office. He sold most of his woodworking products in the store, including hand-carved bed frames, dressers and hope chests as well as smaller items such as carved moose that sold like wildfire, so he was definitely involved.

Lucas put down the window and stuck his head out. "Come on, Fred. Be a sport. It's my freaking birthday, and it's already been a bitch of a day. Have a heart and move your ass, will you?"

Fred eyed him as if he was considering the request.

"*Please?*"

With another loud moo, Fred took one step forward and then another.

"Was he honestly waiting for me to say please?" Lucas asked the universe as he put up the window, put the truck in Drive and headed over the bridge toward home. He hadn't lived in the barn in years, but it would always be home to him and his siblings. As he pulled into the driveway that was already full of pickup trucks and SUVs built to withstand brutal Vermont winters, his grandfather, Elmer, was getting out of his truck.

Lucas parked and went to greet his grandfather, who was waiting for him.

"Oh, hey, Luc." Elmer said his name after giving him a close look to make sure he got it right. Elmer was one of the few people in their lives who almost always got it right. "I couldn't tell what color your truck was in the dark."

His was navy. Landon's was black. Same model. Shocker, right?

Lucas gave his grandfather a hug. "How you doing, Gramps?"

"I'm good." He patted Lucas on the back. "Happy birthday, buddy."

"Thanks."

"I can't believe you guys are twenty-seven. Where does the time go?"

"And still such nitwits."

"You said that, not me."

Lucas laughed as he held the door to the mudroom for Elmer. "Saved you the trouble."

"You boys like to have fun. Nothing wrong with that."

A few days ago, he would've agreed with Elmer's statement. Now he had reason to wonder how a guy transitioned from acting the fool to being an actual adult. That was his goal for the next year. He would be mocked ruthlessly by his siblings and others who had come to expect certain behavior from him, but he wouldn't be deterred in his goal to take his game up a few notches.

Having a plan for himself helped as he hung his coat on the hook with his name on it, which was to the left of Landon's. He'd been born ten minutes before Landon. Since Landon's hook was empty, Lucas realized he'd gotten there first. Taking a quick glance at the hooks, he noted that everyone else was there.

Lucas took off his hat, tucked it into the pocket of his coat and ran his fingers through dirty-blond hair to bring some order to it. This time of year, everyone in Vermont suffered from a terminal case of hat head. He stepped into the kitchen and received a warm, welcoming smile from his mother.

"There's one of my guests of honor."

Lucas wondered what it might be like to have a birthday all to himself and then immediately felt guilty for having the thought. "Hi, Mom."

Molly Abbott, her gray hair in a long braid down her back as usual and her pretty face bright with pleasure over an evening with her family, hugged him. "Happy birthday, Luc. Twenty-seven looks good on you."

He stuck out his chin. "Better than twenty-six did?"

"Much better."

"He had nowhere to go but up," their youngest brother, Max, said when he joined them in the kitchen with his baby son, Caden, in his arms.

Molly tried to hide her smile but failed miserably.

Lucas scowled at his brother and reached for the baby, noting the cacophonous noise coming from the family room where the rest of the family was probably watching the Bruins game.

Max handed the baby over to his uncle. "Don't listen to a word he says, buddy, and don't do *anything* he does."

In light of his recent revelations, Lucas couldn't help being slightly wounded by Max's teasing comments. Not that he hadn't earned the jibes. He certainly had, but that was going to change, effective immediately. He snuggled Caden into his chest and kissed the top of his silky head. The little guy always smelled so damned good. His little fist grasped ahold of Lucas's flannel shirt, catching a bit of chest hair that made his uncle wince from the tug of pain. "Easy, pal. Uncle Luc doesn't need any bald spots. Not yet anyway."

"Hey!" His oldest sister, Hannah, let out a happy squeak when she came around the corner from the dining room and nearly crashed into Lucas. "Happy birthday!"

"Thank you." He leaned down so she could kiss his cheek. "Where's my niece?"

"With her daddy. She's all about him these days, except for when she's hungry. Then Mommy is number one."

Lucas smiled at the face Hannah made to express her displeasure while knowing full well she was madly in love with the daughter she'd waited forever to have—and the husband who'd made her so damned happy. "Fred was being Fred again on the way over here. Blocking the road to the covered bridge."

"He's been ornery lately." Hannah acted as if she had a direct bead on Fred's moods, which she sort of did, not that anyone wanted to admit that out of fear of encouraging her moose-whispering activities. The best part was that she didn't even think her unique bond with a full-grown bull moose was weird. Everyone else did, though, especially Nolan, who was continuously freaked out by her close encounters of the moose kind. "Ever since I took Baby Dexter home with me, he's been out of sorts."

"Has it occurred to you that Fred liked having Baby Dexter around and maybe he didn't want you messing with him?" Lucas asked.

"Of course it has, but he has no business raising a baby moose."

Bouncing Caden, who seemed to have dozed off, Lucas raised his brows in disbelief. "And *you* do?"

"I'm better at it than Fred is. At least with me, the poor baby is getting regular meals and lots of love."

"Which is critical to moose development."

"Every baby needs lots of love. Moose are no different."

It took effort on Lucas's part not to roll his eyes. Knowing she was dead serious kept him from mocking her—that and his newfound intention to act more like an adult than a buffoon. The sound of a baby crying in the next room had Hannah spinning around to go to her daughter. "Speaking of babies…"

When they were alone, Lucas gazed down at Caden's sleeping face. "Auntie Hannah may be nuts, buddy, but she's the best kind of nuts." Lucas admired his older sister more than just about anyone he knew. After enduring the devastating loss of her first husband, Caleb, in Iraq, watching her find new love with Nolan had been inspirational. And now they had baby Caleb, whom they called Callie, and Hannah smiled all the time. If taking care of a baby moose made her happy, so be it. If anyone had earned the right to be happy, it was Hannah.

"Was she going on about the baby moose again?" Nolan asked, his mouth full of cheese and cracker.

"Maybe?" Lucas hesitated to toss his sister under the marital bus.

Nolan groaned. "She's round the bend over that baby. Wanted to bring him in the house the other night because it was *too cold* for him outside. I have to keep telling her he's a *wild animal*, not a house pet."

"He'll be a house pet by the time she's done with him."

"That's what I'm afraid of—having a full-grown bull moose in bed between me and my wife."

Lucas snorted with laughter. "Might be a good idea to nip that in the bud."

"Ya think?"

"What're we nipping in the bud?" Lucas's father, Lincoln, asked as he came from the family room to join them.

"Hannah's affair with the baby moose," Nolan said. "If she had her way, he'd be in bed with us."

"Oh dear," Linc said. "Probably best to not let that happen."

"I hate to tell you this, Linc, but there're times when your daughter is downright unmanageable," Nolan said.

"She gets that from her mother," Linc said.

"I can hear you, Lincoln Abbott," Molly said, "and you *will* pay for that later."

"Sorry, Nolan," Linc said. "You're on your own." Heading toward his wife, Lincoln said, "You heard me wrong, love."

"No, I did not."

"No wonder my wife is nuts," Nolan said. "She was raised in a nuthouse."

Lucas cracked a grin. "You're just figuring that out now?"

"Oh, I've known it for a while." Nolan had grown up with Lucas's older siblings and had been in and out of the Abbotts' barn for decades. Nolan's crush on Hannah had developed years after his close friend Caleb had died. And no one doubted Nolan's fierce love for his wife, despite her moose antics.

The door to the mudroom slammed shut, jolting Caden.

Lucas rubbed the baby's back. "Easy, buddy."

"Quit slamming that door," Molly said to Landon.

"Sorry, Mom." Landon laid a loud smacker on Molly's cheek. "It's my birthday. Don't I get a pass on door slamming?"

"No door slamming in this house, even on your birthday. It's in the Abbott family rule book."

"I never got my copy," Landon said, making his twin smile. Lucas would've said the same thing. "Mom, you remember Amanda, right? I hope it's okay that I invited her to join us."

Lucas froze.

Landon had brought *Amanda* to their birthday dinner? *No way.*

"Of course it's all right," Molly said. "The more the merrier is the Abbott family motto, which you'd know if you'd read the rule book. Welcome to our insane asylum, Amanda."

When Amanda laughed, Lucas wanted to turn to look at her, but remained rooted in place, barely able to breathe, let alone move. "Thank you so much for having me, Mrs. Abbott."

"Please, call me Molly. Everyone does."

Lucas listened to them with a surreal feeling of detachment as his mind raced to catch up. Amanda had come to their birthday dinner. With Landon.

Worst birthday ever.

CHAPTER 2

"A man who dares to waste one hour of his life has not discovered the value of life."
—Charles Darwin

As usual, their mom had made pizza from scratch for their birthday—sausage and onion for him and pepperoni and peppers for Landon, along with special orders for the others. Normally, Lucas loved the traditions and the way his mother still paid attention to the details with each of her ten children, even though they were grown and some had kids of their own.

But tonight, with Landon and Amanda seated directly across the table from him, Lucas could barely swallow the delicious pizza or the beer his father had opened for him. He had nothing to say to anyone, which was rare in and of itself. Lucas Abbott always had something to say, especially in the midst of his boisterous family, all of whom had come to celebrate their brothers' birthday. As the eighth child in a family of ten, one learned to speak up early or be drowned out by the noise.

When everyone was there, they were close to twenty people as his siblings were pairing off, getting married and having babies like wildfire these days. Their elusive, quiet brother Wade had shocked the living shit out of them recently by showing up with a wife none of them had met until after he and Mia had said "I do." No one had seen that coming, but Wade seemed happier than Lucas had ever seen him. Mia's long-lost father was throwing them a big wedding in Boston in June that everyone would be going to. Would Landon bring Amanda to that, too?

The noise level in the dining room was probably registering on the Richter scale. Normally, he'd be right in the middle of the fray. Tonight, he had a splitting headache.

Elmer nudged him. "What's up with you?" Fortunately, his grandfather kept his voice down, so the question wasn't heard by everyone else.

"Nothing."

"Not like you to pick at the pizza. You're more likely to inhale than pick."

"I'm not that hungry tonight."

Elmer's white brows furrowed as he placed a hand on Lucas's forehead. "You're not feverish."

Molly zeroed in on Elmer's hand on Lucas's forehead. "What's wrong?"

"Nothing. The pizza is great, Mom."

Though she accepted his answer, he could tell by the way his mother looked at him that he hadn't fooled her.

Per the tradition, she brought out one big cake, half chocolate for him and half vanilla for Landon, and they blew out their candles together. They'd done that twenty-six other times, and it had never once occurred to Lucas that he ought to have his own damned cake as a grown-ass man. Until now.

"Happy birthday, bro," Landon said, giving him a warm smile.

"Same to you." Lucas could barely stand to look at the face that was a mirror image of his own. He felt naked without the beard that left almost nothing to distinguish him from his identical twin.

Clearly Amanda preferred Landon to him if the way she giggled at every stupid thing his brother said was any indication.

She'd worn her dark hair up tonight, which only accentuated her pretty green eyes and the smattering of freckles across her nose that he'd found both cute and sexy. He didn't recall her giggling so much when they went out and was thankful for that. In general, giggling wasn't something he found overly attractive in a woman.

But damn if he didn't find the rest of her overly attractive. She was downright gorgeous. He'd thought so from the first time he saw her in the conference room, surrounded by sex toys as she indoctrinated the family on the line of products her company produced.

And no, it hadn't been the sex toys that had gotten to him. It'd been *her*. The confident way she spoke about something that most people had trouble talking about in private, let alone in a room full of strangers, had really done it for him. This was a woman who owned her sexuality and her freedom to express it.

That's where his attraction toward her had started. But it had only flourished during the evening they spent together talking with an ease he didn't often experience with someone he'd just met.

They'd covered everything from their families to their hometowns to their favorite sports, movies, books, TV shows, and it had been... easy. Fun. He'd immediately wanted to do it again and had thought she felt the same way, but watching her now with Landon, he could see that she had found a connection with him, too. Perhaps a stronger connection than she'd found with Lucas. If that was the case, there was nothing he could do about it. The choice was hers to make, and she'd clearly made it.

He stood, taking his grandfather by surprise. "Where you going, boy?"

"Gotta get home. I've got an early morning tomorrow."

"Where you got to be?" Landon asked.

"I'm covering for Denny." Lucas referred to one of the paramedics they worked with. "His wife has an ultrasound, and they're going to find out what they're having."

"Oh, cool."

"You didn't open your presents," Molly said.

"I told you guys no presents."

"When do we ever do what we're told?" Linc asked.

Lucas took the time to open the gifts from his parents—some new tools for the shop, a sleeping bag to replace the one he'd trashed after the last camping trip, a pair of the cargo shorts he wore in the summer, a book about Lewis and Clark that he'd been meaning to get and a watch with GPS capability.

"Thanks, Mom. I love it all."

"You're very welcome."

He appreciated that she seemed to get that he wanted out of there. But he hoped she knew it wasn't because he didn't love the time with his family.

Tomorrow, he would do the shift for Denny during the day, and then he had three days off before his next shift at the firehouse. That was enough time to hit the road and get out of town for a couple of days. If his brother was going to be falling all over Amanda, he didn't have to stick around for the show.

After he said his goodbyes to the others, his mother met him in the mudroom.

"You really shouldn't have gotten presents, Mom."

She shrugged off the statement. "It's fun for me to find things I think you'd like."

"Well, thank you. For the gifts, the pizza, the cake. For everything."

"Are you all right, Luc? You aren't yourself tonight."

"I'm all right. Just fighting off a cold."

"Are you sure that's all it is?"

"Yep." The last thing he'd ever do is confess to anyone that he was jealous of his brother. Such a stupid, pointless emotion, and one he'd felt rarely enough to be unfamiliar with how to deal with it. He kissed his mother's forehead. "I've got a few days off, and I'm going to take a run over to Stowe tomorrow." One of his best friends from Bowdoin College lived there, so no one would question why he was going. They didn't need to know that he wouldn't be seeing Craig this time around.

"Supposed to snow tomorrow. Be careful driving."

"I will. Don't worry."

"You know better than to tell me not to worry."

"I'll be fine. If there's one thing your children know how to do, it's take care of themselves. You saw to that."

"True. I'm very proud of that."

"Then don't worry. I have snow in my DNA." He hugged her and headed out the door before he had to see Landon and Amanda again. Was he being ridiculous running from them? Yes, and he knew it, but so be it. He didn't want to deal with it, especially on his freaking birthday.

He got in the truck, started it and cranked the heat, hoping it wouldn't take long to warm up. It was bloody freezing, as per usual for the last week in March in Vermont, where winter tended to hang on until after the first buds of spring appeared on the trees. Keeping an eye on his parents' dogs, George and Ringo, who'd followed him outside, he backed out of the driveway and glanced back at the house to see his mom still at the door, watching him go.

Lucas hoped she'd forgive him for leaving the party early, but he'd needed to get out of there before he gave away how he was feeling to the whole family. This was all new territory for him. He wasn't one to have secrets. What you saw was what you got with Lucas Abbott, and he had no clue how to navigate this situation.

Keeping an eye out for rogue moose, he drove to the family's Christmas tree farm that was shuttered until spring planting. Normally, he loved the isolation and the serenity of life at the farm, but, like everything else the last few days, it didn't bring the usual comfort. He was edgy, out of sorts, off his game and feeling lost in a sea of familiar places and people.

His plan to get the hell out of there for a few days was looking better to him with every passing minute. Inside the loft apartment over the barn, he started a load of laundry and pulled a duffel bag with the Butler Volunteer Fire Department logo from under the bed.

He and Landon were both lieutenants in the department, charged with handling most of the administrative work that earned them small salaries. Lucas's was enough to cover most of his expenses, which were minor thanks to the fact that he didn't have to pay rent. He got to live at the farm in exchange for keeping an eye on the place in the off-season and acting as the caretaker on behalf of the family business. Between his fire department salary and the sale of the furniture and other wood items he crafted, he eked out a pretty decent living, but his needs were minimal.

Would a woman like Amanda be satisfied with the life that had always more than satisfied him, or would she find it lacking? And since when did he care what anyone else thought of his life?

Since the best first date in history, that's when.

He had put his laundry in the dryer and opened a beer when the phone rang. Seeing his grandfather's number on the caller ID, he took the call. "What's up, Gramps?"

"I was thinking about you on the way home and decided to give you a ring. You weren't yourself tonight, and I'm wondering if I know why."

Amused as always by his grandfather, Lucas leaned back against the kitchen counter and smiled. "Knock yourself out."

"I think you and your brother have set your sights on the same woman, and that's got you all turned around."

Lucas knew he shouldn't be surprised that Elmer had figured out his dilemma.

"Am I warm?"

"Pretty warm."

"Ah, thought so. It's a heck of a thing to meet someone who really strikes your fancy. Happened to me once upon a time, and it was the worst feeling in the world."

Lucas stood up straighter. "When did it happen to you?"

"With your grandmother. I met her when she was dating my cousin."

"No way."

"Yes way, and it was awful, I tell you."

"What did you do?"

"Nothing, and that was the hardest part. I loved my cousin. We were as close as brothers. I never would've done anything to hurt him."

"Since I know how this story ends, I have to know how you ended up together."

"She told him she fancied me."

"Whoa! How did he take that?"

"Punched me in the mouth," Elmer said with a low guffaw. "That's how I knew she'd picked me."

"Wow, Gramps. I had no idea."

"We didn't talk about it much after the fact. I remained close to my cousin until the day he died, and I went out of my way to make sure there was never any bad blood between us."

"Did he ever get married?"

"Yep. Married a great gal a couple years later, and the four of us ran around together for the rest of his life."

"I'm glad he ended up happy, too."

"Believe me—so was I. Second-happiest day of my young life was standing up for him at his wedding." After a pause, Elmer said, "You never really know what people go through before they end up with a happily ever after, son. It's not always rainbows and unicorns or straight lines that lead from point A to point B. A lot of times, it's hard and messy and painful."

"Yeah," Lucas said, marveling at how Elmer had homed right in on everything Lucas was feeling.

"But the most important thing is family. Your brother is your closest friend, your soul mate, if you believe in such things. The two of you have been like two peas in a pod from the word go. I'd hate to see anything come between you."

"Me, too."

"Then don't let it, Luc. Amanda seems like a nice gal with a good head on her shoulders. If she's taken a shine to Landon, well, then, there's nothing you can really do about that. But being angry with him over it isn't going to make it better for you. It'll only make everything worse."

Elmer was right. Of course he was. He was always right. "Very true."

"I'm glad you agree. Amanda is only here for a short time. Brothers are forever."

"Especially identical twin brothers."

Elmer laughed. "Especially that. You okay, pal?"

"Yeah, Gramps, I'm good. This helped a lot. I'm going up to Stowe for a couple of days to ski and clear my head."

"That's a great idea. Have a wonderful time."

"Thanks for calling."

"Happy birthday, Lucas. I think this is going to be your best year yet."

"I hope so."

"Love you, son."

"Love you, too, Gramps."

Lucas put down the phone, feeling thankful for the unconditional love of his grandfather, who had always been a steady presence in his life. Elmer had made an excellent point. It would be foolish to allow a woman he barely knew to come between him and the twin brother who was also his closest friend. He wasn't going to let that happen and would use the time away to get his head back on straight.

Amanda was a great person, and he really liked her. However, she certainly wasn't the only woman in the world. If she had decided Landon was the one for her, Lucas would find someone else. Stepping aside was the right thing to do. He had no doubt about that after talking to his grandfather.

He couldn't believe the story Elmer had told him about the early days of his relationship with Lucas's grandmother. He'd never thought too much about how his grandparents might've gotten together, but he hadn't pictured anything like the story Elmer had relayed.

The next day, after putting in a ten-hour shift at the firehouse that had included calls to a couple of snow-related fender benders and one elderly resident who'd needed transport to the hospital, Lucas set out for Stowe. Normally a ninety-minute drive, tonight it was slow going due to the snow that continued to fall. Lucas took his time, keeping the speedometer around forty and following in the tracks left by an eighteen-wheeler that was a mile or so ahead of him.

Driving in snow was second nature to him after growing up in northern Vermont. If Vermonters stayed home every time it snowed, they'd go weeks without leaving the house some years.

He'd called his friend Craig, who'd told him to use the house while he was out of town on business. Lucas had the security code to the house and was eager for some time alone on the slopes. Physical activity always helped to clear his mind, and he hoped it would have the usual effect on him this time.

He hated being out of sorts like this and needed to shake it off and get back to normal. Moping around wasn't his style. At the peak of ski season in Stowe, he could also count on some good nightlife. Perhaps a night with a snow bunny would fix what ailed him. One thing he knew for certain was that getting out of Butler had already made him feel better than he had in days.

Two hours into the ride, he was yawning and guzzling the coffee he'd brewed at the firehouse to keep himself awake. His eyes were tired from staring into the snow that had seemed to intensify as he got closer to Stowe. Finally, he took the exit onto the local road that led to Craig's place and found that it hadn't been plowed.

"Awesome..."

He slowed the truck to a crawl, inching along while hoping he was still on the actual road. As he rounded a bend, he watched with horror as the car in front of him fishtailed wildly before pitching off an embankment into a ditch.

CHAPTER 3

"A baby is God's opinion that life should go on."
—Carl Sandburg

Lucas put on the emergency lights that were wired into his truck and pulled over next to the place where the car had left the road. The road was completely deserted except for him and whoever was in the car. Grabbing his parka and the badge he'd stashed in the glove box after his shift as well as the high-powered flashlight he carried with him at all times, Lucas got out of the truck and zipped his coat as he jogged toward the car.

He carefully navigated his way down the small hill that led to the ditch where the car had landed, illuminated by the red glow of taillights. Even through the closed window, he could hear the driver crying hysterically as she tried to open the door that was jammed against the slope. First order of business would be to calm her.

When he knocked on the window, she startled.

"I'm a firefighter and paramedic." He spoke loudly, hoping she could hear him through the closed window, as he withdrew the leather billfold from his pocket and showed her his badge. "I can help. Put down the window."

She lowered the window about halfway.

"I'm Lieutenant Lucas Abbott from the Butler Volunteer Fire Department. What's your name?"

"Danielle," she said between sobs. "Danielle Rowson."

"Are you hurt, Danielle?"

"I… I don't think so."

A squeak from the backseat got his attention, and that's when he realized there was a baby in a car seat.

He was relieved to see the baby's arms and legs moving.

"I don't have a cell phone," he said. "Do you?" It wasn't unusual for people in Vermont not to have them, since the reception was spotty in the mountains.

"I have one, but it lost service a while ago."

"That's pretty common up here. Okay, then, I guess we're it. If you're sure you're not hurt, I can help you out and then get the baby out. I can drive you wherever you need to go."

As he handed her the billfold containing his badge, he could tell she was trying to decide whether she should allow him to help her. "I know I'm a stranger, but I swear you and your baby are safe with me. I'm the eighth of ten kids. My brothers and I are all certified in cold-weather rescue, and like I said, I'm a lieutenant with the Butler fire department."

After taking a good long look at his badge, she handed it back to him. "Okay." She sounded hesitant, and really, who could blame her? He was a total stranger to her, despite his fancy badge. At least she'd stopped crying.

"Release your seat belt and open your window and the baby's. I'll help you out, and then we'll get your little one."

She followed his instructions and climbed out of the driver's side window into his arms. The first thing he noticed was that she was tinier than he'd expected her to be and curvy, not that he was noticing the supple flesh that pressed against him. He reached back into the car for her coat and purse and handed both to her before going to retrieve the baby from the car seat. Judging by the pink snowsuit, he assumed the baby was a girl.

He gave her a cursory check, determined that in addition to her limbs moving normally, her pupils were responsive to his flashlight. Once he'd ensured the baby was okay, he released the straps and lifted her out, handing her over to her mother. Then he lowered the handle and lifted the detachable seat out of the car through the window.

The baby let out a happy squeal at the sight of her mother.

"Thank God she's all right," Danielle said on a long sigh of relief.

"What else do you ladies need from the car?"

"Our bags in the trunk. The flowered two on top."

Leaning inside the driver's side window, he removed the keys from the ignition and pressed the button on the key fob to open the trunk. He grabbed the bags she'd asked for from a trunk full of stuff, shouldered them both and clicked the lock button, which also closed the windows before the lock chime sounded.

"Everything we own is in that car. Is it safe to leave it?"

"I'll call for a tow as soon as we get to a phone. They'll take it somewhere safe for the night." He wished they were in Butler so he could call Nolan to take care of the car.

He offered Danielle his arm. "Hold on to me and take it slow."

When she hooked her hand around his arm, he could feel her trembling, probably from the shock of the accident as much as the biting cold. Snow continued to fall steadily and was accumulating on the road at an alarming rate.

Lucas powered the three of them up the small hill to the road and guided them to his truck. "We can belt the baby's seat into the backseat."

While Danielle took care of that, he put their bags on the other side of the backseat, next to the work bag that contained the personal protective equipment he kept with him at all times. As a member of a volunteer fire department, he could be called out at any time and had to be ready for anything. He got into the driver's side and blasted the heat.

With the baby settled, Danielle got into the passenger seat and closed the door. "Thank you for helping us."

"It's no problem. Where were you headed?"

"I… I'm not sure. I was hoping to find somewhere to stay when I got to Stowe, but the snow was coming down so hard that I didn't know if I would make it there."

"You don't have reservations?"

She shook her head. "Do you think that's a problem?"

"Normally, I'd say no, but this is the end of ski season. Hotels and inns in these parts are sold out months in advance through March."

"Oh God," she said, sighing deeply.

"I'm heading to my friend's house outside of Stowe. He's away, but the place is huge and has plenty of extra bedrooms. You're welcome to one of them for the night if that would help."

"I… I don't know if that's the best idea."

"I understand. You don't know me at all, and why should you trust me, right?"

She gave him a side-eyed glance full of trepidation. "Something like that."

"I have several ways to prove I'm an actual firefighter, including the lights on my truck, the license plate that identifies me as a member of the fire service as does the gear and emergency equipment in the backseat."

Despite his assurances, Danielle displayed concern that he certainly understood. He could be a predator, for all she knew, and she was right to protect herself and her child.

"How about we do this? We'll go somewhere public like a gas station or convenience store. I'll give you a phone number to call, and you can fully vet me."

"Who would I be calling?"

"My mom," he said with a grin. "I could also give you the number of the fire department I work for, and they can vouch for me as well."

She thought that over for a second, giving him a chance to take a closer look at a pretty face framed by a knitted hat. Strands of reddish-blonde hair escaped the confines of the hat, and her eyes might've been blue or green. He couldn't tell for certain in the murky light inside the truck. "That sounds okay to me."

"All right, then." He put the truck into Drive and headed slowly toward town. "What's the baby's name?"

"Savannah." Hearing her name, the baby let out a little chirp.

"She's adorable. How old is she?"

"Thank you. I think so, too. She's four months."

"What're you girls doing out in the middle of a storm?"

"I had the Bluetooth connected to my phone, so I didn't hear that the storm was coming. I realize now how stupid that was."

He noted that she didn't say why she was out in the first place and chose not to press her. What did it matter? He would help her out tonight and probably never see her again.

"Are you new to Vermont?" He'd seen Kentucky plates on the car, but it could be a rental.

"No, I used to come up here to see my grandparents when I was a kid, but I haven't been here in years. Heck of a welcome back."

Lucas chuckled. "Vermont tends to behave this way from about November to April, when everything starts to melt and we enter mud season."

"Charming."

"Mud season is an acquired taste. You get used to it after a while."

"I'll have to take your word for it."

"Are you planning to stay awhile?" he asked, thinking of all the stuff she had in the car.

"That's the plan. I've applied for jobs in Stowe and Butler. I'm hoping one of them will come through and that I can find childcare."

"What kind of jobs are you looking for?"

"Retail management. That's what my degree is in."

He immediately thought of the family business.

"My grandparents had a home in Stowe when I was younger. We spent a lot of time there every summer, and some of my best memories were made in that house. I've never forgotten it and always hoped to come back sometime."

"It's a great town with so much to do and see. You may find it a little more built up than it was then, but the overall feel of the place hasn't changed much."

"That's good to know." She looked over at him again. "Are you really the eighth of ten kids?"

"Yep."

"What was that like?"

"Loud."

She laughed.

"Still is, especially now that most of my siblings are either married or about to be married. Two of them have kids, with more on the way. It gets louder all the time."

"That sounds wonderful," she said wistfully.

"Do you have siblings?"

She shook her head. "Just me."

"You can't imagine ten kids. I can't imagine one."

"Two extremes."

"Ten is definitely extreme—and we were raised in a barn."

"Seriously?"

"Uh-huh. My parents restored an old barn and turned it into a house. You can get away with a lot in life when you tell people you were raised in a barn. And I live in another barn now."

She laughed again, this time a helpless-sounding giggle that made him smile. He had no idea why he thought so, but he suspected she didn't laugh very often. "And did you get away with a lot?"

"I found my share of mischief."

"I'll bet," she said, chuckling.

"Did you drive here all the way from Kentucky?"

She gasped, and he immediately regretted the question.

He held up his hand to stop her from panicking. "I saw the plates on the car. You don't have to tell me anything if you don't want to. I don't mean to pry."

After a long silence, she said, "I did drive from Kentucky. It was stupid of me not to check the weather, but I was anxious to get here."

He wanted to ask if she was running away from something— or someone—but he didn't dare pose another personal question after her reaction to the last one. A short time later, they reached the outskirts of Stowe. Lucas spotted a gas station-convenience store. "Does that one work?"

"Sure."

He was glad she agreed to stop there, because he didn't think they'd have many open places to choose from at that hour. After pulling into a parking space, Lucas shut off the engine. They got out of the truck, and while she retrieved the baby, he waited by the front of the truck for her and then held the door that led inside.

"Evening," the attendant said.

"Hi there. Do you have a pay phone we could use?" Lucas asked.

"In the back."

"Who should we call for a tow?"

The attendant handed him a business card. "They take twenty-four-hour calls."

"Thanks very much." Lucas gestured for Danielle to lead the way to the back of the store where the phone was located between the restrooms. "I'll call for the tow first if that's okay."

"Okay, thanks, but what is this relic you call a pay phone?"

"You don't have these in Kentucky?"

She shook her head. "We have a modern invention called the cell phone."

"Ah, yes, I've heard of this thing of which you speak, but since it's often useless in my part of the world, the pay phone is still essential."

Amused by the conversation, Lucas made the call, gave the dispatcher directions to where Danielle's car could be found and mentioned it was in a ditch by the side of the road. The dispatcher said he would call Craig's house to let them know where the car had been taken. With that taken care of, he glanced at Danielle. "I'll call my mom, and you can ask her anything you'd like to. I'm an open book." Lucas dropped coins into the phone and placed the call to the most familiar phone number in his life.

"Hey, Mom, it's Luc."

"Hi there. Did you make it to Stowe?"

"Just now, and on the way into town, I witnessed an accident."

"Oh wow. Is everyone all right?"

"Yep. I've got Danielle and her four-month-old daughter, Savannah, here with me. They were hoping to find a place to stay in town."

"That won't be easy this time of year."

"That's what I told her. I offered her a room at Craig's, but she's understandably reluctant to trust someone she's only just met. I thought maybe you might be able to set her mind at ease."

"Of course. Let me talk to her."

"Hang on." Lucas handed the phone to Danielle, who had Savannah propped on her hip. He thought about offering to hold the baby for her but sensed she wouldn't want that. "My mom. Molly Abbott."

"Hello?"

Lucas wished he could hear the other side of the conversation, but he suspected he already knew that his mother would assure Danielle that she could trust him to provide shelter for her and her child for the night and to help her get settled somewhere the next day.

Danielle did more listening than talking, and after about five minutes, she nodded, said thank you and handed the phone back to Lucas.

"Thanks a lot, Mom."

"Always happy to talk about one of my kids."

Lucas smiled at the predictable comment. "Talk to you soon."

"Love you."

"Love you, too." He ended the call and looked at Danielle, realizing in the bright light of the store that her eyes were hazel. She was startlingly pretty, with delicate features and what his grandmother used to refer to as a "peaches-and-cream" complexion. "Would you like me to call the fire department, too?"

She shook her head. "Your mom was very convincing. I appreciate your offer of a place to stay for the night."

"What exactly did my mom tell you?"

Danielle's lips formed a small smile. "I'll never tell."

Lucas desperately wanted to know, but he didn't pursue the line of questioning. "Let's pick up some groceries to get us through the night and morning. Do you drink coffee?"

"Of course I do. I'm not a savage."

Lucas laughed as he grabbed a handheld basket. "Great answer. Cream? Sugar?"

"Both, please."

They picked out a couple of frozen pizzas for dinner as well as eggs, bacon and bread for the morning. Lucas tossed in a package of lunch meat, some chips and salsa, a twelve-pack of Sam Adams, as well as toilet paper and paper towels, just in case Craig was low on either. "You want a bottle of wine or anything?"

She shook her head. "I'm breastfeeding, so no alcohol for me."

"Ah, got it," he said, while trying not to imagine her breastfeeding her child. A tingle of sensation made his skin feel strange, and then she brushed against him, setting off a full-body reaction to her nearness. What the hell? He shook off the odd feelings so he could focus exclusively on her and the baby and making sure they had what they needed. "Diapers?"

"I have plenty, but thanks for checking."

"Anything else you want or need?"

"Chocolate."

Smiling, he led her to the candy aisle. "Pick your poison."

She gave the vast array of options her full attention before choosing a small bag of Nestlé Crunch bars, which happened to be Lucas's favorite, too. When she started to walk toward the checkout, he added a second bag of the candy bars to the basket before following her.

Lucas loaded their groceries onto the counter.

Danielle propped Savannah on her hip so she could get out her wallet.

Lucas put his hand on her arm.

She startled and looked up at him.

"I've got this. I needed to get supplies anyway."

"Can we split it?"

"Nah. It's all good."

"Thank you."

He paid for the groceries and carried the bags out to the truck, stashing them in the backseat while she put the baby in the car seat.

She cast a glance his way, her gaze colliding with his for a brief, charged moment before she looked away.

"You okay?"

"I made a huge mistake by not better planning this trip." She sounded so sad and down on herself that Lucas wanted to object. "I just hope that this isn't going to be another huge mistake."

"I swear to God on the lives of everyone I love—and I love a lot of people—you have nothing at all to fear from me."

"That's what your mother said, too."

"She's somewhat partial to me and my siblings, but I've never once known her to lie about anything. In fact, that was the one thing we got in really big trouble for when we were kids. My sister Charley was a world-class liar, and she got in so much trouble."

"How about you? Did you get into trouble for lying?"

"Nah, with me, it was more about broken windows, fender benders with my father's cars, music that was always too loud and wrestling. I was—and am—a big fan of wrestling with my brothers, sometimes in places such as my mother's dining room where her grandmother's china is kept. That was a bit of a problem for her, to say the least."

"The woman must be a saint."

"That word is often used to describe her."

"How many brothers?"

"Six. One of them is my identical twin."

"Oh wow. That's so cool!"

"Get in the truck and I'll tell you all about it." Most of the time, people expressed dismay that there were two of them, but Danielle just seemed intrigued. That was because she didn't know that he and his twin were largely considered buffoons by everyone who knew them. She didn't know them, so here was a great opportunity to test out his new plan to act like a grown-up.

As they left the parking lot of the convenience store and headed for Craig's house, it occurred to Lucas that he hadn't thought of Amanda, Landon or the mess he'd left behind at home in more than an hour.

CHAPTER 4

"Our truest life is when we are in our dreams awake."
—Henry David Thoreau

Dani hoped she wasn't making yet another huge mistake by letting Lucas help her, but what was she supposed to do? Both he and his mother had confirmed that lodging in Stowe would be hard to come by this time of year, and he'd said the place he was staying had plenty of room.

How could she have been so stupid as to not have anticipated ski season in Vermont? She'd been so consumed with leaving Kentucky, hadn't looked past the logistics of getting to her destination. The trip had taken twice as long as it normally would have, due to having to stop to feed and change Savannah every couple of hours.

Yesterday, she had gotten tired of being trapped in her seat and had begun to scream her head off until Dani had had no choice but to quit early and find a hotel in Pennsylvania. Today had been another long day, and when the car had spun off the road and landed in a ditch, Dani had been immediately convinced she and her daughter were both going to die out there alone in the cold.

Until Lucas Abbott had come along to save the day. After she'd stopped being terrified of the strange man knocking on her window, she'd immediately noticed he was handsome like a movie star. And when he'd lifted her out of the car, she'd discovered he had muscles on top of muscles.

Not that she was in any way interested in him as a man. Not even kind of. However, it was good to know that she was still able to notice a handsome man when she saw one. And Lucas Abbott was the most handsome of handsome men. He smelled really good, too. Like cold winter air, evergreen and woodsmoke, which was one of her favorite scents.

Why she was allowing herself to dissect what he smelled like, she couldn't say. It was better if she didn't let her thoughts go beyond a bed and a roof over her head and Savannah's for the evening. Tomorrow, she would find a place for them to stay before her interviews. She'd arranged the interviews from the hotel room in Pennsylvania the night before and had told the managers that she would need to bring her daughter with her until she found qualified childcare. They had been understanding, but she hoped that being a single mom to a four-month-old wouldn't hurt her chances of securing employment.

Thanks to the life insurance her late fiancé's work had provided, her financial situation wasn't dire. Not yet anyway, but she needed a job and was counting on finding something that would offer long-term security for her and her child. It still tugged at her heart, all these months later, that Jack had made her the beneficiary of his life insurance policy and was taking care of her even after he was gone.

When they got to the house where they'd be staying, she'd ask Lucas if she could use the phone so she could call to let her best friend at home know she'd made it to Vermont. Leslie knew better than anyone how badly Dani needed to get away from the painful memories she'd left behind in Kentucky.

It was sobering to realize how totally screwed she would've been if Lucas hadn't come along to help her.

"I really appreciate you stopping to help us," she said, breaking another long silence.

"Of course I stopped to help you."

"You say that like everyone would do what you did."

"I'd like to think anyone would."

"And yet we both know better, don't we?"

"Yeah, I guess. Most of the people I know would've stopped to help someone in need."

"You must know all the nice people."

"The people you know aren't nice?"

"They are." The people in her world were almost too nice, and that had been her problem at home. It would be so easy, she realized, to pour her heart out to this sweet guy who'd been a lifesaver. But she'd left all that crap at home when she set out to reinvent herself in a place where some of her happiest memories had been made. The last thing she wanted to do now was revisit the many reasons she'd had for pulling up stakes and changing her life—and Savannah's.

Her mother would never forgive her for moving her only child and grandchild so far away, but Dani couldn't breathe with her parents wanting to fix everything for her. They couldn't fix the unfixable. Only she could, thus the decision to move far enough away that her parents wouldn't be able to pop by without notice or interfere with every aspect of her life and the baby's.

She was thankful for everything they'd done for her and Savannah, but she'd gotten to the point where she wasn't doing any thinking for herself, which had worked out well for a while, but that couldn't go on forever. Dani only wished she'd left things on a better note with her parents, who were furious with her after reading the note she'd left for them. She'd gotten an earful when they called her.

Taking a deep breath, she let it out slowly, trying to clear her mind of things that were better left in the past. Imagining what her parents would have to say about her riding in a truck with a man who'd been a stranger an hour ago had her once again questioning her own judgment. If she was wrong about Lucas Abbott, she would never trust herself again.

A few minutes later, Lucas took a right turn into a driveway that wound through thick woods.

Dani's heart beat faster, and her mouth went dry.

Maybe this hadn't been such a good idea.

They traveled at least another half a mile before a large house came into view. It occurred to her in those final moments in the truck that if she had been wrong about Lucas, it would be months before anyone found her and her child.

Terror gripped her, closing her throat around a lump so big, she could barely breathe. *Oh God, no. No, no, no. Please no.*

"Danielle? Are you all right?"

She shook her head, which was the only thing she could do as the panic overtook her with a sudden ruthlessness that reminded her of the first weeks after Jack died, leaving her alone and pregnant and heartbroken. Her throat closed, making it impossible to breathe as she broke out in a sweat.

"Danielle!"

She could hear Lucas calling her name, but he sounded far away.

The baby began to cry, but Dani couldn't move. Tiny dots danced in front of her eyes. This was a bad one, worse than any of the others she'd had in the months since Jack died. Then, as quickly as it had come on, the tightness in her chest loosened, allowing her to take a gulping deep breath that cleared the fuzz from her brain. That's when she realized that Lucas had run around the truck to the passenger door and was standing next to her, telling her to breathe.

She sucked in a greedy breath of frigid air.

"Again," he said, his tone patient and kind.

"Baby," she gasped.

"She's fine. Keep breathing."

Dani closed her eyes and focused on drawing air into her lungs until her heart rate returned to normal, leaving only the clamminess from the sweat that made her shiver in the cold air.

"Are you okay now?"

"I… I think so. Sorry about that."

"Nothing to be sorry about. Let's get you ladies inside where it's warm."

If there was an upside to suffering a panic attack in front of the stranger who'd rescued her… He'd just had a golden opportunity to take advantage of her and had chosen to help rather than harm. That counted for something, didn't it?

On legs that felt shaky and unsteady, Dani carried Savannah's car seat and followed Lucas to the dark front door, where he punched in a code that turned on the outside lights while unlocking the door.

"After you," he said, gesturing for her to lead the way inside.

Dani stepped into a spacious foyer that led to an open-concept living room/kitchen/dining room. A floor-to-ceiling stone fireplace was the centerpiece of the big room. "This is beautiful."

"I know. I love this house. My friend Craig inherited it from his father when he died and usually rents it out during ski season.

This year he's not renting it because he's got a big idea about trying to write a novel when he's not traveling for work."

"Oh wow, that's great." Dani appreciated that he didn't ask a bunch of questions about what'd happened in the truck.

"I can't wait to see what he comes up with. He was a total lunatic in college, but he's grown up a lot since then. We all have."

"Happens to the best of us."

"Let me grab the bags and some firewood and get this place warmed up."

While he left to do that, Dani took off her coat and removed Savannah from the car seat. The baby's face was red from crying and her eyes wet with tears. "There now. Everything's okay. Mommy is sorry she scared you." She kissed her soft cheek and cuddled her into her arms.

Savannah let out a squeak as she rooted around, looking for her dinner.

Dani's breasts tingled in response to the baby, giving her about a minute before her milk let down. She moved quickly to grab a blanket and landed on a sofa, managing to cover herself and the baby before Lucas returned with their bags.

Lucas took a quick glance in their direction, saw that she was feeding the baby and looked away. He went back outside, brought in an armload of wood and had a fire started in the time it took her to finish feeding Savannah. After burping and changing her, Dani walked her around until she dozed off—or at least she thought the baby was asleep. Turning her back to Lucas, she said, "Is she asleep?"

"Out cold."

"I thought so, but I wasn't totally sure." She settled the baby on the sofa with a blanket rolled to keep her in place.

"She's a good baby."

"She really is. Thank goodness for that." The whole time she'd been pregnant, she'd prayed for an easy baby, which had turned out to be one of the few recent prayers that had been answered. Others had gone mostly ignored, such as when she'd prayed for her parents to accept her choices without judgment. That one had gotten a big fat zero in response. So too had the one about keeping Jack safe. Ignored. Don't even get her started on the prayer for a safe trip to Vermont for her and Savannah. Was it any wonder she was thinking about giving up on praying?

"There're two bedrooms down here and four more upstairs." He pointed to a hallway off the main living area. "If you want to take one of the rooms down here, I'll go upstairs."

"Whatever you want is fine with me."

"I'll put your stuff in the bigger of the two rooms down here. First door on the right. There's a bathroom attached and towels in the closet."

"Perfect, thank you."

While he went to stash their bags, Dani ran a brush through her hair to contend with a bad case of hat head. Exhaustion tugged at her after the long day of driving and the stress of the last hour. What would she do if her car was badly damaged? She tried to remember if her insurance provided for a rental. She could figure that out in the morning when she had a better idea of the damage.

"Are you hungry?" Lucas asked when he returned to the room from stashing her bags in the bedroom.

"I could definitely eat something."

"I'll heat up the pizza."

"Sounds good."

He smiled, which only made him handsomer than he already was. In the months since she'd lost Jack, she hadn't so much as glanced at another man. Until Lucas Abbott had come to her rescue and made her aware that while Jack might be gone, she was still very much alive.

She followed him into the kitchen so she could help with dinner prep and still keep an eye on Savannah. "I'm so sorry to bomb into your time alone, and now I'm eating your food, too."

"It's no problem at all. I'm actually glad to have the company." He unboxed two frozen pizzas—one supreme and one pepperoni—and put them in the oven. "I was in a pretty pissy mood when I left Butler. Helping you has taken my mind off the reason why I wanted this getaway in the first place."

She took a seat at one of the barstools that surrounded a huge island, making sure she could still see the baby. "I'm a pretty good listener if you want to air it out with someone. My friends are always coming to me with their problems. I was called Lucy in high school."

"After the Charlie Brown character?"

"Yep. And because you've been so nice to me, I won't even charge you five cents for my advice."

"Well, that's an offer I'd be hard-pressed to refuse." He popped open a beer. "What can I get you to drink?"

"Ice water would be great."

He poured a tall glass of ice water for her and sat on the barstool across from her, taking a deep breath and releasing it. "So it's like this. I told you I'm an identical twin."

"Right."

"My brother Landon and I get along like a house on fire. We always have."

"That's a funny way to put it as a firefighter."

"That's one of my grandfather's many favorite sayings, and Landon and I are both firefighters. Anyway, he and I fought like billy goats with our other siblings but never with each other."

His wording made her laugh. "How do billy goats fight, exactly?"

"Lots of head-butting, kicking and sucker-punching."

"I see."

"Bottom line, Landon and I have always been tight. And then this woman Amanda came to town to sell sex toys at the store, and suddenly—"

"Whoa! *Sex toys at the store?* You're going to need to unpack that for me."

His low chuckle echoed through the big kitchen. "I suppose that does warrant some explanation."

"Ah, yeah. Please proceed."

"My family owns the Green Mountain Country Store."

"What? *Seriously?* I have an interview there this week!"

"Really?"

"Yes! It's my first choice. I devoured the website. I'd love to work there."

"I might be able to help." He leaned in closer, adding in a conspiratorial whisper, "I know people."

"You're turning out to be rather good to have around."

That earned her a huge smile. "Aww, shucks. I do what I can. Anyway, my dad got a big idea to offer an intimate line in the store. Amanda came to do training. Landon and I both asked her out, and she went out with me one night and him the next."

"Why'd she go out with both of you? That's kind of weird."

"I think she was trying to be nice since her company is doing business with our family's store."

"Ah, okay. So what happened?"

"We had a really good time, but I think she likes him better than me. She came to our birthday dinner last night with him, and after that, I just wanted to get the hell out of there for a while. That's why I'm here."

"Happy birthday."

"Thank you."

"So which part is worse for you—that she might like him over you, or that you're at odds with him?"

"That's a good question." He got up to check the pizza. "Probably being at odds with him is worse. I can't stand that."

"So then don't be. If you'd pick him over her, then pick him. If she likes him better than you, so be it. You'll find someone who likes you better. Isn't that what you want anyway?"

"How do you make it sound so simple?"

"Because it is. Your brother is your best friend forever. He comes first over someone you both just met."

"My grandfather said the same thing. You're both absolutely right."

"Duh. I know."

Laughter lit up his gorgeous golden-brown eyes. The man was ridiculously handsome. She couldn't believe that there was another one just like him. The two of them must've left a trail of broken hearts in their wake.

Dani shook off those thoughts. What did their trail of broken hearts matter to her? She had no intention of adding hers to their scrap pile. She'd had enough heartbreak for one lifetime. Allowing herself to be sucked in by a handsome, kind, sexy stranger would only lead to more.

He was providing her with shelter and frozen pizza for tonight and maybe a recommendation to his family's business. That was all this was, and she couldn't allow the pervasive loneliness she'd brought with her from Kentucky to turn this bizarre evening into something it wasn't ever going to be.

The scent of the pizza cooking made her stomach growl.

"Someone is hungry," Lucas said.

"That's embarrassing."

"Don't worry about it. In my family, that's the least of the sounds you'll hear over an average dinner."

"I'm very curious about what it was like to grow up with nine siblings."

"It was loud and crowded and chaotic, but fun, too. There was always someone to hang out with or fight with or wrestle with."

"Wrestling seems to be a key element to life in your family."

"I have six brothers, all but two of them older than me, and one of my sisters could kick my ass until I hit high school. I learned to defend myself at a very young age."

"What's your mother like?"

"She's very cool and was a fun mom, but she didn't put up with our crap. She really is a saint. Everyone says so."

"She'd have to be. And your dad?"

"He's awesome, super laid-back and chill at home, but intense and driven when it comes to the business."

"It's his family's business, then?"

"Actually, it's my mom's family business, but my dad graduated from Yale's School of Management. My gramps hired my dad after he and my mom got married, and he became the CEO when Gramps retired. The two of them are great pals, constantly interfering in the love lives of my siblings and cousins and generally thinking they're in charge of us all. Did I mention that my mom's sister has eight kids?"

Dani's mouth fell open. "Holy crap!"

"The winters in Vermont are long and boring, or so my mom and my aunt always said."

"That's funny."

"It's true." He retrieved the pizzas from the oven, cut them, got out plates and silverware and then joined her at the island.

"You know your way around this kitchen pretty well."

"I come up here to visit a couple times a year. Craig and I were close friends in college, and it's only ninety minutes from Butler when it's not snowing. It's an easy getaway. We've had some great times here."

Dani marveled at how he ate five pieces of pizza in the time it took her to eat two. "Nice of him to let you use the place when he's not here."

"I agree. He's a good friend to have."

"So are you. Thank you for everything tonight. I don't know what I would've done if you hadn't come along when you did."

"I'm glad I could help."

When they finished eating, they worked together to clean up the kitchen while she suppressed one yawn after another. Lucas opened a bag of Nestlé Crunch bars and offered her one.

Dani took a candy bar from the bag and opened the wrapper. "I should explain what happened before… In the truck."

"You don't have to."

"I really should, though." She took a bite of the rich chocolate and tried to collect her thoughts. "Almost a year ago, I started having panic attacks after a traumatic event. They come on out of nowhere, and I don't have a lot of control over when or how it happens."

"You don't owe me any explanation. I'm just glad you're okay. But you should probably go to bed before you fall over."

"I think I will. Today was a long day, and Savannah will be up during the night."

"Go on ahead. I'll lock up and wait for the fire to die down before I crash."

"Thank you again for everything. You really saved my life—and Savannah's."

"Happy to help. Get some sleep, and we'll figure out what's up with your car in the morning."

"I hope it's not a total loss."

"I don't think it will be. From what I could see, it was wedged pretty cleanly in the ditch. Once they get it out, it should be fine, or so I hope."

"Me, too." She really hoped he was right. The last thing she needed was major car trouble when she was trying to find a whole new life for herself and her daughter in the only other place that had ever felt like home to her. Maybe her parents were right, and she was crazy to want to take care of herself when they were more than happy to do everything for her and Savannah. She checked her cell phone and saw that she had no service. "Would it be possible to make a quick phone call to my friend at home to tell her I got here and where I am?"

"Of course."

"I can leave some money for your friend's phone bill."

"No worries. He won't care. You can use the phone over there while I tend to the fire."

"Thank you. I'll be quick."

"Take your time."

CHAPTER 5

"When you take charge of your life, there is no longer need to ask permission of other people or society at large. When you ask permission, you give someone veto power over your life."
—Geoffrey F. Abert

After he walked away, she picked up the portable phone and dialed the number she knew by heart.

Leslie picked up on the first ring. "Hello?" She sounded suspicious of the unfamiliar phone number.

"It's me."

"Oh, thank God! I've been trying to call you for hours."

"The cell service up here is nonexistent."

"I was about to call the Vermont State Police. Your mother has been driving me crazy texting me to ask if I've heard from you."

"Sorry to call so late. You won't believe what happened." Dani conveyed the story of her spinout and how Lucas had rescued her.

"Wait a minute. *Are you telling me you're staying with a guy you just met, alone in a house in the sticks of Vermont?*"

The hysteria in her friend's voice put Dani on edge. "He's a firefighter and paramedic. I talked to his mom, and she told me he's one hundred percent trustworthy. He's been nothing but super nice and helpful. And he's the eighth of ten kids." She had no idea why she added that, but the detail had provided comfort to her. Maybe it would do the same for Leslie.

"That doesn't mean he's not a serial killer!"

"He's not a serial killer, Les. He's a really nice guy, and he saved me and Savannah from spending the night in a ditch by the side of the road. He even fed me."

"I don't like this one bit, Dani. What the hell are we supposed to do if you go missing?"

Dani's stomach dropped. "That's not going to happen. He's going to take me to get my car tomorrow, and I've got my first interviews in the morning."

"I want to know his name, address and telephone number, and the address where you're staying. If I don't hear from you by ten o'clock tomorrow morning, I'm calling the Vermont State Police. I mean it."

Dani tried to put herself in Leslie's place and knew she would feel the same way if she hadn't met Lucas and seen how great he'd been. "Hold on." She put the phone down, picked up a pad of paper and a pen and went into the living room. "Um, Lucas?"

From his perch in a squat in front of the fireplace, he turned to look at her. "What's up?"

"My, ah, friend wants your full name, address, phone number and the address here, and she wants to hear from me by ten in the morning, or she's calling the Vermont State Police."

Amusement had his lips quivering and his eyes sparkling, both of which were a good look on him. Hell, mud would be a good look on him.

He took the pad and pen, wrote down the requested info and handed it back to her. "I put my mother's phone number and the fire department number, too, if she wants to check my references."

"Thank you for not being offended."

"Why would I be? She doesn't know me from Adam, and neither do you."

"I know you a little, and if I'm wrong about you, I'll never trust myself again."

"You aren't wrong about me." The way he looked at her when he said that had butterflies in her belly doing cartwheels.

"I'll, um, just give this info to Leslie."

"Okay."

Dani went back into the kitchen and picked up the phone. "Still there?"

"What took so long? I was about to call the cops!"

"Stop it, will you? Here's the info you wanted. You got a pen?"

"Yep."

She read back the info he'd given her, including the number for his mom and the Butler Volunteer Fire Department. "In case you want to check his references."

"I might just do that."

"Les, come on. He's a nice guy. I swear. He showed me his firefighter badge, he has equipment in his truck and emergency lights, fire department license plates, and he told me to call his department if I wanted to confirm he's legit. He's been nothing but nice to me—and his family owns the store where I'm interviewing in Butler."

"That's all well and good, but you'd better call me by ten, or I'll reach out to the state police. I'm not just saying that, Dani."

"I think you need to stop watching so much true-crime TV."

"Maybe you should watch a little more of it so you'd know how *insane* it is to be alone with your infant in the woods of Vermont with a guy you've never met before today."

"I feel safe with him, Les. If I hadn't felt safe, I wouldn't have taken him up on the offer of a place to stay."

"I hope you're right. Make sure you lock your bedroom door and put something heavy like the dresser in front of it so he can't get in."

"I'm going to bed now. I'll call you in the morning."

"By ten."

"Yes, and Les? Do *not* tell my mother any of this. Do you hear me?"

"I won't tell her, because she *would* call the cops, but I will tell her you got there okay."

"Thank you." Dani breathed a sigh of relief that Leslie wouldn't tell her mother where she was or who she was with. "I'll talk to you in the morning."

"Yes, you will. Or else. Oh, and Dani, you broke my brother's heart when you left."

"What? I did not!"

"Yes, you did. He was looking forward to the date you had planned."

"It wasn't a date, and I didn't plan anything! It was your mother and my mother interfering in our lives, and it's a big part of the reason why I left. But don't tell him that."

"I won't, but I understand even if he doesn't."

"It's got nothing to do with him. Please tell him that. This was brewing long before I found out my mother and your mom were planning to soothe our broken hearts by pushing us together when there's never been anything but friendship between us."

"I know, and eventually he'll figure that out, too. Don't forget to call me in the morning. And I love you."

"I won't. Love you, too." Dani ended the call and returned the phone to the charger. She and Leslie had grown up next door to each other and had been best friends all their lives. Les was married to Mark, a guy they'd gone to school with who was now a doctor, and they were expecting their second child in the fall. Leaving Les and her family had been the hardest part about deciding to relocate, but they would always be in close touch no matter where they lived.

Leslie's older brother, Tom, had recently moved back home after his marriage ended. Hearing her mom and Mrs. Carter plotting to fix them up had been the final impetus for Dani to get the hell out of there before they decided she ought to marry Tom, a man who'd been like a brother to her.

"Everything okay?" Lucas asked when he came into the kitchen.

"Yes, thanks. Sorry about the inquisition."

"I'm glad you have friends who care about you."

"I am, too, even if they can be a pain in the butt sometimes."

"Those are the best kind of friends."

Dani glanced at Savannah, who had thrown her arm over her head the way she did when she was really asleep. "I'm going to take my girl to bed now."

"Let me know if you need anything."

"I will. Good night."

"Night."

She carefully picked up Savannah, hoping she wouldn't awaken during the transfer, and carried her into the bedroom where Lucas had put their things earlier. A dark wood sleigh bed took up most of the space in the cozy room, which also had a matching dresser. The bed was covered by a red plaid flannel quilt that matched the curtains.

After laying Savannah carefully on the bed and rolling a blanket on the far edge so she couldn't fall off, Dani eyed the dresser that was next to the door. Leslie's words bounced around in her mind as she locked the door and then nudged the heavy dresser to the right until it blocked the door.

Just in case.

From the living room, Lucas could hear what sounded like a sliding sound and then a loud thump. What was she doing in there?

Should he check on her?

No, if she needed help, she'd tell him, wouldn't she?

He hoped she would, even after her friend filled her head with all sorts of awful thoughts about him. Not that he could blame the friend. If one of his sisters had done what Danielle had with him, he'd probably freak out, too.

Then he realized what the sliding sound was—the dresser being pushed in front of the door.

That made him laugh quietly, so she wouldn't hear him. She was perfectly safe with him, but she had no way to know that for certain.

The house phone rang, and Lucas got up to answer it in the kitchen.

"Hey," Craig said. "Just checking that you were able to get in okay and have what you need."

"I'm all good, thanks for checking. Where're you?"

"Stuck in Chicago for at least the next two days thanks to another slow-moving snowstorm coming tomorrow. This winter isn't going quietly."

"No, it isn't. We got bombed with snow here today, too." He took a sip from his beer bottle. "So I hope you don't mind, but I have someone staying here with me, probably just tonight."

"I don't mind, you know that, but are you holding out on me?"

Lucas laughed. "Nah, nothing like that." He told his friend about the accident and how he'd brought Danielle and Savannah to the house for the night.

"Good call. You would've been hard-pressed to find anywhere for her to stay in Stowe this time of year."

"That's what I told her. I get the feeling the trip wasn't well planned."

"Sounds that way. All right, brother. I've got to get some work done before more meetings tomorrow. Enjoy the slopes."

"I will. Thanks again for the use of the house."

"My house is your house. Talk soon."

"Later."

Lucas popped open another beer, went into the living room and turned on the TV, flipping through the channels until he landed on *Ridiculousness*, which was one of his favorite shows. He watched the shenanigans for a few minutes, through the lens of the new, more mature Lucas Abbott, and realized the show was far too juvenile for new Lucas. He moved through the channels until he landed on a news show. New Lucas ought to pay more attention to what was happening in the world.

After forty-five minutes of news, he was thoroughly depressed and switched to a home renovation show that sucked him right in. He woke quite a bit later to the sound of a baby crying and realized he'd fallen asleep in front of the TV. The fire had burned down completely, so he shut off the TV and headed upstairs to bed.

Lucas changed into flannel pajama pants and a long-sleeved T-shirt. As he got into bed, he could still hear the baby crying and hoped they were okay. He had the oddest desire to go down there and offer to help her. As if there was anything he could actually do. Hannah had taught him how to change Callie, but other than that and holding her and Caden from time to time, he had zero experience with babies and was the last person Danielle would need if something was actually wrong.

He stayed put, but as he started to doze off, he realized once again that he hadn't thought of Landon or Amanda in hours.

Dani slept fitfully, dreaming of being stalked by a man who wanted to harm her and Savannah. She blamed Les for putting those ideas in her head, when, in fact, they were perfectly safe with Lucas. For whatever reason, she'd never had any doubt that he was exactly who and what he seemed to be. There were times when you had to trust your own instincts, and hers had served her well where he was concerned.

She got up with Savannah around six fifteen, changed and fed her, and then strapped her into her car seat so Dani could shower without worrying about her. That hadn't been a concern when she'd been with her parents, who both worked from home. Someone was always around to watch the baby when Dani needed to shower or run to the store. She would miss that, but she wouldn't miss them making all the decisions for her and her daughter, as if Dani were still a teenager and not a grown, twenty-five-year-old woman with a child of her own.

They'd meant well. She knew that. But even after she'd asked them to back off a little and give her some room to breathe and think, they hadn't. After hearing her mom and Mrs. Carter plotting to make a couple of her and Tom, Dani had come to the conclusion that she had to leave or risk losing control of her own life—and her daughter's. She'd never considered going anywhere other than Vermont, the memory of idyllic childhood summers with her grandparents fueling her long journey.

Because she had an interview at ten and another at eleven, she took the time to blow-dry and straighten her hair while Savannah played with the toys attached to her seat, cooing and squeaking every few minutes. Dani loved her baby chatter and had talked to her all the way from Kentucky to let her know Mommy was there, even if Savannah couldn't see her. She'd been paranoid about keeping half an eye on her in the mirror she'd rigged up and had been thankful for every minute the baby had spent asleep during the trip.

She dressed in black pants and a warm sweater and then got Savannah dressed for the day in a warm one-piece outfit before sliding the dresser back to where it belonged and opening her bedroom door. The scents of coffee and bacon greeted her, making her mouth water in anticipation.

"Looks like our host is up early," she whispered to the baby.

They went to the kitchen, where Lucas was standing watch over the stove while sipping from a coffee mug. "Morning."

"Morning." Damn, the man had gotten even better looking overnight. His jaw was covered in stubble that was on its way to becoming an actual beard. He wore flannel pajama pants and a Bowdoin T-shirt. Yum. She put the seat on the counter and so Savannah could play with her toys while Dani ate.

"Did you ladies sleep well?"

"We did, thank you." He didn't need to know she'd dreamed about serial killers. "You're up early."

"I wasn't sure what time you have to be in town."

"My first interview is at ten and the second at eleven."

"Got it."

"I know you came up here to ski, so you can drop us in town and be on your way. We'll figure it out from there."

"I'm not going to just drop you in a strange town with a baby, Danielle. I can ski anytime. I'll help you get your car sorted and anything else you girls need before we go our separate ways."

"I feel like I keep saying thank you, but you continue to give me reasons to."

"No worries. It's all good." He served up plates of eggs and crispy bacon. "Coffee?"

"I'd love some." She allowed herself one cup a day while breastfeeding. He put the cream and sugar she'd mentioned last night next to the mug of coffee he'd poured for her. She liked that he paid attention to the details. "Are you, by any chance, putting maple syrup on eggs?"

"Uh huh. This is the real deal, right from my family's store. We make our own. Well, I should say my brothers Colton and Max do. The rest of us help out during the sugaring season, and we sell the syrup in the store."

"Wow, that's so cool, although I'd never imagine putting it on eggs."

He grinned. "I love it on eggs."

"Tell me about the store. I'm super curious after seeing the website."

"The website is actually new. My sister-in-law Cameron came up from New York City to build the site and crashed into Fred, our town moose, on the way into Butler. My brother Will rescued her, and they've been together ever since."

"Wait. Butler has a town moose?"

"Sure does. And my sister Hannah is a self-proclaimed moose whisperer, much to her husband Nolan's dismay."

"I love that! What does she do with the moose?"

"Well, for one thing, she thinks she 'speaks Fred.' And now she's adopted a baby moose who showed up with Fred one day."

"No way."

"Yes way, and Nolan is not happy about it, let me tell you. We were teasing him about having a full-grown bull moose in bed between them at the rate she's going. He was unamused."

Dani laughed. "That's awesome. This family of yours sounds quite entertaining."

"You have no idea."

"These eggs are delicious, by the way."

"Thanks. My mom taught us all how to cook the basics when we were still in elementary school. Then we had to take turns making meals for the whole family. She would pair us up with an older sibling to make sure it wasn't a total disaster."

"Am I allowed to say that I'm totally in love with your mom? I want to meet her and have her tell me everything I need to know about raising kids."

"You can meet her while you're in Butler."

That smile of his must've been melting panties all over northern Vermont for years now. Not that *her* panties were melting or anything. Just having the thought made her feel disloyal to Jack, who'd been the love of her life. Yes, Lucas was a sweet, sincere, good-looking man, but she had no business thinking about what it might be like to date him—or anything else, for that matter. She'd had her great love, and now Savannah was her only priority.

Her focus needed to be on her daughter and finding a job as well as a new home for the two of them—and quickly.

"Everything okay?" he asked.

Dani glanced at him. "Why do you ask?"

"You just looked really sad for a minute there."

Thinking about Jack and everything she'd lost wasn't a good idea, especially when she had so many things she needed to do. Allowing the grief to suck her back into the depths of despair wasn't an option now that she was on her own with Savannah. "A lot of changes in my life," she said in response to Lucas's comment. "I'm hoping I did the right thing coming here."

"Why did you leave Kentucky?"

"I… I needed to…"

"It's okay if you don't want to talk about it."

"I know you have questions."

"It's none of my business, Danielle."

"Dani."

"Excuse me?"

"My friends call me Dani."

"I like that. It suits you. Are we going to be friends, Dani?"

"I think we already are. You saved me and my daughter last night."

"You saved me, too. I'd come here to brood, and you ladies have given me something far more productive to do. So thanks for that."

"We're glad we could do something for you, too."

"You did, and your business is your own. I'll only tell you that I'm also a good listener if you need one. No obligations."

"That's nice to know. Let me help you clean up the kitchen."

They worked together to load the dishwasher, and then he washed the pans while she dried them.

She used a hot, soapy dishcloth and wiped down the counters and stove then took a deep breath and said the words before she lost her nerve. "My fiancé, Jack, was killed in an accident six months before Savannah was born."

CHAPTER 6

"Grief can't be shared. Everyone carries it alone.
His own burden in his own way."
—Anne Morrow Lindbergh

Lucas stared at her for a second before he recovered himself enough to react. His heart ached for her and Savannah. "Oh God, Dani. I'm so sorry."

"Me, too. He was the best man I ever knew, other than my dad. He was so excited about the baby, and it breaks my heart that he never got to meet her." It had taken months for her to be able to speak of him without breaking down.

"I can't even imagine how hard that must've been."

"It was." She forced a small smile. "Still is. The thing is… My parents, they were so there for me when it happened, and ever since. I wouldn't have survived it without them and Les and my other friends and family."

"I'm glad you had that kind of support to help you through it."

"I'm very lucky, for sure." Her eyes filled as she recalled the darkest days of her life. The shock of losing her twenty-seven-year-old, perfectly healthy fiancé had left her reeling for months. "But after a while, it got so I couldn't seem to do anything without consulting with them first. They just took over, and I let them because it was easier than fighting back."

When Savannah started to fuss, Lucas deftly removed her from the seat and lifted her into his arms. "Hi there, sweet girl."

The baby automatically reached for his hair, but he was one step ahead of her, giving her a finger to wrap her pudgy hand around.

Dani watched him with her child, her mouth gone dry with emotions that came over her so fast and furious, she could barely process them all. It occurred to her that this man could be dangerous to her in ways that had nothing to do with serial killers.

"You left because they were suffocating you?" he asked, as if he hadn't just stopped her heart with the tender way he handled her daughter.

"Yes," she said, relieved that he got it. "And I had to go far enough away that they couldn't pop in every day and try to fix everything for me."

"How'd they take the news you were leaving?"

"I left while they were out, and they came home to a note. They called to let me know they're furious with me. They said I'm irresponsible and impulsive—two things I've never been in my entire life. Why would they think I'd start being that way now when I have Savannah to think about?"

"Perhaps they're concerned that the grief is messing with your judgment."

"Maybe it is, but I couldn't *breathe* there. I needed to get away to have a chance to figure things out for myself."

"I can understand that. I was doing the same thing, in a way."

"And then you got stuck with us, and you haven't had a chance to think."

"Actually, I have."

"Really?"

He nodded. "Last night when I went to bed, I realized I hadn't thought about Landon or Amanda in hours."

"What do you suppose that means?"

"That maybe I'm not as put out by their relationship when I have some distance and perspective. You were right when you said he's my brother, and he has to come first."

"I'm glad you can see that."

"What's that old expression? Bros before—"

She held up her hand. "Do *not* finish that thought and ruin my positive impression of you."

He laughed. "Gotcha. And for what it's worth, I think you did the right thing leaving home before you reached the point of a permanent rift with your folks."

"I'm hoping the rift isn't permanent."

"It won't be. When they see the two of you happy and thriving in Vermont, they'll know you did the right thing for you, even if it wasn't the right thing for them."

"I really hope you're right. They're not too happy with me at the moment."

"Give them some time to miss you. They'll come around."

Smiling, she said, "Thanks for listening."

"Anytime."

"And now I must call Les, or she'll send the state police to check on me and arrest you."

"We can't have that. Phone is all yours."

The more time Lucas spent with Dani, the more he liked her. The more he talked to her, the more he wanted to say and hear and ask. He wanted to know what kind of accident had caused her fiancé's death and how she'd coped with losing him while carrying his child. He wanted to know how long they'd been together and how they'd met.

But he couldn't ask her any of those things. He didn't have the right to pry. One thing he could say for certain was that hearing what she'd been through made his recent issues seem foolish and insignificant.

He gave her so much credit for taking control of her life—and Savannah's—and for knowing what she needed when it probably would've been easier to stay with her parents and let them help her with everything after the heartbreaking loss of her fiancé.

On the way into town for her interviews, he told her so.

"That's nice of you to say, but it probably was pretty foolish to move so far away from my entire support system."

"Why do you say that?"

"Well, if I get one of these jobs, I'll have to find childcare in a place where I know no one, not to mention housing."

"Do you need the job immediately, or do you have some time?"

"I have time, but I want to get things figured out for both of us."

"I can understand that."

"I hate the feeling of being in limbo. I want my ducks in a row."

"I'm being totally biased, but you should come to Butler. You'd love our little town, and our store is fantastic—way better than anything they have here. And you know *someone* there who can help you find an apartment and *someone* to watch Savannah."

"Hmm, you do make good points."

"Our store is really awesome. I'm not just saying that."

"I know. I saw that on the website. The position they're advertising for is in the new warehouse."

"Ah, yes, the catalog, which is my dad's latest big idea. Guess who he's forcing to model the clothes?"

She glanced over at him, eyes wide. "*No*, really?"

"Yep, us and our cousins and significant others. He says, 'Why would we hire models when we've got all these good-looking young people to choose from right in our own family?' Even the two grandchildren are being recruited. My cousin Izzy is the only one who doesn't have to do it because she's going to take the pictures, which is totally unfair. We had to postpone the shoot when she got a great opportunity in Europe, but she'll be back this summer and has promised her first order of business will be the catalog shoot."

Dani didn't say anything, but out of the corner of his eye, he could see her rocking with silent laughter.

"It's *not* funny. We're dreading it."

"It really *is* funny."

"If you knew my family, you'd know just how unfunny it is. It's going to be a world-class mess."

"You ought to videotape it for the store's YouTube channel. I bet you'd get a million views of something like that."

"I hate to say you're probably right. Our family is a three-ring circus on a normal day. I can't begin to imagine what it'll be like when we become 'models.'"

"It'll be hilarious, and you need to record it."

"I'll mention your suggestion to Cameron and Lucy. They'll probably jump on it."

"Is Lucy one of your sisters?"

"No, she's engaged to my brother Colton. She and Cam were business partners in a web company in New York that has relocated in part to Butler."

"So they both ended up with your brothers. That's cool."

"And it doesn't stop there. Lucy's sister Emma is living with my cousin Grayson, and their dad, Ray, is apparently dating my aunt Hannah. I haven't witnessed that with my own eyes yet, but it sure would be something. Aunt Hannah has been single since her husband left her with eight kids more than twenty years ago. Gray, who's the oldest, was only sixteen at the time."

"Holy crap. And I think I've got problems. He left her with *eight kids*, sixteen and under?"

"Yep. I don't really remember that much about him. I was only, like, six or seven when he split, but I certainly remember how upset my mom was about it."

"That'd be hard to forget. It's amazing if she's found someone after all this time."

"It really is, and by all accounts, Ray is the best. He's been widowed for years. When Emma and her daughter, Simone, decided to follow Lucy to Vermont, Ray said he was coming, too. And now look at him dating Aunt Hannah."

"That's awesome."

"I totally agree."

"Your family is very interesting, Lucas."

"That's one word for what my family is. Others include crazy, loud, annoying, *loud...*"

"I always wished I had siblings."

"I have a few you can have."

"You say that, but you don't mean it. You wouldn't give any of them away."

"Maybe Charley. She's often extra, but she's been better since she fell in love with Tyler. We call him the Charley Tamer."

"Does she know that?"

"Oh hell no."

As she laughed, he pulled the truck into a parking space in the center of downtown Stowe and shut off the engine. "Here we are."

Yesterday's snowfall had been shoveled and plowed, but the snow only added to the town's quaint appeal. The sidewalk was busy with people dressed in ski attire, hustling in the cold air. Though the sun was out, the temperature hovered in the low twenties.

"The general store is that way," Lucas said, pointing, "and one of the many ski shops is over there. Is that the one?"

"Yes, that's it."

"While you're at your interviews, I'll go see what's up with your car."

"You don't have to do that."

"I know I don't have to. I don't mind."

"You're supposed to be skiing."

"I can ski anytime." He would've offered to keep the baby for her while she went to her interviews, but he knew she would refuse, and rightfully so. Even after spending the night in the same house, she didn't know him well enough to leave her child with him. So he didn't offer. "Good luck, or I guess I should say break a leg."

"With the way my luck has been lately, I'd better stick with good luck."

"I'll meet you right back here when you're done."

"Okay. Thanks."

"No problem." Lucas watched until she had crossed the street and entered the store before he started the truck and headed for the garage that had her car. Was it wrong of him to hope that she didn't feel a connection to the stores in Stowe? He wanted to take her to Butler and show her his family's store.

"Why do you even care?" He had no idea, but he liked her and wanted to help her for some unknown reason. If nothing else, helping her kept his mind off the situation at home.

The garage was located on the outskirts of Stowe, and Lucas arrived about ten minutes after he left Dani. Her black sedan was out front, and at first glance, the only damage he could detect was a horizontal crease on the passenger door. Inside, he introduced himself to Bob, the manager, and asked about Dani's car.

"Dude, that thing was *wedged* in that ditch. How'd she do that?"

"She spun out, and that's where she landed."

"Wow, well, it took a hell of an effort to get it out of there."

"I noticed a dent on the passenger door."

Bob nodded. "Matching one on the driver's side, and the front bumper is banged up, too, but remarkably, the rest of the car seems fine. She's lucky the ditch was a perfect fit, or the damage would've been way worse."

Lucas breathed a sigh of relief on her behalf. She had enough on her plate without adding the hassle of totaling her car to the list.

"We can fix the dents if you want."

"That's okay. We have someone who can take care of that." His brother-in-law Nolan would give her the family discount if Lucas asked him to. "What do we owe you for the tow?"

"Two hundred. Like I said, it wasn't easy getting it out of that ditch."

Lucas handed over his credit card and signed the receipt. "Thanks again for your help."

"No problem."

He left the garage and drove back into town to wait for Dani. When she was finished with her interviews, he'd give her a ride to her car. After that, he had no idea what her plan was. Would she stay another night with him, or try to find somewhere else to go? He returned to the area where he'd left her and realized he had some time until she would need a ride. In a spur-of-the-moment decision, he headed back to Craig's to use the phone.

He called his father at work.

"This is a nice surprise," Lincoln said. "I thought you'd be skiing."

"I had a change of plans."

"Your mom told me you rescued someone."

"Yes, a woman named Danielle Rowson and her baby daughter." He told his father about Dani's interest in the warehouse manager job.

"I knew that name sounded familiar. I have her résumé right here. She's well qualified and at the top of our list of potential candidates."

"I'm not asking for favors, but she seems like a really nice person who's had some tough breaks."

"I appreciate you putting in a good word for her, son. It always helps to have a personal recommendation."

"Of course I have no way to know what kind of employee she'd be," Lucas said with a laugh. "But she comes across as genuine and ambitious."

"Says on her résumé that she's from Kentucky. She's a long way from home."

"Her grandparents had a place up here where she spent happy summers. She was in need of a change and headed our way."

"Ah, I see. Well, I'll look forward to meeting her the day after tomorrow." After a pause, his dad said, "So, um, couldn't help but notice you weren't yourself at your birthday dinner. Everything okay?"

"Yeah, I'm fine."

"You can tell me if you're not. You know that."

"I do know that, and I'm okay. I promise. The getaway has been good, even if it didn't work out how I planned."

"Unplanned detours can lead in interesting new directions."

"Now you sound like Gramps," Lucas said with a laugh.

"I guess I do, but it's true. Follow the detour and see where it leads you."

"Thank you for the words of wisdom. I'll see you when I get back to town."

"See you then, son."

Amused by his dad, Lucas put the phone back on the cradle and left the house to go meet Dani.

CHAPTER 7

"Motherhood: All love begins and ends there."
—Robert Browning

"I'm so sorry," Dani said to the manager of the ski shop. "She's never been like this." Savannah had started crying shortly after Dani's meeting began and hadn't let up for twenty minutes. The baby had dozed through the interview at the general store, at which the manager said she had decided not to immediately fill the assistant manager position after all. That hadn't been the news Dani had been hoping for.

The ski shop manager, a woman named Nancy, had tried to be patient while Dani tended to the baby, but Nancy kept checking her watch and was now visibly annoyed.

Dani gave Savannah the bottle she'd brought, and when that didn't soothe her, she tried the pacifier that she saved for emergencies.

Savannah spit it right back out and continued to wail.

Dani stood and patted the baby's back, bouncing her in hopes of salvaging the interview. This was too much to ask of anyone.

"Could we please reschedule?" Dani would have time in the morning before she had to leave for Butler.

"Look, you seem like a nice person, and you're certainly qualified, but we need someone who can give the job their full attention."

"I can do that. I just need to arrange childcare, which I'd do before I start."

"I'm not sure this is going to be the right fit for us."

Dani wanted to argue with her and remind her that she couldn't legally exclude her from consideration because she was a mother. She'd read up on that topic before leaving Kentucky. But did she want to work for someone who would dismiss her simply because she had a fussy baby? Absolutely not. Without another word, she stood, reached for Savannah's seat and walked out.

Nancy could go screw herself.

Anger and fear propelled her out of the back office into the store, where she stopped only to zip Savannah into her snowsuit before stepping out into the cold. Standing on the sidewalk, contemplating her next move, she realized her hands were shaking. What if she couldn't find a job in Vermont that paid enough for her and Savannah to live there? Maybe she should've listened to her parents. The possibility of having to return home with her tail between her legs after proving them right about her inability to take care of herself and her daughter made Dani feel sick.

Of course, the minute they were outside, Savannah finally stopped crying.

From across the street, she saw Lucas coming toward her, and her heart gave a happy leap at the sight of his friendly, familiar face.

"Hey." He took the car seat from her. "How'd it go?"

"The first one was okay except for the part where they decided not to fill the position after all. The second one was a disaster."

He winced. "How so?"

"Savannah decided to have a meltdown, which led to the lady telling me she didn't think we were a good fit."

"Seriously? She can't do that because you have a baby."

"Actually, she can do it because I brought a fussy baby to the interview, and I don't blame her for that. But I asked myself if I wanted to work for someone who has no empathy for working mothers, and the answer to that is a big, fat no."

"Good for you."

"It felt good to walk out of there. Once I was outside, however, I was smacked in the face with the cold and a big dose of reality. Two interviews, and I still don't have a job."

"I talked to my dad while you were interviewing. He said he's looking forward to meeting with you about the warehouse manager position."

"Really?"

"Really."

Dani immediately felt better knowing that.

"And I have other good news. Your car is dented but otherwise seems okay."

"Oh, that is great news. What a relief."

"The guy at the garage said you did a hell of a job wedging the car into the ditch, but they were able to get it out. We can pick it up anytime."

"Thank you for doing that. And for everything else, too. I suppose I should look around in town for a place to stay tonight so you can get back to your plans."

"You're more than welcome to spend another night with me. It's been nice to have the company."

She twisted her lips into an adorable expression as she gave that some thought. "I don't want to impose."

"You're not. I invited you."

"Are you *sure*? Please don't feel obligated. I'll figure something out."

"It's fine. Really. Let's go get your car and get Savannah out of the cold."

Dani walked with him across the street, where he secured the car seat into his truck like an old pro. She settled the baby into the seat, giving her a kiss on the cheek, which felt warm under her lips. Resting her hand on the baby's forehead, she realized the rest of her was warm, too. *Oh no.*

"Is she okay?" Lucas had turned around in his seat to check on them.

"She's warm, and she was super fussy just now, which isn't like her."

"Let's pick up your car and get her home."

Dani got into the passenger seat and put on her seat belt. It was amazing how quickly the disastrous interview ceased to matter when it was possible that Savannah might be sick. Her belly clenched with fear. What had she been thinking leaving the place where Savannah's pediatrician had been hers, too, and she could call for a same-day appointment if needed?

Lucas reached over to place his hand on top of hers, which were clenched tightly together. "Try not to panic. My brother's son Caden got fevers when he was teething. That might be all it is."

"She's young to get teeth." Dani tried not to dwell overly much on how comforting it was to have his large, warm hand covering her freezing fingers.

"He was, too. Started right around two months for him."

"Really?"

"Uh-huh. Caden is advanced. We think he's going to be a rocket scientist."

Dani laughed at that, but hearing his nephew had started teething early helped to ease her anxiety. Hopefully, that's all it was. "How old is he now?"

"He was born November twenty-fifth."

"Oh my God! So was Savannah! They have the same birthday!"

He smiled at her. "That's so cool."

"Which one of your siblings does he belong to?"

"Max, the youngest, if you can believe that. He finally did something first. My sister Hannah's baby, Callie, was born a few weeks after Caden, and there are at least three more on the way that we know of—Will and Cam, Hunter and Megan, and Ella and Gavin are all expecting."

"Wow, that's a baby boom."

"Yep, but that's what happens when your parents have ten kids, I guess."

"I have my hands full with one."

"Not to mention two sets of twins in the mix for my parents."

"I really can't wait to meet your mom."

"You'll like her. Everyone does."

"My mom used to be like yours—cool and fun and chill. But then I got pregnant and Jack died, and she just tried to take over my life. I needed that at first, I really did, but after Savannah was born, I started to snap out of it, only to find my mom was running my life the way she had when I was a teenager. And my dad was letting her because he was so upset about losing Jack and me being alone to raise our child, it was just easier to go along with her."

He took back his hand, and Dani immediately missed the warmth and the comfort. "You're doing the right thing. So your interviews didn't go well and Savvy might have a fever. You'll deal with it. You've got this."

"You called her Savvy."

"Did I?"

"I like it. No one has called her that. You're the first one to give her a nickname."

"I think she's going to be very *savvy*, just like her mama."

It had been, she thought, a very long time since anyone had thought she was savvy. Jack used to tell her she was clever and smart. He'd appreciated the way she found pieces of junk at yard sales and flea markets and turned them into things of beauty for their home.

Dani smiled at the memory of asking him for a corner of his precious garage to use for her projects and how he'd indulged her request and then expressed shock the first time he saw one of her finished projects. He'd called her "wildly talented," which had been one of the best compliments she'd ever received. Her plan had been to turn her hobby into a business while Savannah was little and eventually go back to work outside the home when she started school. That plan, like all her other plans, had died along with him.

Now she needed a job, and her artistic endeavors were on hold indefinitely.

Lucas took a right into the parking lot of the garage, where her car was parked out front. Dani immediately saw the dent running the length of the right side and the mangled front bumper.

"It could definitely be worse. When we get to Butler, I'll have my brother-in-law Nolan take a look at it. He's the go-to guy for bodywork. He'll have it looking good as new in no time, and he'll give you the family discount as a favor to me."

"I can't ask him to do that."

"You won't. I will. Don't sweat it. He'll be happy to help you out."

"You're very sweet to want to help me."

"It's no big deal." He put the truck in Park and released his seat belt. "I'll move Savvy's seat to your car."

She appreciated that he never suggested leaving her with him, probably because he knew she wouldn't. "That's okay. I have to run in and pay, so I can take her with me."

"I, ah, already paid them, so you're good to go." Before she could process that, he was out of the truck to remove Savannah's seat. "Let's go, sweet girl." He carried her to Dani's car and looked over his shoulder to see if she was coming.

Dani hit the unlock button on her key fob, got out of his truck and shut the passenger door. "You can't *pay* for my car."

"I knew you'd pay me back."

"How do you know that for sure?"

He finished buckling Savannah's seat into the car and then stood upright to face her. "I figured if you'd come all this way to keep from relying on your parents, you wouldn't want to overly rely on a new friend. It never occurred to me that you wouldn't pay me back."

"I will. As soon as we get back to the house."

"No rush."

"How do you know how to put in a car seat anyway? It took me weeks to get the hang of it."

"We run car seat clinics at the firehouse once a month. Most people have no idea how to do it. We make sure they're installed correctly so they can work the way they're supposed to."

"Oh. Well. Thanks. I, um, I guess I'll see you back at the house?"

"Follow me. I know a back way."

"Okay."

As Dani followed Lucas through winding back roads, she decided that spinning off the road into a ditch might turn out to be the best thing to happen to her in the months since Jack died. Right around the time the accident had happened last night, she'd run out of the outrage that had fueled her trip from Kentucky to Vermont. Exhausted after hours of driving and having to stop frequently to care for the baby, she'd been close to tears as the visibility dropped and the roads got slipperier by the minute. Who knew what might've become of them if Lucas hadn't found them in the ditch?

Her eyes filled with tears. After having run away from her overly involved parents, here she was relying on a stranger to help solve all her problems. What did that say about her ability to take care of herself? Not much, apparently, if she couldn't even take the time to check the damned weather forecast before heading to Vermont this time of year. If she'd only done that, none of this would've happened.

But then she wouldn't have met Lucas either, and that would've been unfortunate. A girl could never have too many friends, especially a girl on her own in a new place with a baby and a possibly misguided plan for their future.

She took a series of deep breaths, the way the counselor she'd seen after Jack's death had taught her to do when things got to be too much for her. Which was often. She'd done a lot of breathing in the last year, trying to stay calm, to avoid the panic attacks that frightened everyone around her, to be the mother Savannah needed her to be, to keep up a line of defense so her parents wouldn't make every decision for her.

Dani was exhausted from the effort it had taken to keep her head above water and to carry on without Jack. Her heart had been shattered, but Savannah had helped to tape it back together somewhat. Nothing would ever be the same, but she refused to give up, even on the days when the stress and heartache became almost too much to bear.

After a ten-minute ride, Dani followed Lucas into the driveway and parked next to him. Before she could get her seat belt off, Lucas had Savannah's seat out of the car and was carrying her and the diaper bag into the house for Dani. Gratitude filled her soul. People had been so incredibly nice to her since Jack died, especially her parents, who had to be frantic with worry even though she'd tried to reassure them when they called her after reading her letter.

She needed to call them and would as soon as she got Savannah settled.

"Thank you for carrying her," she said to Lucas.

"No problem. That basket is heavy."

"I know. I have bruises from it banging against the back of my leg."

"You're a heavy load, sweet Savvy," he said to the baby, who cooed in response to the handsome man giving her his undivided attention.

A shaft of pain to her chest made her gasp. Jack would never be able to give his daughter his undivided attention. He would've been such a marvelous father.

"You okay?" Lucas asked, gazing at her with concern.

"I'm fine, thanks," she said, shaking off the sadness the way she did so often these days. "Time to feed my little bean and get her down for a nap."

"While you do that, I'll make us some lunch."

"That'd be great."

Dani freed the baby from the car seat and removed her snowsuit. In the bedroom, she changed Savannah's diaper, gave her a dose of baby Tylenol for the slight fever and settled into a pile of pillows to feed her. She stroked the wispy strands of light blonde baby hair and ran a finger over a cheek so soft, it felt like cotton. Fortunately, she didn't seem as warm as she had earlier. "Your daddy would've loved you so much," Dani whispered. "So, so much."

The sadness hit at strange times, coming at her out of nowhere and leaving her flattened, sometimes for days. An event, such as the interviews gone wrong, that reminded her of the many ways her life had changed forever could trigger the sadness. Jack had insisted that she wouldn't have to work after the baby came. He said he would work overtime if he had to so she could be home with the baby.

As soon as they found out she was pregnant, he'd made her the beneficiary on his life insurance at work, which she hadn't known until after he died and his company had notified her. That money was her lifeline, and knowing Jack had seen to that prescient detail had meant everything to her in the midst of unrelenting grief.

After Savannah was born, the blues had only intensified. Other than feeding Savannah and tending to her during the endless nights, Dani spent a lot of time in bed, weeping for her lost love and everything he would miss with their baby.

She didn't need her mother or Les or anyone else to tell her that lying in bed crying wasn't healthy for her or her child. In fact, if one more person tried to tell her what was best for Savannah, Dani might be tempted to punch them. They meant well, but she knew what was best for her child. It was up to her to make sure Savannah got the best of everything. And she would see to that, even if she ached on the inside.

When she'd surfaced from the worst of the grief, she'd made the decision to leave Kentucky, hoping to make a life for herself and her child far away from the painful memories and her parents' unrelenting need to fix that which could not be fixed.

Soon it would be one year since the day that had changed everything, and Dani continued to believe that shaking things up was the best thing for her and her child. She would feel better, however, once she landed a job, found the best possible childcare for Savannah and secured a place for the two of them to live.

CHAPTER 8

"All love that has not friendship for its base,
is like a mansion built upon the sand."
—Ella Wheeler Wilcox

When she finished feeding Savannah, she carefully transferred the baby to the bed, propping her up with a blanket to keep her in position. She was too young to roll over on her own, but Dani wasn't taking any chances. While she waited for Savannah to fall asleep, she wrote a check to Lucas to reimburse him.

Only when she was certain the baby was fully asleep did she leave the room, leaving the door open so she could hear if Savannah awakened. Most of the time, she slept for at least two hours at this time of day. Dani went into the kitchen, where Lucas was putting the finishing touches on two sandwiches.

He put handfuls of chips on each plate and pushed hers across the island to her and then filled glasses of ice water for both of them before joining her on the stool next to hers.

"This looks great," she said.

"One thing I can 'cook' is a sandwich."

Dani laughed at the silly comment. "And frozen pizza."

"That's one of my specialties. When I'm home, I like to doctor them up with all kinds of extra stuff."

"Like what?" Dani asked between bites of ham and cheese.

"Onions, for one thing. They make everything better. Extra cheese is a must. Fresh veggies and meat. Lots and lots of meat."

"In other words, you take the concept of supreme to a whole new level."

"Yep."

She put the check on the countertop next to his plate. "Thanks for fronting me on the car. I left the amount for you to fill in."

He tucked the check into his shirt pocket. "No problem, and it was two hundred."

"You should take off and go skiing. We'll be fine here by ourselves. I hate to think that we totally derailed your plans."

"It's fine, really. Skiing was an excuse to get out of town. I can ski anytime right in Butler."

"Are you feeling better about things with your brother and the Amanda situation?"

His smile lit up his golden-brown eyes. "I like that. 'The Amanda situation.' And yes, I do feel better. What you said, what my grandfather said, about my brother being more important than a woman we both just met is very true. She's a nice person, but he's my brother. End of story."

"For what it's worth, I think that's the right way to think. I would've given anything for a brother *or* a sister growing up. It must be awesome to have nine of them—and eight close cousins."

"It is, most of the time. My parents were forever telling us that our siblings and cousins were our best friends. They wouldn't have been happy about me getting mad with Landon over a woman."

"I'm sure they'd understand if they knew you both liked her."

"Oh, they know. Somehow, they know everything."

Dani laughed. "I suppose they'd have to in order to stay ahead of ten kids."

"I want to have a big family like they did." A second after he said the words, he clapped a hand over his mouth. "I've never said that out loud before."

Though his words were muffled by his hand, she had no trouble hearing them. "You want, like, *ten* kids?"

"Maybe not ten, but at least six. I think. I really love being an uncle, and I think I'll enjoy fatherhood."

"Six kids. *Whoa.*"

"Or seven," he said, winking and smiling.

"I can picture that for you. A man who'd think nothing of taking in a strange woman and her child when he was supposed to be spending time alone and skiing would make a good father."

"You really think so?" he asked, looking and sounding madly vulnerable.

Dear God, the man was *adorable.* "Yes, I really do. Why wouldn't you think so?"

He fiddled with the plate, spinning it in a slow circle. "I'm sort of known as a clown, I guess you could say. Landon and I… We never miss a chance to go for the laugh."

"Nothing wrong with keeping people entertained."

"No, there isn't. It's just… That's not *all* I am, you know?"

"Ah, yeah, I definitely know that. You rescued me, remember?"

Waving his hand, he said, "That's nothing. I do that stuff all the time."

Dani wasn't sure what made her do it, but she reached for the hand he'd waved and wrapped hers around it. "You may do it all the time, but that was the first time I've ever needed that kind of rescuing, and you were kind, caring, compassionate, competent and incredibly supportive of a single mom and her child when we desperately needed help. Those are all special and important qualities in anyone, especially a father of six—or seven—kids."

Lucas smiled and gave her hand a squeeze.

Dani's heart did a weird little lurch when she realized she was staring at Lucas and holding his hand.

He directed his glance at their joined hands. "Thank you for that."

"I meant every word. You may have a fun and funny personality, but you know when to be serious and how to stay calm in an emergency. To me, that sounds like the definition of a responsible adult. You're not giving yourself enough credit."

"Probably not. But I want people, especially the people who matter most to me, to take me more seriously."

"That's an admirable goal, but you can't stop being you. You can still be fun and funny and be an adult, too."

"I suppose so."

Dani gave his hand a squeeze and then removed hers from his grip, feeling self-conscious about touching a man who wasn't Jack. She'd never touched any man who wasn't Jack. They'd been together since her sophomore year of high school, which had been his senior year. Even while they were in different colleges, they'd stayed together. Theirs had been a forever kind of love, until he was gone and she'd been left to figure out how to go on without him.

She folded her arms, giving herself a little hug. Someday she would have to do a whole lot more than touch another man, but for today, holding Lucas's hand had been enough for her.

"So what do you like to do when you're not running away from home?" he asked.

Smiling at his choice of words, she said, "I used to love to read romance novels. I devoured them, three or four a week even when I worked full time."

"Past tense?"

She shrugged. "Romance novels are known for their happy endings. I found out that not all endings are happy, and now I can't bear to read them anymore." Before he could form a reply, she continued. "I also like to restore furniture that I find at yard sales and flea markets. I had a nice little hobby going that I hoped to turn into a business, but that, too, kinda fell to the wayside in the last year or so."

"Since you lost Jack?"

"Yeah. It's hard to be creative when you're heartbroken."

"I imagine so. I'm into woodworking, so we have that in common."

"What kind of woodworking?"

"I make furniture mostly—beds, cribs, cradles, dressers, hope chests—as well as kitschy stuff like wooden moose and ornaments of moose, the state of Vermont, a maple syrup bottle. That kind of stuff. We sell it all in the store."

"I can't wait to see your work."

"I can't wait to show you. If you end up staying in Butler, I can 'lease' you a corner of my shop for your refinishing business, if you want."

"That's nice of you to offer, but I'm not sure I'll have time for that with a baby to care for. Single parenthood doesn't allow much time for anything else."

"She won't be a baby forever. The offer stands."

"Thank you."

"You feel like watching a movie?"

"Sure, that'd be fun. But first… I really need to call my parents. Would that be all right?"

"Of course. Go right ahead. There should be an extension in the bedroom if you want some privacy."

"I'll just check on Savannah and then call from out here so I don't bother her."

"Sounds good."

He got up and started collecting their plates, loading them into the dishwasher.

Dani went into the bedroom to look in on Savannah, who was right where she'd left her.

When she returned to the kitchen, Lucas was wiping down the counter. His back was to her, which allowed her a longer look at his broad shoulders, tapered waist, muscular legs and backside. He certainly was beautiful to look at, and if things had been different for her, she might've been attracted to him.

But that wasn't an option. Not now anyway. Not with her life in an uproar, her heart still broken and a child depending on her for everything.

"All yours," Lucas said of the kitchen as he moved to the family room and turned on the TV.

Dani watched him sit on the sofa and stretch his long legs onto the coffee table as he flipped through the channels. She licked lips that'd gone dry and reached for the phone, forcing herself to punch in the familiar number before she lost her nerve.

Her mother answered on the first ring. "Hello?"

"It's me."

"Dani," her mother said on a long exhale. "Why haven't you answered my texts?"

"Because there's hardly any cell service up here. Didn't Les tell you I called her last night?"

"She did." Two little words that said it all. Her mother was pissed that Dani hadn't called her.

"I'm sorry if you were worried. Everything is fine. I had two interviews today in Stowe, and I have another one the day after tomorrow in Butler."

"Dani, listen to me. There's no need for you to move hundreds of miles away."

"I've already moved, Mom."

A sniffling sound came through the phone. "I don't know why you're doing this to us."

"I'm doing it for me, and for Savannah. We need a fresh start."

"You'll have no support there."

Dani glanced at Lucas and his big feet, encased in rag wool socks. He was running his fingers through his thick dirty-blond hair as he watched a home renovation show. "I'll make friends and figure things out."

"We're worried about you—and Savannah. A few weeks ago, you couldn't get out of bed, and now you live in Vermont?"

"I know it's hard for you to understand, but the reason I didn't have to get out of bed was because I knew you and Dad and Aunt Ellen were there to take care of me. I'm never going to get back on my feet again if I let other people do everything for me and Savannah." They'd already had this conversation, easily a dozen times, but they would keep having it until her parents understood why she'd had to leave.

"You're going to let strangers take care of your child while you're working? That's better than your own family?"

"Of course not, but other working mothers pay for childcare. There's no reason why I can't do that, too."

"You don't have to!"

Dani closed her eyes, trying to contain the tears that would've spilled down her cheeks. She'd cried enough for one lifetime. She didn't want to cry anymore. "This is what I want, Mom, and I hope you can accept my decision. I'm sorry if it's not what you want for me. I'm not doing this to hurt you. I'm doing it because I need to. For me."

Her mother was silent for a long time, so long that Dani wondered if she'd hung up.

"I won't pretend to understand what you've been through—"

"I hope you never know that kind of pain."

"It broke our hearts to lose Jack, Dani. You know we loved him like a son. And to watch you suffer the way you have…"

"I know, Mama." Dani closed her eyes, hoping to contain the tears. "I'm not doing this to hurt you. I swear I'm not. It's just what I need right now. We had such good times here with Nana and Papa. I was happy here. Maybe I will be again."

"You have to call me every day or two, or I'll worry."

"Trust me on that," Dani's dad said. "And she'll drive me mad worrying about you."

Dani laughed through her tears. She should've known he'd be listening in. "Hi, Daddy."

"Hi, sweetheart. It's good to hear your voice."

"Yours, too."

"How's Savannah?"

"She's great. She was a trouper in the car."

"You'll send lots of pictures?" her mom asked.

"Every day, and we'll FaceTime all the time. And once we're settled, you guys can come visit."

"That sounds good," her mom said. "We'd love to visit."

"We'll make that happen soon. Try not to worry. Everything will be all right." As she reassured them, she only hoped it was true. If they ever found out about how she'd landed in a ditch on her first night in Vermont, they'd freak out.

"We love you girls," her dad said.

"Love you, too. I'll call in a day or two."

"We'll look forward to hearing from you," her mom said.

Dani pressed the button to end the call, feeling relieved that she had smoothed things over with them. She'd hated leaving when they were at odds. But she'd feared if she didn't go then, she might not go at all, and that hadn't been an option. This was the best thing she could've done for herself and Savannah. Maybe if she kept telling herself that, she'd start to believe it.

Lucas came into the kitchen, his hair standing on end after running his fingers through it. Even a little disheveled, he was still beautiful to look at. Dani felt a pang of distress at realizing she was somewhat attracted to him. How could that be? Panic gripped her, making her chest feel tight and restricted.

"Dani? Are you okay?"

She forced a nod and took a deep breath.

"And your folks? Everything good there?"

Swallowing the lump that had planted itself in her throat, Dani said, "It will be. Eventually."

"That's good. Nothing worse than family drama. Sucks the life out of you."

"Yes, it certainly does."

It helped that he understood, that he was close to his family like she'd always been to hers. "They only want the best for me and Savannah."

He filled his glass with ice and water from the door of the fridge. "Sounds like they're great parents."

"They are. I don't know how I would've survived... every-thing... without them."

"You'll want to get a landline as soon as you're settled so you can keep in touch."

"How do you people *live* without cell phones?"

Lucas shrugged. "You don't miss what you've never had."

"I may go into convulsions without mine. Do you know the emergency protocol for cell phone depravation convulsions?"

His lips quivered with amusement. "There's a whole section on that in the manual. We treat it a lot in my corner of Vermont, where the only reliable cell service is on my brother Colton's mountain."

"Your brother has a mountain?"

Laughing, Lucas said, "Well, it's not his technically, but don't tell him that. He's lived up there for years now, running the family sugaring facility."

"What's a sugaring facility?"

He feigned horror. "How can you not know that's how maple syrup is made?"

"Oh, okay. I see."

"No, you don't, but I'll show you while you're in Butler. It's something you need to see."

Dani wasn't so sure about that, but she took his word for it. She realized she was looking at him the way a normal young woman would look at a sweet, handsome, sexy man. And after talking to him for a minute, she felt calmer. More settled.

Only one other person had ever had that effect on her.

Dani swallowed hard. She was venturing into dangerous territory when it came to her sexy rescuer and that couldn't happen. It just couldn't.

CHAPTER 9

"You can't blame gravity for falling in love."
—Albert Einstein

She's so beautiful. Every time Lucas glanced at Dani, that was his first thought. With the sun streaming in the window, her reddish-blonde hair glowed with highlights in both shades. When he'd entered the room, he'd seen the remnants of tears in her soft hazel eyes and had wanted to console her. Whatever it took to make her smile again, a thought he hadn't had before about a woman who wasn't one of his sisters or cousins.

It pained him that she'd obviously suffered so much over the loss of her fiancé and her decision to leave home to find a new life in Vermont. Other than the devastating loss of his brother-in-law, Caleb, in Iraq, Lucas hadn't experienced anything remotely close to what she had and wanted to know the details. However, he still didn't feel he had the right to ask, and the last thing he wanted to do was upset her any further.

"Not sure what you think of *My Best Friend's Wedding*," he said, "but it's coming on in five minutes."

"I love that movie. Doesn't everyone?"

He made a face. "Um, not *everyone*…"

She laughed, and he wanted to wallow in that sound. He wanted to make it happen over and over again until she forgot she was supposed to be sad. Why he wanted that so badly was something he'd have to think about later, when he had time to ponder the extraordinary last twenty-four hours.

As they moved into the living room to watch the dreaded chick flick, Lucas thought about something his dad had said many times over the years—the day he'd met their mother, he had known, almost immediately, that she would change his life. Not that Lucas thought anything like that would happen to him. Still, he couldn't deny that he'd felt… different… since he'd first encountered Dani and Savvy the night before. He couldn't articulate what was different, but something was.

Not that he could allow himself to go "there" with Dani when she was dealing with so many other things. She'd lost her fiancé and the father of her child tragically, and now she was trying to establish a whole new life for herself and her daughter. This was no time to have a guy sniffing around, not that he would sniff, per se, but he had noticed she smelled incredibly good.

He'd have to be dead not to notice the scent that followed her around like a cloud of sweetness.

"Have you seen this before?" she asked.

Lucas was so deep inside his own thoughts that he had to remind himself they were watching a movie. "Unfortunately, yes. My sisters love everything about it, but then, they also love *The Bachelor*."

"I've seen every season of *The Bachelor* and *The Bachelorette*."

Lucas rolled his lip in distaste. "Ewww. Not you, too."

"'Fraid so. I'm addicted to the train-wreck element of it."

"How is that entertaining?"

"Watching women catfight over a guy who is dating all of them at the same time? It's nonstop entertainment. I always wonder what happens to them when they try to go back to their real lives as office managers, or whatever they do, after having behaved that way on national TV."

"That would make for a good reality show. *Rejoining My Life After I Made an Ass of Myself on National TV.*"

She laughed, and again, he wanted to wallow in the sound because he sensed that she hadn't had much to laugh about recently. "I would so watch that. Like, are the guys in her town suddenly more interested because she was willing to catfight other women on TV?"

"I wouldn't be."

"But you know there are guys who'd be all kinds of attracted to that."

"I just can't imagine that. I hate drama of any kind and would avoid that like the plague."

"That's why the situation with Landon and Amanda was so upsetting to you. You're not used to that kind of thing."

"No, I'm not, and I have no clue how to deal with it."

"Yes, you do. You took yourself out of the situation, which is one way of dealing with it."

"I guess that's true."

"I think you were very wise to do that. The last thing you want is trouble with your brother, so you walked away. It takes a big person to realize trouble is brewing and to step away from it before it gets out of hand. I wish I'd done that with my parents."

"How do you mean?"

"I realized months ago I had ceded everything to them after Jack died. My mom was even paying my bills and organizing

Savannah's pediatrician appointments, and I let her because it was easier than doing it myself."

"You were devastated. It's only natural to let people help you at times like that."

"For a while, yes, but months of that?" She shook her head. "I never should've let it go that far."

"You went through an awful thing, and there's probably no sense critiquing how you handled it. I think it's amazing you could see the problem through the haze of grief."

"After a while, the haze cleared a bit, and I didn't like what I saw. I had worked really hard to separate myself from my parents after Jack and I moved in together, and it was like none of that progress had happened. I was right back to being sixteen again and firmly under their thumbs, not making any decisions for myself or my child."

"Then you did the right thing by making a change."

"I hope so." She rolled the right side of her bottom lip between her teeth. "Part of me agrees with them. It was insane to move away from my entire support network."

Lucas tried not to stare at the way she worked that poor lip, but he found himself fascinated. "You'll get a new support network, one that doesn't tell you what to do or how to do it."

"They mean well. I don't want you to think they're bad people. They're not."

"Say no more. I get it. I have parents, too. Mine like to know what we're up to and aren't afraid to speak up if they see us going in the wrong direction. But they're not out to live our lives for us."

"That must be nice. I love my mom, I really do. She's awesome, but she had five miscarriages before she had me. I'm like the miracle baby she thought she'd never have. Letting go now that I'm an adult has been hard for her."

"Wow, *five* miscarriages."

"I know. It was a nightmare, from what I was told, not that they ever said much about it. I heard most of it from my aunts and grandmother. My mother doesn't talk about it at all."

"That had to be so incredibly painful."

"I can't imagine what she went through, so I try to give her a lot of space when she needs to hover."

"Which is good of you to do."

Lucas couldn't believe how much of the movie they'd missed by talking—and he noted how easy she was to talk to. That had been one of the things he'd liked about spending time with Amanda. The conversation had flowed effortlessly with her, but talking to Dani was even better for some reason. Maybe because his brother wasn't also in the mix—not that there was a mix with Dani.

Watching her sing along to "Say a Little Prayer," he realized in a moment of clarity that he truly liked her.

Dani's cell phone rang, startling them. "I thought I didn't have service here."

"You never know from one minute to the next."

She took the call. "Oh, hi," she said, giving Lucas a side-eyed look. "I'm so sorry she was disruptive. That's not like her. I think she's teething, but of course that's not why you called."

Lucas turned down the TV and smiled at the grimace she sent his way.

"Really? That's really nice of you. There's no need to apologize. I know it wasn't ideal to bring a baby to an interview." She listened for another few minutes, her brows furrowing in concentration.

She's beautiful, Lucas thought once again, his heart doing something weird that made him lightheaded and slightly uncomfortable. Was the woman on the phone offering her a job? If so, why did the idea of her living and working ninety minutes from him make him feel unsettled? What the hell was wrong with him? This time yesterday, he hadn't even known she existed, and now…

Now, what?

He didn't know, and that made him anxious as she ended the call.

"That was the lady from the ski shop, apologizing for the way our interview ended and offering me a job if I'm still interested."

"That's cool. Do you suppose she consulted with legal counsel and found out she has to be really careful dismissing a mom because of her child?"

Dani's eyes widened with shock. "Oh my God, do you think that's what happened?"

Lucas immediately regretted his flippant comment. "Of course not. She probably realized how lucky she'd be to have you. I doubt they even have legal counsel."

"Hmm, I think you may be right about the legal counsel, but it's nice to have an offer on the table."

"You're, um, still coming to Butler to interview at our store, right?"

"Absolutely. I'm super excited to see it."

"Oh, good," he said, filled with unreasonable relief.

He would have more time to get to know her and hopefully figure out why the thought of never seeing her or Savannah again filled him with anxiety the likes of which he'd never before experienced.

The next morning, Dani loaded the baby into the backseat of her car for the ninety-minute ride to Butler. She'd timed the departure to coincide with the baby's morning nap time and hoped she'd sleep most of the way. Savannah had a full belly and a clean diaper, so they should be good to go.

Yesterday after the baby's nap, the three of them had taken a ride over to check out her grandparents' former home, which had been just as Dani remembered it. The house had been sold after they passed away, and Dani had been happy to see kids playing on the tire swing her grandfather had hung for her. After that, Dani had insisted on treating Lucas to dinner at a local restaurant to thank him for all his help.

Lucas pulled his navy truck out of the driveway and waited for her so she could follow him to Butler. The sides of his truck were nearly white from the salt and sludge of a Vermont winter. He'd joked the day before that between winter and spring mud season, he saw the true color of the truck only about three months a year.

Speaking of true colors, she'd certainly seen his in the last two days. What a great guy he'd turned out to be and how lucky she was to have met him, even if the circumstances had been less than ideal. Since Jack died, there'd been times when she seemed to have exactly what she needed when she needed it, giving her reason to believe he'd stayed close to her in the afterlife, continuing to care for her the way he had when he was alive.

The thought, as it always did, made her teary-eyed. It would be just like him to want to stay close, to make sure she was okay, and it gave her great joy to think that maybe he could see the beautiful daughter they'd created together. She looked up at the mirror where she could see Savannah's face, her eyes heavy with sleep. "God, I hope he is watching over you, sweet baby."

Dani sniffled and dabbed at the tears that still came with startling frequency, making her wonder if there would come a time when she would simply run out of tears. If so, she must be getting close to her quota.

Rather than dwell on the past, she tried to stay focused on the present—on the bright, sunny day, the gorgeous scenery, the little girl in the backseat and the new friend leading the way to a place she'd never been before but couldn't wait to see.

On the drive from Kentucky to Vermont, her thoughts had been full of Jack and memories of their life together. But now, as she followed Lucas to Butler, she found herself thinking of him, of the time they'd spent together in Stowe and the immediate friendship they'd established. In addition to being fun, funny and easy to talk to, the man was drop-dead gorgeous to look at. Though she felt guilty for having such a thought about another man, Dani was wise enough to know that eventually, she would meet someone who made her want to take a second chance on love. Certainly not now or anytime soon, but someday.

The possibility of one of them dying had been so remote as to be impossible to imagine before tragedy struck with swift and sudden finality. They'd never discussed what one would do without the other. But she had to believe that Jack wouldn't want her to spend the rest of her life alone, mourning for him and what had been lost for them, as well as their daughter.

She hoped he would want her to find someone to love, someone who could be a father to Savannah while also honoring the man who had given her life. It would be a tall order for any man, but Dani wouldn't settle for less than what she'd had with Jack. She knew what true love felt like and would hold out until she found that again. Being a single mom didn't intimidate her, nor did the idea of being alone. She'd rather be alone than be with the wrong person. Several of her friends had settled for men who were convenient and had ended up unhappy as a result.

After having had the real thing, Dani couldn't imagine settling for less.

The ride passed quickly, with so much breathtaking scenery to take in as she went. She saw pine and aspen trees coated with snow, picturesque little towns, winding roads, frozen rivers, places she now knew were called sugaring facilities and barns of all shapes and sizes dotting the landscape.

From the time she'd first come to Vermont as a small child, she'd absolutely loved it and had even asked Jack if he'd ever consider relocating. But with both their families close by and a baby on the way, she'd agreed with him that moving away would be silly. But Dani had continued to dream about the place she'd once loved so much, and now she was here with the possibility of a whole new life standing before her.

They finally entered the town of Butler, which was nothing but more winding roads at first. Then the town itself came into view, and Dani took in the sight of the adorable shops, restaurants and cafés. In the middle of it all was the Green Mountain Country Store and the Butler Inn. Lucas signaled to take a right turn into the parking lot behind the store.

Dani followed him and parked next to him, glancing in the mirror to see that Savannah was still asleep. She got out of the car and stretched muscles stiff from far too much time in the car over the last few days. "This town is awesome," she told Lucas when he joined her outside her car.

"We like it."

"I can see why."

He tipped his head to see inside the backseat. "Your little passenger is still sacked out."

"She probably will be for a while longer." Dani eyed the big white building next to the store. "I should go see about a room."

"I'll carry her for you if you'd like."

"Oh, thank you. I'm sure you have other stuff to do, though."

"I'm off until tomorrow, so I don't mind helping you get settled."

"You've been so great. I'll never be able to thank you enough."

"I enjoyed the company. No need to thank me."

"Then I'll just say I'm glad it was you who found us and kept us safe."

"That was entirely my pleasure." He gave her a small smile that didn't reach his golden-brown eyes. She wondered if he felt as sad as she did at the thought of not seeing each other again after they went their separate ways. Although, if she ended up working for his family's business, they would probably see each other again. Or so she hoped.

Lucas deftly removed Savannah's seat from the backseat of Dani's car and carried it as they walked toward the inn.

"I hope they have rooms." She should've taken care of lodging before she set out, but she'd been so hell-bent on leaving before her parents got home from a night out with friends, that she hadn't taken the time to do proper preparations.

Lucas held the back door of the Butler Inn for her and led the way to the front desk, where an older woman was working.

"Hi, Mrs. Hendricks."

She eyed him carefully. "Hello, Landon."

He shook his head. "Lucas."

"Darn, I thought I had it right this time. I'm sorry."

"No problem. Happens every day. This is my friend Dani and her daughter, Savannah. Dani is looking for a room."

"Oh, honey, we're completely sold out through the weekend."

Dani's stomach sank. "Is there anything else nearby?"

"I can call over to a few places in St. Johnsbury, but it's tough this time of year with the mountain open for skiing. I doubt they have anything either."

"That's okay, but thanks for the offer." Lucas hoisted Savannah's seat from the counter. "We'll figure something out. Thanks, Mrs. H."

"Sorry I couldn't help, but check back after the weekend. I should have some rooms open up early next week."

"Will do, thanks again." With his hand on Dani's lower back, he guided her toward the back of the inn.

"What am I going to do now?" she asked.

"My mom and dad have a barn with seven bedrooms, and only my brother Max and his son live at home. They'd be happy to have you."

"I can't stay with your parents, Lucas. I'm here to interview with your dad."

He'd hoped she might feel that way. "There's an extra room at my place, too. It's all yours if you want it."

"I suck at this," she said, looking and sounding dejected.

"At what?"

"Being independent. Running away from home to find a life of my own. If I hadn't been rescued by you, Savannah and I would've frozen to death in Stowe. They would've found our bodies in a week and had to defrost us."

Lucas brushed his free hand over his mouth, clearly trying not to laugh. "You would've figured something out."

"*What* would I have figured out? Vermont isn't like where I'm from where there's a chain hotel on every corner and no way this ever could've happened. I didn't even take the time to figure out where we would stay before getting in the car and heading north. Who does that with an infant? What kind of mother am I?"

"You're a great mom trying to do the right thing for yourself and your child. Maybe you didn't plan it as well as you could have, but you haven't been to Vermont since you were a kid. How were you supposed to know there's not a chain hotel on every other street corner?"

"I should've taken care of lodging before I left."

Lucas stopped walking and turned to her. "If you'd taken the time to check, you would've learned that everything was full during ski season. You wouldn't have come, Dani. You wouldn't have made the change you needed for yourself and Savvy."

When he put it that way, her lack of proper planning seemed fated.

"You and Savvy can come home with me and stay for as long as you need to. I've got a spare bedroom, plenty of space, and I'd be happy to have you, so no more fretting, okay?"

Savannah chose that moment to wake, coming to life with an indignant wail that meant a wet diaper and an empty belly. "I need to change and feed her."

"Come with me. I'll set you right up." He led the way across the parking lot, where she stopped to grab the baby's diaper bag from her car, and into the Green Mountain Country Store.

Dani wanted to stop to look at everything she saw, but Savannah wasn't having it. Her cries were getting louder and more furious by the second. Dani followed Lucas up a long flight of stairs to the second floor, where they encountered a reception area.

"Hi, Emma," he said to a pretty blonde woman at the desk.

Emma eyed him closely before she replied, "Hey, Lucas."

"This is my friend Dani and her daughter, Savannah. Could she borrow the conference room for a few minutes?"

"Sure. There's nothing scheduled in there until later this afternoon."

"Great, thanks." He gestured for Dani to lead the way toward a closed door on the far side of the lobby.

"Will this work?" he asked.

"This is perfect. Thank you for solving all my problems."

He grinned. "My pleasure. I'll be out there. Come find me when you're ready for some lunch." Winking, he added, "I know a place."

Dani's stomach growled loudly, making him laugh.

"Well, that was mortifying."

"Nah, you girls are ready for lunch, and so am I. Take your time. I've got nowhere to be."

"Thank you, Lucas. Seriously. You're the best."

"No worries."

He closed the door behind him, and Dani got busy freeing the baby from the car seat and the lightweight blanket she'd wrapped her in for the ride because she would've been too warm in her snowsuit. These were the things she had to think about now that she was a mother with a child depending on her to know what was best.

"What do you think is best for us?" she asked the baby as she put the blanket on the table to change her wet diaper. "Should we stay with Lucas for a little while longer?"

Savannah cooed and gurgled, which Dani took as approval.

As she brought the baby to her breast and felt her latch on eagerly, Dani gave silent thanks for the man who had been so good to both of them. Since she lost Jack, she'd had ample reason to feel spectacularly unlucky. But perhaps her luck had changed on that snowy night in Stowe when her car went off the road and led her to a new friend.

CHAPTER 10

*"Old friends pass away, new friends appear. It is just like the days.
An old day passes, a new day arrives."*
—Dalai Lama

Lucas exited the conference room and returned to the reception area, taking a seat in one of the chairs that were there more for show than actual use. "Where is everyone?" he asked Emma as he stretched his legs out in front of him, glad to be out of the truck after the long ride.

"Ella and Charley are at lunch. Your dad, Hunter, Will and Wade are over at the warehouse." Emma glanced at the closed door to the conference room. "You have a new friend?"

"She was in an accident in Stowe that I witnessed. I helped her out."

"Wow. She was so lucky to have someone with your training right there when she needed help."

"Yeah, it worked out well. She's interviewing here tomorrow."

"For the warehouse manager job?"

"Yep."

"Oh, cool. They're eager to get someone in that position. Charley and Ella have been handling most of it on top of their regular jobs."

"Dani would be great. She has a degree in retail management and lots of experience."

"Where's she from?"

"Kentucky."

"She's a long way from home."

"Uh-huh. How's Grayson?" Lucas asked of his cousin, looking to steer the conversation away from Dani.

Emma's pretty face flushed with color. "He's great. Wonderful, in fact."

Lucas rolled his eyes, as he knew she expected him to.

"What?" Emma asked, laughing. "He's great *and* wonderful."

His cousin was a good guy—one of the best—and Lucas was thrilled that he and Emma had found each other. "How does Simone like Vermont?" he asked of Emma's daughter.

"She loves it. Colton has been teaching her how to ski, and she's taken to it like a natural." Colton would become Simone's uncle when he married Lucy in May.

"That's great. Glad it's working out so well for you guys."

"It is. We love it here. Moving to Vermont was the best thing we ever did."

Lucas glanced at the conference room. "Maybe you can tell Dani that if you get the chance."

"Sure, I'd be happy to. Of course, I had a very *enticing* reason to move to Vermont."

Lucas scowled at her. "You're not allowed to refer to my cousin as enticing."

Emma laughed. "He's *extremely* enticing."

"Stop it. Right now."

They were still laughing when Dani emerged from the conference room, carrying Savannah in one arm, the car seat and diaper bag hooked over the other.

Lucas jumped up to relieve her of the seat and bag. "All set?"

"For now," she said, smiling up at him.

Lucas liked seeing her smile. That was so much better than the despair he'd felt coming from her when she learned the inn was sold out. "Emma and I were just talking about how she and her daughter, Simone, are recent transplants to Vermont."

"We love it," Emma said. "If you ever need someone to talk to about pediatricians, dentists, childcare and all that, I'd be happy to help."

"That'd be amazing. I'll definitely take you up on that if we end up staying in Butler."

Emma smiled warmly. "I hope you do."

"We're going to hit the diner," Lucas said to Emma. "Can we bring you something?"

"No, thanks. Grayson made me a delicious lunch that I can't wait to eat. He's the best."

Lucas wrinkled his nose and left her laughing as he escorted Dani down the stairs. "Emma and her daughter live with my cousin Grayson," Lucas reminded her. "They're ridiculously happy together, as is her sister Lucy and my brother Colton. Their dad, Ray, is the one who is seeing my aunt Hannah."

"Wow, that's a lot of family cross-pollination."

"It's all because Will met Cameron. And Cameron's dad, Patrick, is now traveling the world with our former office manager, Mary."

"All that came from one person's decision to take a job out of state," Dani said, amazed.

"I know. It's crazy."

"It's really awesome."

"They're all super happy. Will and Cam have a baby on the way. Lucy and Colton are getting married in May. And I'm sure Emma and Grayson won't be far behind them."

"How does Grayson get along with Emma's daughter?"

"They're crazy about each other. Simone's father has never been part of the picture, so Grayson is like the first dad she's ever had. They're super cute together."

"That's so sweet," she said, sounding wistful. "I hope I can find that for Savannah someday."

"I'm sure you will. Anyone would be lucky to be a dad to her."

She looked up at him, her eyes bright with unshed tears. "You really think so?"

"Of course I do. She's adorable, and I'm sure she's going to grow up to be a sweetheart just like her mom." As soon as Lucas said the words, he realized how revealing they were. He hadn't meant to tell her so much in one statement. And judging by the way she held his gaze, she was equally stunned.

"Um, let's cross." He led her to the crosswalk. "My sister-in-law Megan runs the diner. She's my brother Hunter's wife."

"I'll never be able to keep all the names straight."

"If you stick around, you'll have them all down before long." He hoped she decided to stay in Butler. He'd become invested in her and Savvy over the last few days and wanted to keep them close so he could continue to see them both.

They stepped into the lunchtime rush at the diner and headed for the one open booth in the back, which was unfortunately right next to the booth his sisters Ella and Charley were sharing.

"Ladies." They took a careful and extensive look at Dani. "Quit your gaping. This is Dani and her daughter, Savannah. These are my sisters Ella and Charley. Ella is the nice one."

"Oh, bite me," Charley shot back at him as she shook hands with Dani. "Nice to meet you. Where'd you pick up this one?" She used her thumb to point at Lucas.

"Actually, he picked me up—out of a ditch when my car spun out near Stowe."

"Oh my God," Ella said. "How scary with the baby in the car."

"I know. I was freaking out, and then Lucas was there, and everything was okay."

Her words had a strange effect on him, leaving him with an ache of longing. For what? He couldn't say, but for something.

"You were so lucky he was there," Charley said. "Despite their many other failings, Luc and Landon are first-rate paramedics and firefighters."

"Gee, thanks, Charl."

Charley laughed at his acerbic comment. "I mean it!"

"You don't have to convince me," Dani said. "I've seen the proof firsthand."

"You guys want to join us?" Ella asked.

"That's okay." Lucas nudged Dani toward the vacant booth. "We have some stuff to talk about, but you should know that Dani is interviewing with Dad about the warehouse manager job tomorrow."

"No way!" Ella said. "If he offers you the job, *please* say yes. We've been looking for someone for weeks now, and he hasn't found the right fit yet, or so he says."

"If he doesn't find the right fit soon, I'm gonna quit," Charley said.

"You can't quit the family business," Lucas said, knowing Charley was all talk as usual.

"Watch me. Doing one job is enough. Doing half of another job that requires me to interact with people is another thing altogether."

"She hates people," Lucas said for Dani's sake.

Dani giggled helplessly.

"No, she really does," Ella said, dead serious.

That only made Dani laugh harder.

Her delight at their foolishness filled Lucas with a feeling of elation at knowing, at least for this moment in time, she was happy. "Come on. Let's eat. I'm starving."

"It was nice to meet you both," Dani said.

"You, too," Ella said. "Really nice to meet you and your adorable little girl." She gave Lucas a meaningful look that he purposely ignored.

"When they said I hate people, that doesn't mean you," Charley added.

"Good to know," Dani said, leaving them with a smile as she slid into the booth across from Lucas. She had Savannah in her arms and gave her a toy to keep her entertained.

Megan came over with menus, stopping short when she realized Lucas was with someone she hadn't seen before.

"Dani, this is my sister-in-law Megan. Megan, this is Dani and Savannah."

"Oh hey, nice to meet you. Are you visiting?"

Dani nodded. "I'm interviewing at the store tomorrow."

"Welcome to Butler." Megan rattled off some specials and left them to peruse the menu.

"Are all the women here exceptionally beautiful, or just the ones you're related to?"

Lucas crinkled his nose. "Ella and Charley are *not* exceptionally beautiful."

"Um, I hate to break it to you, but yes, they are."

"No. Just no."

"Stop it. They're your sisters. Be nice."

"This is me being nice."

She laughed again. "What should I get to eat?"

"The turkey club is my favorite here, and Megan makes a mean veggie burger, from what I'm told. I've never had it, but my brother Wade, the vegan, loves it."

"That sounds good actually. I'm trying to watch what I eat while I'm breastfeeding."

Megan returned to take their orders, and Lucas got the turkey club while Dani asked for a veggie burger.

Savannah started banging her toy on the table and then did it again when she seemed to realize it made a loud noise.

Dani covered the baby's hand with hers to stop her, and Savannah let out an indignant squeak. "My daughter does not like being told what to do."

"Sounds like my sister Hannah's daughter, Callie. She's the same way." Lucas glanced toward the door and saw Hannah coming toward him, carrying her daughter. "Speak of the devil. There's Callie and her mom now."

Dani turned to look at Hannah, who smiled as she came toward them. "It's official. They're all gorgeous."

"Hannah is definitely *not* gorgeous."

"You need to get your eyes checked. She is so!"

Hannah said hello to Ella and Charley before continuing on to his booth, where the goings-on would be much more interesting to Hannah than anything happening with Ella and Charley. Standing next to Lucas, she said, "Move over."

"What if I don't want to?"

"I can make you."

"Whatever. You cannot."

"*Move it.*"

"I'm only moving because Callie is here." He slid over to make room for Hannah. "*You* are not welcome."

"Whatever." Hannah sat next to Lucas and handed Callie over to him before extending a hand across the table to Dani. "I'm Hannah, this rude dude's oldest and wisest sister."

"You're the moose whisperer."

"Awww, is that how he described me?"

"It was in a crazy, unhinged kind of way," Lucas said. "Not a compliment."

"Ignore him," Hannah said, "and tell me everything, starting with your name and your beautiful daughter's name."

"I'm Dani, and this is Savannah. Your Callie is adorable."

"Thank you. I quite like her. So how'd you meet my baby brother?"

Lucas scowled at her.

"What? Did I or did I not change your diapers?"

Lucas picked up the butter knife from the setup on his napkin and gave it careful consideration. "Nope, not sharp enough to do the job."

"Oh, be quiet." She leaned in closer to Dani. "I did change his diapers, but not recently. He's been doing really well with the potty training lately."

"Hannah! Oh my God!"

Dani and Hannah lost it laughing. Lucas didn't mind because Dani was having such a good time, even if her laughter was at his expense.

"Your mom is ridiculous," he told Callie, who replied with a gummy smile. In his opinion, she was tied with Caden for most beautiful baby ever. He'd never thought much about babies until his siblings started having them, giving him new people to love and spoil.

"She knows I'm ridiculous," Hannah said. "Doncha, baby girl?"

Callie reached for her mother, who took her from Lucas.

Hannah had waited such a long time to be a mom, and seeing her with Callie never got old for Lucas. He adored them both, not that he could ever say as much to Hannah. But he suspected she already knew. She was ten years older than him and Landon, had doted on them both when they were little and had in fact changed their diapers, not that either of them liked to dwell on that fact of their lives.

Megan came by to see if Hannah wanted lunch.

"Just iced tea for me, please, and put it on Lucas's tab."

"Sure," Lucas said dryly. "No problem."

Hannah stuck her tongue out at him.

"Wait until Callie does that to you," he said.

"My Callie will never do that to me."

"*Right*," Lucas said, snorting with laughter.

"So what brings you to our fair town?" Hannah asked Dani.

"I'm interviewing at the store tomorrow."

"For the warehouse manager position?"

"That's the one."

"Ella and Charley are *dying* to get someone in that job," Hannah said.

"I heard they've been picking up the slack," Dani said.

"It's been a lot for them." Hannah lowered her voice so her sisters wouldn't overhear her. "Ella is pregnant, so she's tired all the time, and she and Charley have been doing double duty. But enough about them. How did you two meet?" She blinked innocently at Lucas, who wanted to muzzle her.

"You showed real restraint in waiting ten whole minutes to ask that, Han."

"Thank you. I thought so, too. Now spill it."

"I was on my way to Stowe when I skidded off the road and landed in a ditch. Lucas came to my rescue in more ways than one."

"Is that right?" Hannah asked, perking up.

"Not like that," Lucas said. "Get your mind out of the gutter. She didn't realize every hotel in town would be booked because of ski season, so I gave her a room at Craig's."

"We would've been screwed if Lucas hadn't come along," Dani added.

"I'm so glad he was there and that you're both all right."

"Thank you. It was pretty scary, but Lucas was awesome. He took good care of us."

Hannah gave Lucas a curious look that meant he was in for further interrogation when they were alone.

Was it his imagination, or was Savvy reaching for him?

"It was my pleasure to help you ladies." He extended his hand across the table, and sure enough, Savvy curled her pudgy hand around his finger. Glancing at Dani, he found her watching him with a curious expression that had him wondering what she was thinking.

The moment was broken when Megan arrived with their food, forcing him to release Savannah's hand.

She let out a cry of protest that went straight to his heart, making him realize he was getting attached to the two ladies who had entered his life in such dramatic fashion the other night. It had only been a couple of days, but he already couldn't fathom the possibility of never seeing them again.

He really, really hoped his dad saw the potential in Dani and hired her to work for the company so the two of them would settle in Butler.

That would make him happy, although he couldn't say why, exactly. All he knew was that he liked them both and didn't want them to leave.

CHAPTER 11

*"Being twins goes way beyond my relationship with my brother.
That's a lot deeper bond."*
—Stan Van Gundy

After the entertaining lunch with Lucas and his sisters, Dani followed him to the Abbott/Stillman Family Christmas Tree Farm, where he lived in a loft above the barn.

"I wasn't sure what to expect when you told me you live in a barn, but this is amazing."

The loft had wood beams across the cathedral ceiling and a big, open stone fireplace. The two bedrooms with adjoining bathrooms were located on either end of the rectangular space, with an open-concept living room, kitchen and dining area in the middle.

"This is really nice," she said.

"Thanks. I like it. And the price is right. I live here rent-free in exchange for keeping an eye on the place between seasons. Landon is responsible for the farm itself. He didn't want to live 'at the office,' as he put it."

"Does he live in town?"

"Uh-huh. Not far from here. He bought a run-down cabin for next to nothing and fixed it up a couple of years ago." While carrying Savannah's seat for Dani, Lucas led her to the bedroom on the right side of the loft. "The bed isn't made, but I'll get you some sheets and towels and anything else you might need."

She glanced up at him. "I'm not sure what I ever did to deserve a new friend like you. Saying thank you seems so inadequate."

Moved by her kind words, he said, "I'm glad you both are here." He set the car seat on the floor next to Dani. "It's no problem at all."

Savannah chirped and waved her arms and legs as if trying to get his attention.

Lucas bent to free her from the seat and lifted her into his arms.

She let out a happy squeal that made him smile. She was so damned cute.

"Sure it isn't," Dani said. "Thanks to us, you missed two days of skiing on fresh powder."

"I ski all the time. I really don't care about missing out this time. The last few days have been fun and just what I needed to get my mind off my own problems, which hardly even count as problems."

"Don't do that."

"Do what?"

"Make it sound like the things that were bothering you were silly."

"Well, it was kind of silly to get so wound up over my brother dating someone that I liked, too. With a few days of hindsight, it all seems rather ripped from the hallways of junior high."

"Don't do that either."

"What now?" he asked, amused.

"Don't discount emotions that were very real to you, even if they were uncomfortable. My therapist taught me that after Jack died. She said I needed to feel everything there was to feel so I could experience it and put it behind me. Letting in all those emotions can be painful at the time, but she was right. Once I had wallowed in whatever the pain of the moment was, it didn't seem to have the same power over me as it had before I wallowed. If that makes sense."

She amazed him with her strength and courage.

"What?" she asked.

Christ, he'd been staring at her like a lunatic. "That makes all kinds of sense."

"Does it?"

He nodded, still unable to look away, even when Savannah grabbed hold of his shirt and managed to snag some chest hair under the fabric. Wincing, he grasped her hand and gently redirected her attention to his shirt pocket. "I think you're very wise."

"No, I'm not," she said with a laugh. "Look at what a mess I made of my trip to Vermont. Not only did I skid off the road and end up in a ditch, I failed to do even the most basic planning."

"We're not going to fight about that again." He scowled playfully at her. "We've already decided that your quick escape and lack of planning were meant to be."

"Did we?" she asked, gazing up at him wistfully.

He nodded as that odd sensation came over him once again, making him lightheaded with the realization that if she hadn't slid off the road, he never would've met her or Savvy. The thought of never meeting them made him incredibly sad for reasons he couldn't comprehend. He needed a minute to himself, to collect his thoughts and get back his equilibrium, so he handed Savvy over to her mom.

The baby didn't approve of that at all and let out a howl of outrage.

"I think she likes you," Dani said.

"I like her, too." He cleared his throat. "Um, let me see about getting you some sheets and towels." Lucas turned away and headed for his own bedroom at the other end of the loft, rattled for reasons he couldn't articulate. What the hell was wrong with him? Why were his hands shaking and his palms sweaty? He rubbed his hands on his jeans and opened the linen closet his mom had helped him stock with what she referred to as "the essentials"—sheets, pillowcases, towels, washcloths and hand towels, all of it from a shopping trip to the store that had been full of laughs as he'd protested the things she thought he had to have. Some of it had never been used in the five years he'd lived here.

He removed a new set of queen-sized flannel plaid sheets and three fluffy white towels from the shelf above the one he normally used, thankful to his mom for making sure he had what he needed for his unexpected guests. He'd have to tell her that she'd been right the next time he saw her. There was nothing she loved more than when one of her children told her she was right about something.

With the linens tucked under his arm, he leaned against the vanity to try to get his thoughts in order. Two days ago, he'd fled Butler to get away from what was happening between Amanda and Landon. Now, he'd barely given either of them a thought and was instead completely sucked into the needs of a woman and child who'd been strangers to him forty-eight hours ago.

You like her. You like Dani.

So what? Of course I like her. She's nice and sweet and pretty and… Oh God. I like her.

How was that even possible when he'd thought he was interested in Amanda as recently as two days ago? What the hell was happening to him? He had no idea, and that was the craziest part of all this. He always knew his own mind and was never confused about things such as emotions.

From the other side of the loft, he could hear Savvy crying and wanted to go to her, to offer whatever comfort he could to the baby who'd taken a shine to him, as his grandfather would say. Instead, he forced himself to stay right there so as not to get more involved than he already was. As her cries intensified, he had to grit his teeth to stop from moving.

He needed to take a big step back from both of them—and he needed to do it right now. Moving quickly, he took the linens to Dani's room, where she was sitting against the pillows feeding Savannah, who was now quiet and tucked under a blanket. Not wanting to intrude, Lucas stood awkwardly in the doorway. "I'll leave this stuff on the sofa. If you need anything else, help yourself to whatever. I've got to run a couple of errands. I'll be back in a little bit." He was talking fast, and he knew it, but he needed to get the words out so he could leave.

"Are you okay?" Dani asked, brows furrowed with concern he didn't want or deserve from her.

"All good. I'll be back." He turned and put the sheets and towels on the sofa, grabbed his coat and keys and got the hell out of there before he did something really stupid, like kiss her.

Dani watched Lucas go, wondering what was wrong, because something was off. He'd been in an all-fired rush to get the hell out of there, which made her feel terrible about invading his space. The poor guy was probably sick of her and her baby, even if he'd pretend otherwise so as not to hurt her feelings.

As soon as she'd fed Savannah and had her down for a nap, she went looking for a phone book and a landline. She found both in Lucas's kitchen and flipped to the back of the phone book for hotels and inns and began calling, starting with the Alpine Inn and ending twenty frustrating minutes later with the Zephyr Motel.

No room at any of the inns.

God, I'm so stupid. How could I have come all this way without knowing where I was going to stay? Dani dropped her head into her hands and fought through the urge to bawl like a baby. That wouldn't solve anything. If she got the job tomorrow, she would quickly find an apartment and get out of Lucas's space. And she would let him know that she'd called every place in the area and struck out so he wouldn't think she hadn't at least tried to find somewhere else to stay.

Maybe her mother had been right when she said Dani wasn't ready to be out on her own. If the last few days were any indication, that was true.

But a funny thing had happened on the way to Vermont and since she'd been here. Despite the string of disasters with the accident, the lodging, the interviews gone wrong in Stowe... Despite all that, for the first time since she'd lost Jack, she felt like she could *breathe* again. The tightness in her chest that had made her feel like she was constantly on the verge of a panic attack was gone, and she was thinking clearly again.

Her heart would always ache over the loss of her beloved Jack, but the fog that had surrounded her for so long since that dreadful day had lifted, and she felt... better. That was a huge improvement over the months in which she'd struggled to get out of bed for even a short time every day. Then Savannah had arrived, forcing Dani to rejoin the land of the living so she could take care of her daughter, all the while feeling as if she was on a million-mile hike through hip-deep mud.

The simplest things took tremendous effort, and when she was in Kentucky, she would fall into bed each night overwhelmed and exhausted, even with her parents helping every step of the way. Since she'd been here, she'd taken care of Savannah on her own, and it had been fine. Better than fine, actually. She didn't have the luxury of too much time to wallow in her grief, because her little girl needed her.

Having Lucas around helped, too. He was fun to be with and interested in what she had to say. Not to mention easy to look at and funny. He'd kept her well entertained when she wasn't tending to Savannah, who was crazy about him.

He was the first new friend she'd made since losing Jack, and he'd been so great to her and the baby.

Dani wished there was something she could do to properly thank him for the way he'd helped her. She thought about that for a few minutes before she arrived at an idea that she would execute as soon as Savannah got up from her nap.

In the meantime, she threw a load of baby clothes into the washer she located off the kitchen and tried to lose herself in the book she'd been reading at home but hadn't touched since leaving. But the words ran together as she wondered where Lucas was and when he might return.

He went to the barn and lost himself in the work that soothed his soul. Running the planer over a cedar plank that would eventually be a headboard, Lucas concentrated on what he was doing and tried not to think about anything else. Easier said than done. The only image in his mind was the one of Dani sitting on the bed, feeding the baby and looking at him with big eyes full of confusion.

Lucas felt bad about leaving her confused and hoped she wasn't wondering if he didn't want her and Savvy in his home. He did want them there. He wanted them there too much, and that was the problem.

"Hey, you're back."

The familiar voice of his twin jarred him out of his thoughts. Lucas looked up to find Landon leaning against the door. He hadn't heard it open or close, which proved how distracted he was.

"I'm back."

"How was Stowe?" Landon wore a tan Carhartt work coat and a black hat over hair the exact same color as Lucas's.

Lucas returned his gaze to the wood. "Good."

"You ski?"

"Not this time."

"Thought that's why you went."

"It was, but the plans changed."

"Is that right? What happened?"

Lucas told him about Dani's accident and how he'd come to her rescue.

"Wow, she's lucky it was you and not a serial killer."

"I had to prove I wasn't a serial killer before she'd let me put her up at Craig's house."

Landon came closer, stopping a few feet from where Lucas was working. "How'd you do that?"

"I called Mom and asked her to vouch for me and offered to call the firehouse, too, but she said Mom was convincing enough."

Landon chuckled. "Why am I not surprised?" After a pause, Landon said, "Are you pissed at me?"

Lucas was unprepared to answer the blunt question. For a second, he thought about blowing it off, but then decided to level with his brother. "I was, and it was stupid. I realize that now, and I'm sorry."

"Because of Amanda?"

"Yeah, and that's the stupid part. I hardly know her. Why would I be pissed with you over her?"

"Because you like her?"

"I did, but I'm over it. Clearly, she likes *you*, so that's what matters."

"I'm not so sure she does. We've had some fun, but it's all somewhat platonic. I can't really get a read on her, to be honest."

That surprised Lucas. "It seemed to me that she was into you the other night at Mom's."

"You think so?"

"Yeah."

Landon shrugged. "She decided to stick around for a few more weeks. She's helping to write new catalog copy for her company. She can do that from anywhere."

"And you don't think she's sticking around because she wants to spend more time with you?"

"I have no idea if that's why she's staying."

Lucas snorted out a laugh. "You're so stupid."

"Why does that make me stupid?"

"*Because*. There's no reason for her to stay here except for *you*, you idiot."

"You really think so?"

Lucas laughed again. "Yes, I really think so, and here's a big idea. Have you thought of actually asking her why she's staying in Butler when she can work on her project anywhere?"

"Um, no?"

"You really are kinda stupid, but we've always known that."

"I'm no more stupid than you are."

"True, but I'm trying to be smarter than I've been in the past. You ought to give it a whirl and see how it goes."

Landon kicked at one of the many piles of sawdust on the floor.

Lucas needed to get around to cleaning them up one of these days.

"What's with the sudden need to be smarter?"

"Everyone has to grow up eventually," Lucas replied. "Don't you think it's time?"

Landon looked at him with horror etched into the face that was almost an exact replica of his own. "No, I don't think it's time. What the hell is wrong with you?"

"Nothing." Lucas returned his focus to the headboard that he planned to give Ella and Gavin as a wedding gift. It matched the dresser he'd made for her when she moved into her first apartment.

"That's it? There's nothing wrong except you suddenly want to be a grown-up?"

"Don't you ever get tired of being a fool, Landon? Of no one taking either of us seriously?"

"No, I don't get tired of it. That's who we are. It's the role we play in our family."

"Forever? We're destined to be a couple of sixty-year-old jackasses?"

Landon's brows narrowed. "Who you calling a jackass?"

"You. Me. Both of us."

"Just because we like to have fun doesn't make us jackasses."

"Often it does."

"Where's this coming from, Luc? Since when are you such a drag?"

"I'm a drag if I want to start behaving more like an adult?"

"Yes! We're all about the fun. That's what we've always been about. That doesn't make us jackasses."

"A lot of the time it does. And I never said I don't want to have fun anymore. I said I want to behave like an adult more often, since I am, in fact, an adult."

Landon shook his head. "I don't know what's gotten into you, man."

Lucas realized there was no point in trying to further explain his recent metamorphosis to his twin, who clearly wasn't there yet. "No worries. Just forget it."

"So Dani, the woman you helped out in Stowe... Anything up with that?"

"She's interviewing at the store tomorrow, so they're staying with me at the loft. She wasn't thinking of ski season when she headed for Vermont."

Landon stared at him, agog.

"What?"

"You're playing *house* with some chick you just met who has a baby?"

"We're not playing house. I gave her a place to stay because she was in a jam. That's all it is."

"Huh."

"Huh what?" Lucas was beginning to be seriously annoyed and wished Landon would take off, which was odd because Lucas hardly ever felt that way about him.

"Nothing." Landon rubbed a hand over his clean-shaven jaw. "It's just you tell me you've decided to grow up, and now you've got yourself a little family, too. It's a lot to process."

"Shut the fuck up and get out of here, will you?"

"Did I strike too close to *home*, where you've suddenly got a wife and kid?"

Lucas forced himself to stay put so he wouldn't be tempted to punch Landon. "She's a nice person who's been through some tough stuff. I'm just doing her a favor. Don't make it into something it's not."

Something it would never be... If he'd met Dani under different circumstances, he'd be interested in her. But her heart still belonged to the man she'd loved and lost. He couldn't compete with that and didn't intend to try.

He looked up at his brother. "Don't you have a woman to see who stayed in town because of you?"

Landon waggled his brows. "I probably should go make her tell me she stayed because of me."

"Are you really going to come right out and ask her that?"

"Why not? What do I have to lose?"

"Nothing, I suppose."

"Hunter said something about organizing a boys' night out in the next few weeks. You up for that, or are you too married now?"

"I'm up for it," Lucas said, gritting his teeth.

"Cool. I guess I'll see you at the firehouse tomorrow."

"See you then." *And don't let the door hit you where the good Lord split you...* Another of his grandfather's sayings.

"Later."

Lucas breathed a sigh of relief when the door closed behind his brother. He couldn't remember another time in his life when he'd felt so out of sorts. One minute, he'd been upset about Landon and Amanda, the next, he met Dani and Savvy. In just a couple of days, his head had been turned all around by them.

And he was out of sync with Landon for the first time ever. That truly sucked.

CHAPTER 12

"There is no greater name for a leader than mother or father.
There is no leadership more important than parenthood."
—Sheri L. Dew

Lucas checked his watch, saw that it was close to six and decided to head out to hit the grocery store since they needed something for dinner. After locking up the barn, he drove to the store and wondered what Dani and Savvy were up to at home. He couldn't wait to get back to see them, even if he knew he shouldn't feel that way.

They were ships passing in the night, and it wouldn't be appropriate or prudent to hope for anything more than a brief friendship.

But if she got the job at the store and stayed in town…

"Don't get ahead of yourself, pal," he muttered, grabbing the first parking space he found in the grocery store parking lot.

The place was busy with people stopping on their way home, and as he trudged through the sloppy remnants of the latest snowfall, he hoped he could get in and out fairly quickly. At the prepared food counter, he decided on barbecue chicken and mashed potatoes that he put in his cart before hitting the salad bar. Hopefully, Dani would like what he'd chosen.

He tossed in some brownies at the bakery and went to the back of the store to buy coffee, eggs, bacon, milk and bread so they'd have stuff for breakfast, too. On the way to the checkout counter, he spotted a familiar face in the cereal aisle and nudged him with his cart.

"Hey there." Elmer's face lit up at the sight of his grandson. "This is a nice surprise."

"I'm sure you run into one of us every time you leave the house."

"Almost, but it's always a delight to see one of my grandbabies."

"Who are not babies anymore."

"Always will be to me. How was Stowe?"

"Good."

"Your mom told me you were in rescue mode over there."

"Something like that."

"A mom and her little one?"

"Uh-huh."

Elmer leaned against the shelf, settling in for a chat. "Just uh-huh?"

"I guess."

His grandfather tilted his head. "What's going on?"

"I don't know! First, I'm pissed off because Landon is seeing Amanda, and then, I meet Dani and Savvy and it's like Amanda never happened, and Landon is pissed because I want to be an adult, and Dani is… Well, she's amazing, but she's broken inside because her fiancé died in an accident before the baby was born. And the baby is just…" Lucas sighed. "She's beautiful, and she really likes me."

Elmer stared at him with eyes gone wide. "All that since I saw you last?"

"I know, right? I wish I could figure out what the hell is happening."

"*Life* is happening, Luc."

"Does it have to be so freaking confusing?"

Elmer let out a guffaw. "Unfortunately, that's how it works."

Lucas leaned on the handle of his carriage, thankful to have run into the wisest person he knew when he was in bad need of some wisdom. "I'm in seriously uncharted territory with Dani, Gramps. I really like her, but things are so up in the air for her. Not to mention the dead fiancé she can't talk about without crying…"

"It sounds like you're being a very good friend to her when she needs one. That's a great place to start."

"Yeah, I suppose."

"I'm going to say something, and I don't want you to take it the wrong way."

"Okay…"

"You're accustomed to 'things' coming rather easily to you with the fairer sex. And I mean no disrespect toward the ladies in your life, son, but you've never had one you had to *work* for. They tend to, how shall I say this… Throw themselves at you and your brother?"

"They do not," Lucas said, mortified.

"Ah, yes, they do, and they always have. From the time you two were the littlest of tykes, people have talked about how handsome and charming you are. And as you got older, the rest of mankind could only sit back and marvel at the female attention that comes your way. You two boys are like honey to the bees."

"Could I please unsubscribe from this conversation?"

Elmer laughed. "My point, dear boy, is that if you've got your heart set on wooing your Dani, for the first time, you're going to have to *work* for it."

"A, she's not *my* Dani. And B, I don't have my heart set on her."

"Don't you? Are you or are you not standing in the middle of a grocery store with a cart full of food for more than one person, trying to figure out what to do about the woman who has stormed into your life, toting some rather heavy and precious baggage along with her? Or did I get this all wrong?"

Lucas directed a teasing glare at his grandfather. "You think you're so smart, don't you?"

"Am I wrong?" Elmer asked, grinning smugly.

"No," Lucas conceded, because how did one ever win an "argument" with Elmer Stillman?

"Be her friend, Luc. That's what she needs more than anything right now."

"We're already friends. We talk about stuff."

"That's a real fine place to start, son."

"Yeah, you're right."

"I know you're not used to being 'friends' with women—"

"Gramps! I'm not a total man-whore. I have friends who are women."

Elmer lost it laughing. "If you say so."

"I do!"

"Okay, okay, sorry." Elmer wiped the laughter tears from his eyes.

"You just crack yourself up, don't you?"

"I really do."

Lucas laughed, because how could he not? "Despite your low opinion of me, I appreciate your advice."

"My opinion of you is extremely high, my boy. You're every bit the fine man your father and brothers are. Don't you ever think otherwise."

Lucas stepped around the carriage to give his grandfather a quick hug. "We're all going to need you to live forever, Gramps. You know that, don't you?"

"I ain't going anywhere anytime soon. I got eighteen grandbabies who need constant supervision. And now there're great-grandbabies to see to as well. I got a lot left to do."

"I have a feeling the great-grandbabies are going to outnumber us all before long."

"You may be right about that."

"Thanks, Gramps. Seriously, I appreciate you so much."

Elmer squeezed his arm. "I love ya, son. I'm here if you need me."

"Thank God for that."

They walked to the checkout together, and Lucas made sure Elmer was safely in his truck and on his way home before he walked to his own truck. Driving home, he thought about the things his grandfather had said, laughing to himself and shaking his head over parts of it.

But one thing had resonated above the rest—be her friend. That he could do, and for now, he would keep any additional thoughts about her to himself.

She had a lot going on. The last thing she needed was a guy making her feel in any way uncomfortable. If she moved on with someone new, that someone new would be the first since Jack, which would be a huge big deal. He already knew her well enough to know that much, and after talking to his gramps, he knew he had to play his cards carefully where she was concerned.

Perhaps if he continued to make himself essential to her, they might one day be more than friends. His grandfather was right about something else—he'd never had to put forth that kind of effort with any woman, but this one...

Something told him she would be worth the effort.

In the middle of planning a nice dinner for Lucas, a terrible thought had occurred to Dani—what if he'd gone to visit Amanda now that he was back in town? He wouldn't do that, would he? What if by being here, she was causing trouble for him?

God, she would hate that after all he'd done to help her.

Hopefully, he liked chicken stir-fry and rice and would appreciate the offering from a grateful houseguest. Ugh, she hated this feeling of uncertainty. It'd been so long since she'd had anything to do with a man who wasn't Jack that she couldn't remember how to behave properly. The rules had undoubtedly changed in the ten years she'd been with him.

They had met her sophomore year of high school. He'd been a senior, captain of the football team and headed for a scholarship to play at the University of Tennessee. Dani could still recall that fateful first meeting at a party she wasn't supposed to be at, when he'd zeroed in on her, turning his formidable gaze her way and changing her life forever.

Her groove in high school had been more along the lines of band and chorus, so she hadn't recognized him without his football helmet. But her friends had known who he was and had gone crazy when they realized he was showing interest in her. They'd pushed her to talk to him when her preference would've been to pretend it wasn't happening.

She'd been rooted in place, afraid to move until he came over to her and introduced himself.

"Hey, I'm Jack. What's your name?"

Her friend Marissa had nudged her forward. "Her name is Danielle, but everyone calls her Dani."

He'd seemed amused that Marissa was speaking for her. "Nice to meet you, Dani."

Marissa had poked Dani in the back.

"Oh, um, you, too."

"You want to get a drink?"

She didn't drink, but something told her to keep that info to herself. "Um, sure." As she walked away with him, she glanced back at Marissa, who had given her a thumbs-up as a giddy smile lit up her face.

Dani had zero experience with boys and had no idea how to act around the handsome, charismatic Jack, who seemed to sense her reticence from the get-go. He was tall and broad-shouldered with blond hair and blue eyes that crinkled in the corners when he smiled, which he did often. Everyone wanted to talk to him, but he shook his head repeatedly to discourage them from approaching. That he was giving her his full attention only made her more nervous.

When they reached the keg on the back porch, he expertly filled a red cup for her. "So, Dani, why haven't I seen you around before now?"

Dani took the cup from him. "Um, I'm a sophomore." *Ugh, what a stupid thing to say.* All these years later, she could still recall her extreme awkwardness that first night and how he'd seemed to find it endearing rather than off-putting. She'd expected him to be a typical jock, out for one thing and one thing only, but from the beginning, he'd been different—at least with her.

The door opened, startling Dani from her thoughts of the past as Lucas came in, bringing a blast of woodsmoke-scented cold air with him.

"Hey." He deposited cloth grocery bags on the counter. "What smells so good?"

"I made dinner."

"Oh, cool. Thanks. I got a chicken from the grocery store, but we can have that tomorrow."

"I, um, I wanted to do something to thank you for everything you've done."

"I told you that you don't need to thank me."

"Before, you seemed…" Dani wanted to take back the words. Who was she to say how he seemed?

"What?"

"Unhappy, and I was afraid we were the cause. We've totally bombed into your space, and the baby cries a lot and…"

Lucas put his coat on one of the barstools and came over to her, shocking her when he placed his hands on her shoulders. "You aren't the reason I was upset."

"Oh, um, okay."

Then he flashed that devastating grin that made her go stupid in the head. "Well, you kinda were, but not for the reasons you think."

"I'm not sure what that means."

He dropped his hands from her shoulders and jammed them into the pockets of his jeans. "It's just that I really like having you and Savvy here."

"You do?"

Nodding, he said, "I like you, Dani, and I know the timing is awful for you when you're in the midst of a move and trying to figure out your life. But maybe when things are settled, you might, you know... Go out with me?"

Dani stared at him, wondering if she'd heard him correctly. "You... you..."

"Like you. A lot."

"*Really?* I'm a disaster with breast-milk stains on my shirt and stretch marks and..."

"And I like you." He shrugged. "I don't see a disaster when I look at you. I see strength, resilience and courage that remind me so much of my sister Hannah after she lost her first husband in Iraq. Before I met you, she *was* the most courageous person I ever knew. I see a mother taking exceptional care of her beautiful child."

If he kept this up, she was going to ugly cry. "You're very kind to say such things about me."

"Instead of thinking about the things that have gone wrong, you should focus on what's gone right."

"None of it would've gone right without you."

"That's not true. You would've figured something out."

"I wanted so badly to do this on my own."

"There's nothing wrong with accepting a little help along the way, Dani. That doesn't make you any less of an adult or mother. I'm somewhat new to maturity, but I already know that sometimes the mature thing is to admit you can't do it all on your own."

She took a step closer to him, and empowered by the information he'd shared, she rested her hands flat on his chest and looked up at him. "I like you, too, and not just because you've rescued me in every way possible."

"No?" He flashed the lopsided grin that sent flutters through her.

Dani shook her head. "I like that I can talk to you about stuff I hardly talk to anyone about and that you listen to me and don't try to tell me what to do the way everyone else does."

"You don't need anyone to tell you what to do. You got this."

"I'm glad you think so. I'm not so sure."

"You'll get there."

"I don't know if I'm ready for..."

He leaned in and kissed her forehead. "I'm not going anywhere."

"You should find someone with less baggage."

"I like your baggage."

Savannah chose that moment to let out a squeak, letting them know she was awake.

"Want me to get her?" Lucas asked.

"I'll do it. She'll need to be changed."

"I can handle that. Hannah showed me how to change Callie so I could watch her one day when she had a dentist appointment."

"That's above and beyond the call of duty."

"I don't mind." He turned and headed for the bedroom where she and Savannah were staying.

Dani watched him go, noting the rangy way he moved, eating up the ground with the impatient energy that was so much a part of who he was.

He *liked* her.

He wanted to *go out* with her when the time was right.

He was *happy* she and Savannah were staying with him.

As she checked the stove to see if their dinner was ready, Dani felt happier and lighter than she had since losing Jack, and it was all thanks to her sexy rescuer.

Lucas emerged from the bedroom with Savannah, who cooed at the sight of her mother, but when he tried to hand her over to Dani, the baby gripped his shirt.

"Yo, little girl." Lucas winced as he freed himself from her grip. "Watch the chest hair." He no sooner freed one hand than she had a fresh hold on him. "You're going to give me bald spots."

Savannah gave him a big gummy grin as he continued to free himself and she continued to grab him. Then she let out a deep guffaw, and Dani nearly dropped the beer she'd gotten out for him.

"Oh my God! That was her first real laugh!" She fumbled in her purse for her phone, powered it up and switched it to video, hoping the baby would do it again.

Lucas sped up the game, and Savannah lost it laughing.

Dani's eyes filled with tears as she recorded the moment, wishing Jack could be there to see their little girl laugh for the first time. When she thought about all the things he would miss, her heart broke all over again for him, for herself and mostly for Savannah, who would never know the father who'd adored her from the first second he'd heard she was on the way.

Lucas kept up the game until Savannah let out her hungry cry.

Dani put down the phone and took the baby from him. "If you want to go ahead and eat while I feed her, feel free."

"I'll wait for you."

"Put some foil over that to keep it warm."

"It smells amazing."

After she fed the baby and set her up on a blanket with some toys to keep her occupied, Dani served the meal.

"This tastes as good as it smells," Lucas said between bites.

"Glad you like it."

"How'd you manage to pull this off? I was only gone a few hours."

"Savannah and I went to the store after her nap." She took a closer look at him. "What's that in your hair?"

He ran his fingers through it, and particles spilled onto his shirt. "Sawdust."

"How did you end up with sawdust in your hair?"

"I was working at my woodshop."

Better that than visiting Amanda, she decided. "I'm jealous. I can't wait to get back to my furniture restoration hobby. I miss it."

"I love to do restoration, too, but my primary gig is furniture. I made the dresser in your room."

"It's beautiful! I was admiring it earlier."

"Thanks. I love doing it, so it's nice to hear that people like what I make."

"I bet your stuff sells like wildfire at the store."

"I do all right," he said with characteristic understatement.

They finished dinner, worked together to clean up the kitchen and spent some time playing with Savannah before tucking her in for the night.

"How about another movie?" Lucas asked when she joined him in the living room.

"That'd be fun, but I warn you—I'll probably fall asleep halfway through."

"That's okay. We can finish it tomorrow."

She sat next to him, but not too close.

He tossed a blanket her way, and she snuggled under it. "*Speed* is on TV," he said. "What do you think of that?"

"It gives me anxiety, but I do love Keanu."

Lucas rolled his eyes. "What is *with* that guy? You sound like my sisters. They *love* him."

"He's very sexy, especially in *Speed*."

"Whatever you say." He put the movie on, and they got lost in the action. "I always forget about the beginning with the elevator."

"I know! I was scared of elevators for years after I saw it for the first time—and buses." As the movie progressed and the anxiety increased, Dani moved closer to Lucas without realizing she was doing it until her leg bumped up against his.

He laughed and put an arm around her, drawing her in close. "Don't worry. I've got you."

The gesture brought back a sweet memory of Jack doing the same thing after he talked her into watching the dreadful movie *Saw*. Ugh, she'd had nightmares for weeks.

"Is this okay?" Lucas asked quietly.

With her head on his chest, she nodded. "It's quite necessary if I'm going to get through this."

His low chuckle made her smile.

Then the bus nearly took out the baby stroller, and she buried her face in his chest, suppressing a squeak. "I forgot about that part!"

"The baby is fine. You can look now."

"I think I'd rather stay here."

"You won't hear me complaining."

Dani felt his fingers slide through her hair, and it was all she could do not to sigh with the pleasure of being touched by a man. It'd been so long that she'd forgotten what it was like. Heavenly… That's what it was like. Wrapped up in his arms, absorbed in the appealing scent of fresh air, woodsmoke and sawdust that clung to him, Dani was able to forget her worries for a minute and just breathe.

Chapter 13

"Maturity is achieved when a person postpones immediate pleasures for long-term values."
—Joshua L. Liebman

This was *torture*. Having her warm and soft and fragrant in his arms, Lucas had to remind himself that she was different from every other woman he'd ever been close to. Usually, a situation like this would lead to much more than platonic snuggling.

Not this time.

If he had a prayer of anything more than friendship with Dani, he had to be very careful and take it as slowly as possible. She was still grieving the loss of her love and her baby's father. Part of her would always be in mourning for him, and Lucas could never forget that. Anything that happened between them would need to be initiated by her, which again was a whole new ballgame for him.

In the past, the women he'd associated with liked it when he took the lead, expressed his interest and made the first move.

None of the usual "moves" would be appropriate with Dani.

Ironic, wasn't it, that he'd no sooner decided to give being an actual grown-up a whirl when he'd been confronted with the ultimate test of his maturity—or lack thereof.

Perhaps if I do the opposite of what I think I ought to do, then I'll do the right thing, he thought, laughing to himself. At least he was wise enough to recognize his own limitations in navigating a situation like this.

"Hey, Dani?"

"Hmm?"

"In June, we're all going to Boston for my brother Wade's wedding. I'd love for you to come with me as my date. I have to send back the RSVP this week, so that's why I'm asking now."

For a long moment, she didn't reply. In fact, she barely seemed to breathe. "I, um, I have Savannah and—"

"She can come with us. Max is bringing Caden, and Hannah will have Callie. Savvy will fit right in. Wade's father-in-law hired a nanny for them so their parents can enjoy the wedding. I'm sure they'd be happy to have sweet Savvy, too."

"I couldn't impose on them that way."

Lucas turned down the TV. "Let me tell you about my sister-in-law Mia and her father, and then you can decide. She recently found out that her mom took her from her father in the midst of a divorce when she was a baby, and her dad, who is *loaded*, is so happy to have her back in his life that he's throwing this huge wedding for her and Wade. He's putting up our whole family in a fancy hotel. He would do *anything* Mia wanted, including add another nanny if need be. It's gonna be a blast. My dad even rented a bus so we can all go to Boston together. That'll be a total shitshow." He realized he might be overselling the trip, so he decided to quit while he was still ahead. "Anyway, I'd love to have you come with me, but only if you feel up to it."

"It's so sweet of you to ask me, but I'm not even sure where I'll be. If I don't get the job at the store, I'll have to figure out what's next."

"No worries. We can wait and see what transpires."

She looked up at him, her eyes dancing with amusement. But he also saw the sadness that was always present. "You know you can't just show up to a fancy wedding in Boston with a surprise guest, right?"

"I can't?"

Dani shook her head. "Doesn't work that way. I was… I was planning our wedding when Jack was killed."

"I'm sorry. I didn't think. If it's too painful—"

She rested her finger over his lips.

Every part of him went rigid from her touch.

"It's fine. I swear." She dropped her hand from his lips, and he immediately wanted her to put it back. "I'd love to go to Boston and the wedding with you if I can make it work."

"My dad would be crazy not to hire you, and I told him so."

"You did?" She wasn't sure how to feel about that.

"Of course I did. Why wouldn't I put in a good word for a friend who wants to work for our company?"

Dani considered that. "I'm going to be honest with you."

"I wouldn't want you to be any other way."

"My first inclination is to be annoyed that you did that without consulting me, but as always, you were only trying to help me, so thank you."

"I'm sorry if I was out of line talking to him without asking you first. But trust me. If my dad doesn't think you'd be great for the job, he won't hire you—friend or no friend. He takes the business very seriously."

"That's good to know." She appreciated that he was letting her know that if she got the job, it would be on her own merits and not because he put in a word for her. "A girl and her baby can never have too many friends."

"Selfishly, I really hope you get the job. I want you girls to stay in Butler."

"That would be nice. It seems like a great little town."

"It is, and we have a lot of fun here. I could teach Savvy how to skate and ski and how to rock-climb. My brothers and I are into all that stuff, and we're crazy-good at it, if we do say so ourselves."

Dani smiled up at him. "Let's get her walking, and then we can see about skiing and rock-climbing."

"I'm not going anywhere. I'll be here whenever she's ready."

"I just want you to know... I heard what you said earlier and..."

He kissed her forehead. "It's okay. I'm not in any rush."

"The thing is, I don't know if I'm there yet. Actually, I don't know if I'm coming or going. Until I have a job and a place for Savannah and me to live, I can't really think about much beyond that."

"Hopefully, you'll have a job by tomorrow, and you can stay with me as long as you need to."

"That's very nice of you, but I'm sure you want your space back."

"Actually, I don't really. I like having you girls around, and I'd miss you both if you left."

"I can't stay here indefinitely, Lucas."

"Why not?"

"Because! You can't just take us in!"

"You still haven't told me why not."

"Lucas…" She dropped her forehead to his chest. "You're being exasperating."

"I'm told that's one of my superpowers."

"I can see why. Let's just take it a day at a time and see what happens. Okay?"

"Sounds like a plan, as long as you know you're more than welcome to stay here for as long as you want."

She surprised the shit out of him when she kissed his cheek. "In case I forget to tell you, you're the best rescuer I've ever had."

"Rescuing you was the best thing I ever did—for myself."

Hours later, after Dani had gone to bed, Lucas sat up watching late-night TV and trying to settle himself enough to sleep. Having her snuggled up to him had felt so *right*. Nothing had ever felt so right. He'd wanted to keep her there with him for as long as he could, and he'd never wanted that with anyone else. Not that long ago, feeling that way about a woman would've freaked him out and had him running for the hills to get away from anything that smacked of commitment.

Now? He wanted her. It was that simple and that complicated.

How did people deal with having feelings that took over their hearts and minds and made it impossible to think about anything else?

Of course, he'd seen this happen to his siblings, but he'd managed to maintain an air of separation from the proceedings. His brothers had gone stupid over the women they loved, all of whom were awesome people he would've hand-chosen for them.

Was that what was happening to him since he'd met Dani and Savvy? Was it possible for her and her daughter to work their way into his heart and soul in just a few days? Did things like that actually happen to people?

Part of him was annoyed that fate had intervened and taken the wheel of his truck to steer him in a direction he hadn't seen coming until he was right on top of it. But then he recalled the way Dani had looked at him when she told him she liked him, too, and any annoyance he felt disappeared like wisps of smoke dancing up the chimney.

He was about to get up and go to bed when Dani emerged from the guest room, carrying Savvy. The baby was red-faced and wide awake, her fingers in her mouth.

"Poor thing is teething and very unhappy. I left the baby Tylenol out here. Hope we didn't bother you."

"Not at all." As if it was the most natural thing in the world, he reached for Savvy. "I'll take her while you find the medicine."

"Oh, thanks." Dani handed the baby over to him.

Savvy snuggled up to his chest and immediately began grabbing handfuls of T-shirt and chest hair.

Lucas chuckled as he freed himself from her grip only to have to do it again a few seconds later. She was so damned cute and pleased with herself every time he reacted to what she was doing.

"You're so good with her," Dani said when she returned with the medicine, which she administered to the baby using a dropper.

Savvy sucked the stuff up and smacked her lips.

"Thank God she likes it." Dani brushed a hand over her daughter's forehead, brows furrowing with concern. "She's warm. I should take her temp." She went into the bedroom to get the thermometer and ran it over the baby's forehead. "Ninety-nine point nine."

"Up just a little," Lucas said. "The medicine will help."

"You think so?"

"She doesn't seem sick."

"I've got to get that pediatrician info from Emma, just in case it's more than teething."

"Try not to worry. She'll probably feel fine in the morning."

"Since she was born, I've learned that motherhood is a metaphor for nonstop worrying."

Lucas smiled up at her. "My mom says the same thing. And the bad news is that it never ends, according to Mom."

"She's got a lot to worry about with ten of you."

"She's pretty chill, but she does worry."

"I can't wait to meet her."

"I'll bring you to Sunday dinner this week before my shift."

"When do you work again?"

"I'm on the next four nights."

"Oh."

"If you don't want to be here by yourself, I can have someone come stay with you. I've got plenty of people I could ask."

"Don't be silly. I'll be fine. Besides, I'm still hoping Mrs. Hendricks will have a room open up at the inn."

"You don't have to pay to stay there, Dani. I mean it when I tell you I like having you ladies here with me." He looked down at Savvy, who had rested her head on his chest, her little fist curled up next to her cheek and her eyes heavy with sleep. "Tell her, Savvy. You'd rather be here with me. Wouldn't you?"

"If it were up to her, we'd never leave."

"That'd be okay."

"Lucas..."

"I know. Too much too soon." With his free hand, he reached for Dani's hand and brought it to his lips for a quick kiss that made her gasp. "You've got enough to worry about with your little one and the interview tomorrow. Don't fret about staying here. If I didn't want you here, I wouldn't have invited you."

"I am fretting."

"Don't." He released her hand and reluctantly turned Savvy over to her.

The second he let go of the baby, she started fussing, her cries escalating quickly. Lucas stood and took her back, cradling her into his chest. "Shhhh. Sleepy time, little girl."

To his astonishment—and Dani's—Savannah immediately settled.

Dani laughed softly. "I'm feeling a little jealous."

Lucas smiled. "Go lie down while you can. I'll bring her in soon."

"You don't have to do that."

"I know I don't. I want to." He brushed his lips over the baby's soft blonde hair. "We've got this, don't we, baby girl?"

"If you're sure…"

"I'm sure." In fact, he'd never been surer about anything in his life and was beginning to realize that everything had changed, whether he'd wanted it to or not.

He wanted it. He wanted Dani and Savvy.

CHAPTER 14

*"The meeting of two personalities is like the contact of two
chemical substances: if there is any reaction, both
are transformed."*
—Carl Jung

Dani got into bed, feeling unsettled and uncertain she'd done the right thing leaving Savannah with Lucas. Not that she didn't trust him completely.

She did. And it wasn't like she was allowing him to take the baby somewhere. They were in the next room, and still, she felt funny about it. But she was also completely exhausted and had a big interview in the morning for a job she wanted badly. It wouldn't do to show up with suitcases under her eyes.

So she closed them and tried to relax to the sound of Lucas's soft voice talking to the baby. He was adorable, sweet, kind, funny and sexy. It was no surprise to Dani that Savannah was crazy about him, that they both were.

A few days ago, the idea of being attracted to a man who wasn't Jack would've been inconceivable to her.

But tonight… Snuggling up to Lucas while watching TV had felt natural and comfortable. She hadn't wanted to leave the warm comfort of his embrace.

So much for trying to stand on her own two feet. Here she was, right back to relying on someone else, even if relying on Lucas didn't come with the same kind of suffocating sensation she'd had while with her parents.

No, this was different, but she was still torn about accepting his kind offer to continue staying with him indefinitely.

She must've dozed, because the next thing she knew, Savannah was crying.

Dani sat up straight, pushing the hair back from her face.

"Sorry," Lucas whispered. "I was trying to put her down, but she's not having it." In the glow of the nightlight she'd left on in the bathroom, she could see him stretched out on the other side of the bed. He put Savvy on his chest and covered her with a baby blanket. "Don't mind us. Go back to sleep. I'll scoot out when she settles down."

Don't mind us… Right, as if she'd actually sleep with him close enough to touch.

If she'd been standing, she might've been tempted to swoon at his tenderness toward her daughter. Her father had always said that the measure of a man was how he treated those who couldn't do anything for him. He'd loved Jack like a son, and she had little doubt that he'd like Lucas, too.

What was not to like? The man was irresistible in every possible way, and she was falling for him, regardless of whether she was ready for him or not.

In the morning, Lucas woke to Savannah pulling a handful of chest hair out by the roots. "Yowza," he said gruffly, shaking off the sleep.

The baby's husky giggle reduced him to pudding.

"You're a devil, aren't you?" He whispered so they wouldn't wake Dani. A glance his watch showed it was only a few minutes after six. Holding the baby, he got up, found a dry diaper and a package of wipes on the dresser and took her with him to the living room, hoping Dani would get to sleep a little while longer.

As he changed the baby, he couldn't believe he'd spent the entire night in Dani's bed, serving as a mattress for Savvy—or how much he'd liked sleeping near them.

Savvy was active in the morning, bicycling her legs and trying to grab anything she could reach.

Though he wasn't well practiced with babies, he managed to get a clean diaper on her and get her sleeper back on. For the next hour, he kept her entertained with the toys that were still on the blanket from the night before. But then she started fussing, and he picked her up to take her to her mother.

Dani sat up in bed, her hair a halo around her sweet face, her eyes wild. "Oh my God! I overslept!"

"No, you didn't. The interview isn't for two hours yet."

"I mean I slept through her waking up."

"Nah, we snuck out so you could sleep in a little."

"Oh." She ran her fingers through her hair and held out her arms to take the baby from him. "Thank you."

"It was fun."

Dani smiled at him and then the baby. "Did you play with Lucas?"

Savvy's arms and legs went nuts with excitement. Did hearing his name cause that? Jeez, the kid was going to have him completely wrapped around her little finger in no time at all at this rate.

"I'll, ah, leave you girls to do your thing while I make breakfast for us."

"Thanks again for the extra sleep. It's much appreciated."

"It was entirely my pleasure."

He went into the kitchen and made a pot of coffee. While it brewed, he cracked eggs into a frying pan and scrambled them before putting four pieces of bread in the toaster. Tomorrow, when they had more time, he'd make pancakes for her. Growing up Abbott, they all had been taught to make light, fluffy pancakes from a very young age, always served with the family's own maple syrup.

Twenty minutes later, Dani came out of the bedroom, showered and dressed in a white blouse and formfitting black pants. She had her hair up and had applied makeup that made her pretty eyes even more so.

"Wow, you look gorgeous."

"Thank you."

"I would've taken her while you showered."

"Thanks, but we have a routine. She sits in her car seat while I rush through the motions."

"Coffee?"

"Yes, please."

Lucas poured a mug for her and put it on the counter along with cream and sugar.

"God bless you and coffee," she said after her first sip.

"I'm honored to rank ahead of coffee."

Her eyes lit up with amusement he could see over the mug that blocked the rest of her face. "That's not a distinction I just throw around. I hope this is dressed up enough for your family's store."

"Absolutely." He plated eggs and two pieces of toast for her. "That'd be considered formal wear by some of the people who work there."

"Smells delicious. Thank you." Dani put Savannah's seat on the island countertop and sat to eat while the baby played with two rattles.

"Someone is in a happier mood today," Lucas said.

"Probably because she got to sleep with her new best friend."

"I do what I can for the ladies."

"I bet you do," she said under her breath but loud enough for him to hear her.

He cocked a grin. "What's that you said?"

"I said this is very good, thank you for cooking."

Lucas laughed as he filled his own plate and soaked his eggs in maple syrup. She sure was fun to have around. He liked everything about her and was more comfortable with her after only a few days than he was around women he'd known for years. He liked that she could still be playful and funny after what she'd been through, that despite her losses, an aura of light surrounded her.

"You're going to kill it with my dad. I have no doubt. So don't be nervous. He's a nice guy."

"If he's anything like his son, I should be in good hands."

"Thank you," he said softly. "That's one of the best compliments I could ever receive."

"It's true. I'll make sure to let him know he can be very proud of the fine man he raised."

Lucas was stunned by the emotional wallop that accompanied her comment. "I, uh, thank you."

She reached across the counter to put her hand on top of his. "You know what you said about needing to act more like an adult?"

He nodded, overwhelmed by her touch, her presence, her words.

"You're fine just the way you are. You don't need to change anything."

"That's kind of you to say, but you don't know the buffoonish side of me."

"I don't need to see that to know that in addition to what you refer to as your buffoonish side, there's a fully grown, responsible, caring, thoughtful man. Nothing says you can't be silly when you want to be and mature when you need to be. Right?"

Lucas hadn't thought of it that way before now. "I suppose so." He tipped his head. "Does this mean you won't think less of me if I let out my inner buffoon every now and then?"

"After everything you've done for me and Savannah, I could never think less of you."

"You say that before you've seen my full potential."

"I say that no matter what."

He turned his hand palm up and gave hers a squeeze. "Thank you. Means a lot to me that you see me that way. I've been in a weird place lately and, well… Meeting you ladies has really helped me, too."

"We're glad we could do something for you."

"You have. More than you know."

A million thoughts went through Lucas's mind in the time it took for her to realize they were staring at each other as they held hands. Her face flushed adorably in the second before she looked down and released his hand to finish eating.

Among those thoughts was one in particular—was she the one he'd always been meant to find? And if so, what did he intend to do about it?

This is not good, Dani thought as Lucas drove them into town for her interview. Something had happened between them over breakfast, something big and important and *necessary*, and now... Now, she was reeling and had an important interview with his father in thirty minutes. Dani wished she had a bag to breathe into, as she feared hyperventilating or worse—another panic attack at the most inopportune time.

The last thing she needed was for Lincoln Abbott to see what a hot mess she was on the inside when she wanted him to see only a cool, competent professional who would be a valuable asset to his management team.

She shouldn't be having these thoughts about Lucas. It was too soon after losing Jack and certainly too soon after meeting Lucas. And she most definitely shouldn't be having these thoughts when she ought to be one hundred percent focused on landing this job.

"I really hope you're not nervous," Lucas said. "My whole family is super chill. Well, except Charley, but you'll figure her out soon enough. Stay on her good side, and she doesn't bite."

"Well, that's a ringing endorsement."

Lucas laughed. "She's cool, but kind of a pain, although much less so since Tyler declawed her. But if you care about me at all, don't tell her I used the word *declawed* in the same sentence as Charley and Tyler."

Dani smiled at him and pretended to turn the key to her lips. "Your secret is safe with me."

"Oh, good, because she can still kick my ass, especially now that her knee is all healed."

"What happened to her knee?"

"She fell off a mountain."

Dani gasped. "Seriously?"

"Uh-huh. She and Tyler were out running in a snowstorm, and she slipped off the side of the trail. Landon and I were on duty that day. Major freak-out to find our own sister badly hurt at the bottom of that ravine."

"Wow, I bet it was."

"But something good came of it. Tyler felt so bad about her getting hurt after he'd dared her to go running with him that he took her home, nursed her back to health and got her to fall in love with him."

"Awww, that's awesome. What a great story."

"We're very thankful to him," he said in a grave tone that had her giggling helplessly and forgetting she was supposed to be nervous about her interview.

"She can't be that bad."

He glanced at her. "Just you wait. If you get the job, you'll be working closely with her as the director of inventory."

"Gulp."

"Don't worry. She'll be nice to you. She saves the worst of her evil for her brothers."

"Good to know."

As the small town of Butler came into view, Dani thought again how pretty it was with the colorful storefronts, the diner, the café and the requisite white steepled church that her grandmother used to say was a staple of every New England town. But the crown jewel of the Butler downtown was the Green Mountain Country Store, with its rustic exterior, rough-hewn front porch adorned with a dozen rocking chairs and the painted sign over the door.

A beat of excitement went through her at finally getting to explore the store she'd read about online. The website boasted of hard-to-find products from a simpler time. With the store planning to roll out its first catalog in time for the holiday season later that year, the warehouse manager would be responsible for overseeing everything from inventory to order fulfillment. It would be a challenging job, especially since the warehouse and catalog were new, but Dani wanted something she could get excited about.

Lucas had offered to take care of Savannah for her during the interview, which was why he'd also ended up driving them to town.

He took Savannah's car seat and diaper bag. "I've got her. You don't want to work up a sweat before your interview."

"True."

She followed him inside, trying not to pay too much attention to the way the denim hugged his ass, but she'd have to be dead not to notice that Lucas Abbott was very finely put together. Dani wondered if his ass was as muscular as the rest of him, which was a wholly inappropriate thought to be having before her interview with the man's father.

"Lucas."

He stopped his trajectory toward the stairs that led to the offices upstairs and turned to her.

"We have a few minutes. Would it be okay if I took a look at the store before we go up?"

"Of course." He hung the diaper bag on the newel post and took Savannah out of her car seat so he could carry her. "We should've done that yesterday when we were here."

"It's no problem. I'm looking forward to seeing it, but I can take her."

"No need, I've got her. Come on, I'll give you the grand tour."

They started in the housewares department, where Dani admired the woven tablecloths the store was known for, before moving on to the apothecary, where cures for just about any routine ailment known to mankind could be found.

"This department is my brother Wade's pride and joy."

Dani took in the dark wood shelves, the nooks and crannies full of products in bottles and jars of all shapes and sizes. "Oh, Tigress perfume." She waggled her brows at him as she took a sniff of the fragrance. "Wonder if it turns anyone who wears it into a tigress."

Lucas swallowed hard. "Uh, I could ask Wade."

Dani laughed. "Don't do that!"

"He can seriously tell you anything you want to know about any of these products. He's a total geek for this stuff."

"I could wear Tabu lipstick with my Tigress perfume," she said, winking at him. And yes, she was enjoying flustering him.

"You're doing this on purpose," he muttered.

"Doing what?" she asked, the picture of innocence.

He scowled playfully at her. "Time to move on, tigress."

"You're no fun."

The look he gave her told her otherwise, but she decided to quit poking the bear before he poked back. And if he did? How would she feel about that? She didn't know, so she needed to proceed with caution.

"That's the jewelry my sister Hannah makes."

"It's beautiful. I want to come back to take a closer look when I have more time."

They cut through an aisle full of toys, where Lucas found a talking sheep he wanted for Savvy, before proceeding to the cheese counter. Olga, the older woman working there, greeted them with warm smiles.

"It's Lucas, right?" she asked hesitantly.

"Yep." He stroked the beard that had thickened overnight. "The fur gives me away this time of year."

"That's the only way I'm certain," Olga said.

"These are my friends Savannah and her mother, Dani, who's interviewing for a job with the company this morning."

Olga wiped her hands on a towel and reached across the counter to shake hands with Dani. "So nice to meet you and your adorable daughter. This is a great place to work, and I'm not just saying that because his folks own the joint."

Dani laughed. "If cheese samples are part of the package, I'm all in."

"You'll have all the cheese, maple syrup, fudge and penny candy you can handle working here."

Dani looked up at Lucas. "Did I just gain five pounds by walking in the door?"

He laughed and shook his head. "Not yet, but you do have to be careful. The ladies that work the floor are like dealers, getting us hooked on whatever is being featured each day."

Olga cut a larger than usual sample and slid the cheese across the cutting board to Dani.

"See what I mean? They're very good at their jobs."

"You're the devil, Olga," she said as she popped the cheese into her mouth.

When the flavorful sharp cheddar attacked her taste buds, Dani moaned with pleasure. Her gaze connected with Lucas's, which had heated at the sound of her moan.

Oh, hello.

"That's some good cheese. Can we get some to take home?"

"Um, sure." His Adam's apple bobbed. "We can grab it on the way out." He checked his watch. "We should head upstairs so you're not late for your very important date."

"Oh jeez!" Dani had been so charmed by the store that she'd almost forgotten the interview. "I definitely don't want to be late. Thanks again, Olga."

"Good luck with the interview. Hope you get the job."

"Me, too!" The place was magical, and she'd love to work there.

She followed Lucas upstairs, smiling at the way he chattered with Savannah the whole way up, making a big production out of bouncing her on each step while the baby giggled with the usual glee she exhibited whenever Lucas was around. It occurred to Dani that Savannah was getting attached to him. Hell, she was, too.

They'd slipped so easily into life together over the last few days, it felt as if she'd known him much longer than she had. When they reached the reception area, Dani forced her thoughts about Lucas to the side—for now—so she could focus on landing this job that she wanted even more after having seen the store.

Emma greeted them with a warm smile. "Welcome back. Linc is in the conference room and said to send you in when you arrived."

"Oh, um, okay, then." She looked up at Lucas. "You're sure you're okay with her?"

"I'm fine. We're going to bother my siblings at work while you're in the meeting, aren't we, Savvy?"

She reached up for a handful of his beard.

He caught her hand before she could pull. "Look at how quick she is. She's a genius, I tell you."

Emma and Dani laughed.

"Lucas," Emma said, "why don't you show Dani to the conference room and introduce her to your dad?"

"Why didn't I think of that? Right this way." He gestured in the direction of the conference room and walked with her to the closed door. After knocking, he stuck his head in. "Can we come in?"

"Of course."

Lucas opened the door and ushered Dani in ahead of him. Right away, she noticed Lincoln Abbott was an older version of his son, and every bit as handsome in his own right. He had silver hair and bright blue eyes, made more so by the light blue dress shirt he wore, the sleeves rolled up to his forearms. His face lit up with a warm, welcoming smile.

"Who've you got there, son?"

"This is Savannah and her mom, Dani."

Lincoln stood to greet them. "Wow, what a cutie you are." When he reached out to her, Savannah curled her pudgy hand around his index finger. "And strong, too!"

"She's super smart," Lucas said. "I'm convinced she's a genius."

Lincoln's brows knitted with curiosity as he took in his son's obvious affection for the baby.

"We'll get out of here so you can talk to Dani. She really loves the store and wants the job, so you'd better hire her."

"Lucas!" Dani couldn't believe he'd said that. "There's absolutely no pressure, Mr. Abbott."

"Call me Linc, and don't mind him. He's not the boss of me."

Lucas surprised her when he kissed her forehead on his way out. "Knock him dead."

Flustered by the unexpected affection from him, Dani had to force herself to remember where she was and why she was there.

"Have a seat, Dani, or do you prefer Danielle?"

"Dani is fine, and thank you."

She sat next to him at the table, and he poured glasses of ice water for both of them from a pitcher on the table.

"Your daughter seems quite fond of my son."

"She's crazy about him. He's been… Well, he's amazing, but I'm sure you already know that."

Linc sat back in his chair, his body language relaxed and welcoming. "I do know that, but I'd love to hear why you think so."

Dani told him the story of how Lucas had rescued her and Savannah after the accident and provided them with a place to stay in Stowe and in Butler. "I'm usually much more organized than I was coming up here. I never gave a thought to ski season or that the hotels would be jammed."

"Ah, right. An easy mistake to make if you don't know the area."

"I promise you, I'm much more on top of it at work than I was in planning this trip. It was somewhat spur-of-the-moment, and I've learned my lesson about being spontaneous in Vermont."

"You can be spontaneous in Vermont, as long as you're mindful of the weather and the seasons. Right now, we're headed into mud season, which is slow at the store. Most people who aren't from here don't realize that the fall is our busiest season because the leaf peepers come from all over to view the colorful foliage."

"See? I never would've thought of that either."

"You're safe in mud season, however. Lots of lodging to be found then, but mud season brings other challenges. Just ask my daughter-in-law Cameron about that."

"Lucas told me about what happened to her with Fred. I can't wait to meet him."

"If you stick around for long, you'll have an encounter with him."

"I'd love to stick around in Butler. It's the most adorable little town, and your store is just… Well, you know. It's amazing."

Smiling, he said, "We're proud of it." He propped a pair of reading glasses on the end of his nose and picked up her résumé. "Let's talk about the position at the warehouse and what you think you could bring to the role."

Dani realized he'd used small talk to put her completely at ease and could see where Lucas came by his natural charm. "I'd be happy to."

CHAPTER 15

"To love is nothing. To be loved is something. But to love and be loved, that's everything."
—T. Tolis

Lucas took Savvy in to meet Hunter, who was, as always, face-first in his computer. As the chief financial officer of the family's many businesses, Hunter was the glue who kept it all humming along, or so he liked to tell them. In truth, Lucas gave his oldest brother credit for all he did and was thankful he didn't have to spend his days face-first in a computer.

"Hunter, I want you to meet Savannah, but you can call her Savvy."

"Hi, Savannah. What're you doing with my degenerate brother?"

Lucas faked offense and covered the baby's ears. "Don't say that. She's in love with me."

"Someone's gotta be."

Though he knew the comment was said in jest, he couldn't help feeling slightly wounded by it.

"What's the story with you and your little doll?" Hunter made kissing noises to get Savvy's attention.

"Her mom is interviewing with Dad for the warehouse manager job. They're friends of mine."

"Oh yeah? Since when?"

"Since I rescued them when their car went off the road in Stowe the other night."

"Yikes. That's scary."

"Yeah, it was. I was right behind them and saw it happen."

"Does her mom know how lucky she was to crash with you behind her?"

That was the story of his life with his siblings—a jab followed by a compliment. "I think she does now. I'm just glad I was there when they needed help."

Savvy rested her head on his chest, her eyes heavy.

He rubbed her back and kept moving, hoping to sway her into taking a nap.

"Look at you. You're like an old pro."

"She's a sweetheart. She makes it easy."

Hunter gave him a probing look. "You getting into something with her and the mom?"

Lucas tried not to squirm. "I don't know. I like them both."

"Hmmm. Interesting."

"What is?"

"You with a baby in your arms. Didn't expect to see that for a while yet."

"Neither did I." Lucas hadn't expected anything that'd happened since he left Butler the other night, looking for some time to himself. He hadn't had much time to himself since meeting Dani and Savvy, and that was fine with him. It wouldn't have been fine with him at this time last week.

Lucas shut the office door and sat in Hunter's visitor chair. "How do you *know*, Hunter?"

"Know what?"

Lucas gave him an imploring look. "With Megan… How did you know?"

"*Oh*. Well… I guess it was when I couldn't stop thinking about her, even when I knew she had a big crush on Will."

"Damn, I'd almost forgotten about that."

"Seems like a distant memory now, but at the time, it was painful."

"I bet it was, especially since no one had any idea how you felt about her."

"I went to enormous lengths to keep it private, which, with hindsight, was probably not the smartest thing I ever did. Look at all the time I wasted that could've been spent with her."

"It was worth it, though, right? All the rough stuff."

Hunter's entire face went soft as the right side of his mouth lifted into a small smile. "Yeah. It's the best thing ever, to know you've found the one you were meant to be with and that she loves you as much as you love her. It's everything."

"I've never really wanted that before." He glanced down at Savvy, who was out cold on his chest, with a handful of his flannel tight in her little fist. His heart gave a weird little lurch at the sight of her sweet face, the tiny little lips pursed into a kiss and the way she held on to him. "But now, this little lady and her mom are here, and I'm just… I don't know what I am, but it's something."

"You're invested. That's what you are."

"Yeah, I guess maybe I am."

"What's the deal with the baby's dad?"

"He died in an accident almost a year ago. They were together since high school and were planning their wedding when he died."

Hunter winced. "Jeez. That's awful."

"Yeah, she's been through a lot."

"If you care about her and her daughter, and it's obvious that you do, let her set the pace. This situation is unlike anything you've confronted before, and you should proceed with caution. That's my best advice."

"Gramps said the same thing when I talked to him about it."

A knock on the door interrupted them. "Come in," Hunter said.

Amanda stuck her head in. "Sorry to disturb you."

Lucas found it curious that he had no reaction whatsoever to seeing her. *Very interesting.*

"Hey, you've got a baby," she said in a whisper.

"She's my friend's daughter."

"She's beautiful."

"Yes, she is. We were just leaving. I'll talk to you later, Hunter."

"See you."

Lucas left Hunter's office and ducked into the one Will shared with Cameron. The two of them were hard at work—Will on the Vermont Made line he oversaw and Cameron on the website she'd built for the store. Their feet were intertwined under the desks that faced each other.

A week ago, he would've cracked a joke about the two of them being joined at the foot, but now it just struck him as incredibly sweet.

Will looked up and waved him in. "What's up?" He did a double take when he realized Lucas wasn't traveling alone. "Who is trusting you with their child?"

"My friend Dani. She's in with Dad interviewing for the warehouse manager position."

"Oh great," Cameron said. "We needed someone in that job a month ago." She stood for a closer look at the baby. She and

Will were expecting their first child in the summer. "What a cutie! What's her name?"

"Savannah."

Probably hearing there was a baby in the building, Charley and Ella came in to say hello.

"Shhhh, don't wake her. She was fussy last night because she's teething."

Ella gave him a warm smile. "She looks good on you, Luc."

"Thanks," he said, pleased by his sister's comment. "She's already got me wrapped around all her fingers."

Wade wandered in, and Charley stepped aside so he could see the baby. "Adorable." As he was the most taciturn of the Abbott siblings, the one-word comment didn't surprise Lucas.

"Hey, Wade, can I still add a plus-one for the wedding?"

"I'm sure it'd be no problem. Cabot has gone stark-raving mad over this event. Sky's the limit, he says. I can let Mia know you'll be bringing someone."

"We might need in on the nanny action, too."

"No problem. Word is he hired two of them, one for Caden and one for Callie." Wade rolled his eyes. "He wants everything to be perfect for Mia."

"Can't say I blame him after waiting so long to find her," Ella said. "Imagine what it was like for him. All those years not knowing where she was." Ella shuddered. "The poor guy has been through hell."

"I know," Wade said. "That's why Mia is being super patient and letting him do whatever he wants. Like she said, who cares if it's a three-ring circus? We're already married."

"And she married *into* a three-ring circus, so there is that," Lucas said.

Wade snorted out a laugh. "Exactly. The wedding will be nothing compared to life with the Abbotts."

"How's your house shaping up?" Will asked Wade.

"Coming right along. Plenty to do if anyone feels like stopping by to lend a hand."

"I can give you a few hours on Saturday," Will said. "If it's okay with my lovely wife."

"Of course it is," Cameron said. "I'm going fixture shopping in Rutland with Mia. We're looking forward to spending a fortune on countertops and farm sinks and other fun stuff."

Wade groaned. "There goes the budget."

Cameron grinned and placed a hand over her growing baby bump. "I'm practicing for when we add on to the cabin this summer to make room for Will Junior."

"You are not naming him Will Junior," Charley said.

"Probably not, but that's what we're calling him for now," Cameron said.

"So you're having a boy?" Lucas asked.

"We have no idea," Will said. "We just started saying *him*, and it caught on."

"Whereas we say *her*," Ella said. "Watch us have the exact opposite."

"Wouldn't matter to me," Will said. "As long as he or she is healthy and my baby mama is okay, I'm good." Cameron's mother and grandmother had both died in childbirth, so Will and Cam had taken the extraordinary step of having her fully examined at Mass General before she became pregnant. The doctors there had said there was no reason whatsoever to expect the same fate for Cam, but Lucas knew that they would worry anyway until the baby arrived.

"Same," Ella said. "No one told me nine months takes *forever*."

Ella had been dying to be a mother for as long as Lucas could remember, and looking at her now, he could see that she fairly glowed with happiness. She finally had everything she wanted—the man she'd loved for years and a baby on the way.

"That's because it actually takes *ten* months," Cameron said. "Hello, *forty* weeks. Why do they say nine months when it's ten?"

"It's an eternity," Ella declared.

Lucas rubbed Savannah's back, happy that she was warm in his arms and he didn't have to wait nine—or ten—months to see her. That would be an eternity, especially after the time he'd already spent with her.

"Um, excuse me. Is Lucas in there?"

"Let her in, you guys."

His sisters moved apart, and Wade stepped closer to Will's side of the office to make room for Dani in the crowded space.

"Everyone, this is Dani. Dani, this is what it's like to be one of ten kids. Meet my brothers Will and Wade, Will's wife, Cameron, and you've met Ella and Charley."

"It's so nice to meet you all and to see you again."

"And this isn't even all of them," Lucas said.

"Wow."

"Right?" Cameron said. "I'm an only child, so the Abbotts were overwhelming at first, to say the least. But you get used to it."

"I'm an only, too."

Cameron stepped forward to put her arm around Dani. "Stay with me, little grasshopper. I'll protect you."

Dani laughed. "Thank you."

"Not necessary, Cam." Lucas stood to put his own arm around Dani. "I'll protect her from the evil Abbotts." He was well aware that he was making a statement—a big statement—and he did it anyway.

Dani smiled up at him. "I got the job."

Lucas let out a whoop that woke Savannah, who came to with a loud cry of protest. "Shhh, sorry, sweetheart. Mommy had good news."

Dani took the baby from him, and he immediately felt lost without her weight and heat against his chest.

"Congrats, Dani," Cameron said. "We need you badly."

"That's what Linc said. He told me you could show me the first draft of the catalog?"

"Yep. I've been working on it with Lucy for weeks, and we're getting close to having most of the text done. I've got a printout you can have. We'll be working on photography this spring and summer, with a plan to drop it in September."

"Reminder," Lucas said. "Lucy is our brother Colton's fiancée, and she's also Emma's sister."

"The head spins," Dani said.

"I'll show you pictures when we get home."

"Visuals would help."

Cameron handed Dani the thick printout of the catalog, held together with the biggest binder clip Lucas had ever seen. "When do you start?"

"Monday. Now I just have to line up childcare. Do you guys know anyone who might be able to do it?"

Lucas and his siblings exchanged glances before they all spoke at once.

"Hannah."

As they drove back to Lucas's place, through the picturesque town and the outskirts that included Butler Mountain in the distance, Dani felt a sense of calm come over her. She had gotten the job. Lucas and his siblings were convinced that his sister Hannah would want to watch Savannah for her, and she felt like she'd made a bunch of new friends in the last few days, particularly Lucas, without whom none of this would be happening. Tomorrow, Ella was going to show her the apartment where she'd once lived that was now available again.

Things were falling into place, and the pressure on Dani's chest, which had been so much a part of her daily existence since Jack died, had eased up, allowing her to breathe freely again. For a long time, she'd wondered if she would always feel as if an elephant was standing on her, making it difficult to do the simplest things such as breathe. Food had lost its taste. Life had lost its purpose.

Then Savannah had arrived and given her a purpose again, but even she hadn't helped to move the elephant.

Only since she'd been here in Vermont, away from home and the constant reminders of what she'd lost, had the elephant gotten its fat butt off her chest.

"What're you thinking about over there?" Lucas asked.

"Elephants."

"What about them?"

"How heavy they are."

"Okay…"

Dani knew she needed to explain it better and took a second to get her thoughts together. "Since Jack died, I've felt like I had an elephant sitting on my chest."

"Oh, I see."

"It's kinda hard to breathe with an elephant sitting on your chest."

"I bet it is."

"It's hard to do anything when you feel that way."

To his credit, Lucas stayed quiet and let her talk.

"I was just thinking that for the first time in a long time, it feels like the elephant is finally gone." She looked over at him. "And so much of the reason for that is thanks to you."

"No, Dani. It's thanks to *you*. I wish you could see yourself the way I do. When I look at you, I don't see a weak, helpless woman. I see someone who suffered an unimaginable loss, but who has picked herself and her daughter up and relocated far away from her safety net because she wants to be in charge of her own life when it would be *so much easier* to let her parents take care of everything for her. That takes guts, babe."

"I don't know about that," she said, moved by his kind words and the conviction behind them as well as the term of endearment. He almost made her believe the things he said about her, but she knew better. While she might seem to have things together on the outside, on the inside, she was still a hot mess.

But not as hot of a mess as she'd been a month ago or two months ago or three, when she could barely get out of bed in the morning after having Savannah and being hit with a massive case of postpartum depression when it sank in that Jack would never meet the child he'd wanted so badly.

"I know how strong you are, even if you don't know it yet, and I'll keep reminding you so you don't forget."

"I don't know what I did to get lucky enough to find a friend like you right when I needed you most, but whatever it was, I'm thankful for you."

"Well, basically, you were lucky enough to spin off the road right in front of me, and for what it's worth, I'm thankful for you, too."

"What've I done?"

"You and Savannah have given me something I didn't know I was missing." He reached across the center console and curled his much larger hand around hers, setting off a jolt of excitement that caught her by surprise. "Now that I have you girls in my life, I hope you know you're stuck with me." He punctuated his words with a squeeze of her hand.

"We're okay with that."

"That's good, because you need someone to keep the elephants off your chest."

"It would be nice to have an elephant wrangler around."

"Does that mean I'm hired for the job?"

They were talking in metaphors, but the implications were clear. "How exactly would you view your job description, should you be hired for the position?"

Lucas appeared to give that significant thought. "My duties would include, but not be limited to, taking care of you and Savvy in every way possible while encouraging and supporting your professional goals and aspirations."

He took her breath away.

"And you... you want that job?"

Bringing her hand to his mouth, he brushed his lips over the back of her hand, his beard tickling her sensitive skin. "Very much so, but only if it's what you want, too. I'd never want to push you into something you aren't ready for."

"I... I'm not entirely sure I'm ready, but something tells me I'll never be entirely sure."

"What you've been through is a very difficult thing, Dani. You'll mourn him the rest of your life."

"I will, for sure. More than anything, I mourn that he never knew his beautiful daughter."

"He knows her."

"You really think so?"

"Definitely. He's watching over both of you. I have no doubt about that. Maybe he was the one who made sure I was right behind you when your car went off the road."

"Wouldn't that be something?"

"Sure would."

A few minutes later, they arrived at his place, and Dani was busy with the baby for the next hour, feeding and bathing her after she spit up. The whole time she was focused on Savannah, she thought about the things Lucas had said on the ride home. He had made his feelings about her and her daughter plainly obvious and had tossed the ball into her court.

She believed him when he said he wouldn't push her for anything she wasn't ready for, and she appreciated that he'd come right out and said that.

What did she want?

More than anything, she wanted to be the kind of mother Savannah deserved and not in a constant state of mourning that would make it impossible to experience joy and every other emotion that'd been dormant in her for so long now.

She wanted to be happy again.

Lucas made her happy. Would that always be the case? She had no way to know, but she wanted more of what she'd already had with him. How much more? She didn't know that either, but she liked the way she felt when he was around, and for now, that was more than enough.

CHAPTER 16

"Love is the voice under all silences, the hope which has no opposite in fear; the strength so strong mere force is feebleness: the truth more first than sun, more last than star."
—E.E. Cummings

While she was busy with the baby, Lucas was dying a slow, miserable death from uncertainty as he second-guessed everything he'd said to her in the truck. He'd gotten caught up in the moment and had laid down a gauntlet that might end up scaring her off.

As he ran an iron over one of the light blue uniform shirts he wore to work, he replayed the conversation in his mind over and over again, wincing at the parts where he'd upped the ante.

"Stupid," he said out loud. "She's got enough going on without you panting over her."

He ironed the hell out of that shirt and then did a second one for tomorrow night's shift, which was wildly out of character for him. Planning ahead was hardly his forte. But he was desperate to stay busy so he wouldn't be tempted to go find her, to press her against a wall and kiss her face off, which was what he wanted to do.

"Can't do that," he muttered. "No matter what, you can't do that."

"Do what?"

Dani's voice from the doorway startled him, and he nearly dropped the iron. She had her arms crossed as she leaned against the doorframe.

He stared at her, unable to put two words together to answer her question. Did she have any idea how freaking gorgeous she was?

"Lucas? What can't you do?"

Faced with the choice of telling the truth or lying, he went with the truth. "Kiss you."

"Oh." She tipped her head adorably. "And you want to do that?"

"Ah, yeah. Kind of a lot, actually."

"Come here."

He hesitated to leave the safety of the ironing board, which he hoped was hiding his immediate, almost painful reaction to her. "Where's Savvy?"

"Sleeping."

"Oh."

"Lucas."

He forced himself to look at her.

"Please come here."

He'd never been more powerfully drawn to another human being in his life, a fact that he acknowledged as he left the sanctuary of the ironing board and went to her, fully aware that she could probably see how badly he wanted her. That he didn't care if she saw everything there was to see about him indicated just how far gone he was over her. "I'm here," he said when he was a foot from her.

"Closer."

He took another step.

Her hands landed on his hips and gave a gentle tug, bringing his body into contact with hers.

He sucked in a sharp deep breath. "Dani…"

"Yes, Lucas?"

"What're you doing?"

She moved her hands from his hips to his chest and then up to curl her arms around his neck. Then she went up on tiptoes to press her lips to his. "This," she said, "is what I'm doing. Is that okay?"

He'd kissed a lot of women, but her soft, sweet, innocent kiss electrified him the way no other kiss ever had. In that moment, he realized he was in big, big trouble with this woman, and he had never loved trouble more. "It's okay," he said gruffly.

"Is it okay if I do it again?"

"God, I wish you would."

This time, he was ready for her. Lucas wrapped his arms around her and brought her in as close to him as he could get her. And when her lips parted, he took the kiss to the next level, with gentle strokes of his tongue against hers.

She fisted a handful of his hair in an apparent attempt to keep him from getting away.

No worries. He wasn't going *anywhere*.

He lost track of time and anything that didn't involve her soft lips and sweet flavor. And when her tongue brushed up against his, he groaned.

She broke the kiss and looked up at him, seeming as stunned as he felt.

Lucas stared down at her, noting the splash of color in her cheeks and the damp lips that beckoned him back for another taste. Though he had to be at work in less than an hour, that was the last thing on his mind with her warm and soft in his arms. He ached for more of her in a way he never had before. In the past, these sorts of things had been all about fun and games, lighthearted encounters in which everyone got what they wanted and no one got hurt.

This, however…

This was something else altogether.

As her hands slid over his back, he moved his up to cover her full breasts, running his thumbs back and forth over nipples that tightened under his touch.

And then she pulled back suddenly, covering her breasts with her hands. "I, uh… I'm… I don't want to leak on you."

He brought her back. "I wouldn't care."

"It's weird."

Shaking his head, he kissed her neck and breathed in the alluring scent of her skin. He couldn't identify the scent that was so uniquely hers. "Not weird."

"Yes, it is."

"No."

"*Yes.*"

Lucas chuckled softly. "It's totally natural. Don't worry about it." Looking over her shoulder, he saw the time on the stove clock and groaned. "I have to go to work."

"I know."

"Will you be okay here by yourselves?"

"Of course we will."

"I'll leave the number at the firehouse in case you need me."

"I won't."

"You could call me around nine or so if you wanted to need me just a little."

Smiling, she said, "I'll see what I can do."

He framed her face with his hands, noting the light sprinkling of freckles across her nose, her lush lashes and pink lips gone slightly puffy from their kisses. "I wish I didn't have to leave."

"I wish you didn't either."

"You'll be here when I get home, right?"

"Where else would I be?"

"You could be anywhere." He smoothed her hair, which had gotten messed up during the heated make-out session. "I'm just very thankful you're here with me."

"So am I." She gave him a gentle push. "Get ready for work."

"Don't wanna."

"Go."

"If you're gonna be that way about it…"

"I am. I don't want you to get in trouble because of me."

"I'm one of the bosses."

"Go to work, Lucas. I've got a catalog to read."

"Oh boy, that sounds exciting."

"I can't wait to check it out. I'm so happy to have gotten this job and that I get to stay in Butler."

"You have no idea how happy I am that you're sticking around."

"I think I have a small idea," she said with a playful grin.

"Nothing *small* about it," he muttered.

"*Lucas!* Go to work."

He walked away laughing and counting the hours until he could kiss her again.

After Lucas left, Dani settled on the sofa with the catalog printout Cameron had given her and tried to concentrate on the pages of products that would soon fall under her purview as the manager of the warehouse that would fulfill orders. But she couldn't stay focused on work when all she could think about was kissing Lucas and how he'd responded to her.

He'd kissed her like a man who'd been starving for a taste of her.

Dani touched her lips, which were still tender and sensitive. She smiled when she thought of the way he'd held her and touched her, as if she were precious to him. A week ago, she wouldn't have been able to picture a scenario where she'd want to kiss any man who wasn't Jack.

But now...

She wondered what would've happened if Lucas hadn't had to work.

Her heart quickened when she thought of what it might be like...

"Don't," she said, shuddering. "Don't think about that."

Why not? She was a healthy young woman who had suffered a devastating loss, but she had to believe that Jack wouldn't want her to be alone for the rest of her life. Eventually, she'd have to "go there" with someone else. Would that someone else be Lucas?

She was starting to hope so. He'd shown her who he really was in the first minutes and hours she'd known him, and nothing she'd seen since then had changed that initial impression. He was a good guy, a decent guy, an *honorable* guy... She'd heard enough horror stories from her friends at home to know those qualities were hard to find in this crazy world. Her friends had seen almost everything with the guys they'd dated. They'd made her feel lucky to have found her true love in high school.

Until she lost him, that was.

Dani shook off that thought. Today had been a great day—the best day she'd had since she lost Jack, and it was a day for celebration and looking forward, not backward.

That said, she did need to check in with her parents and let them know the good news about her job. She put down the catalog that she'd barely glanced at and went to the kitchen to get the portable phone, taking it with her when she went to look in on Savannah.

She was still asleep with her arms tossed over her head. Dani would have to wake her in half an hour so she wouldn't be up all night.

Taking the phone to the sofa, she punched in the familiar number.

Once again, her mother answered on the first ring. "Hello?" She sounded stressed, like she so often did since Jack died.

"Hey, it's me."

"Oh, thank goodness you called! It's Dani!"

Her father picked up the extension. "Hi, honey."

"Hi, Dad."

"Why haven't you called?" her mother asked.

"I didn't have anything new to tell you until today, when I landed a job at the Green Mountain Country Store in Butler. I'm going to be their warehouse manager, and I'm so excited. It's the greatest store and company. You can look it up online."

"What'll you do with Savannah?" her mom said.

"I am working on childcare. My friend Lucas's sister has a daughter around the same age, and he thinks she'd love to watch Savannah so her daughter will have a playmate."

"So she's not a licensed provider?"

"No, Mom, she's a mother with a child of her own who comes highly recommended by my friend and his siblings."

"Where will you live?"

"I'm looking at an apartment tomorrow. I know this isn't what you guys wanted for me, but I'm happy, and I want you to be happy for me."

"We are, Dani," her dad said. "Of course we are."

Her mother remained stubbornly silent on the subject, not that Dani was surprised. She must be having trouble filling her time now that she didn't have Dani's life to run along with her own.

"Well, I should go and get Savannah up from her nap. I'll check in soon."

"Is this the number where you're staying?"

"For now, yes."

"We'll look forward to talking to you soon, honey," her dad said. "Give our granddaughter kisses from us."

"I will for sure. And I'll FaceTime you soon so you can see her. Love you guys."

"We love you, too," her dad said.

The line went dead before her mom could reply. She'd probably been the one who pushed the button to end the call.

Dani returned the phone to the cradle. It'd been nice to hear their voices, but once again, she was happy to be several hundred miles away from their suffocating need to take care of her and Savannah.

Speaking of that little peanut, it was time to get her up. The first two months had been difficult while the baby had her days and nights confused. Dani had wondered if she'd ever get a full night of sleep again. And then, right around the three-month mark, she'd suddenly slept through the night.

Dani had woken up early the next morning, gripped with fear that something awful had happened while she'd been sleeping.

But Savannah had been awake and smiling and biting her own toes. Motherhood, she'd discovered, was full of tiny panics that had only fueled the bigger panic attacks she'd had since Jack died, each one more terrifying than the last.

They came out of nowhere and left her deeply shaken in the aftermath. She'd been afraid she'd have one while driving to Vermont and had remained constantly vigilant for the telltale signs of impending panic. Thankfully, she hadn't had one while driving. But she did live in fear of having an attack when she was home alone with Savannah and unable to tend to her.

She took a deep breath, found her center the way the counselor she'd seen for a few months after Jack's sudden death had taught her and went to wake up her daughter. Savannah hadn't moved from where she'd been the last time Dani checked her. After placing her hand on the baby's back, she was startled by the intense heat coming from her tiny body. She felt her forehead and gasped at how hot she was.

"Oh my God." She picked her up. "Savannah, wake up and see Mommy."

She was like a ragdoll in her mother's arms.

"Sweet baby girl, don't make your mommy cry. Please wake up and talk to me." With shaking hands, Dani took her into the bathroom, turned on the cold water, wet a washcloth and ran it over the baby's red face. "Savannah!"

The baby came to with a sharp cry of outrage that turned into shrieks that were at once a relief and further cause for panic. She'd never cried like that. Ever. Over the next hour, Dani tried everything she could think of to calm her, but nothing worked. She got some baby Tylenol into her that she promptly threw up all over herself and her mother, who was now in tears, too.

Dani changed her diaper and tried breastfeeding her, but Savannah couldn't stop crying long enough to latch on. Only when the baby had cried for more than ninety minutes did Dani get desperate enough to find the number Lucas had left for her and call him at work. She thought the man who answered was him.

"Lucas, it's me, Dani. Savannah... She won't stop crying."

"Hey, this is Landon. Let me get him for you."

Lucas came on the line a minute later. "Dani? What's wrong?"

"She won't stop crying and she's burning up. Where can I take her to be seen around here?"

"Northeastern Vermont Regional in St. Johnsbury has an ER."

"Can you give me directions?" She could barely hear him over the baby's crying, but she couldn't depend on GPS in the mountains.

"I'll come get you."

"No. You're working. I'll take her. I just need to know how to get there."

"Dani, it's dark, wet and cold, which means black ice and other hazards. It's safer for me to take you than for you to try to get there on your own. Trust me on this."

Once again, she was forced to acknowledge she had no business trying to stand on her own two feet. But now was not the time to try to prove anything to herself or anyone else. Savannah needed help, and that was all that mattered. "Okay."

"I'll be there in ten. Get her ready."

The line went dead, and Dani got busy shoving a reluctant baby into a snowsuit. She fought her mother every step of the way, her limbs rigid and her face so red that Dani feared her little head would explode.

"Please, Jack... If you can hear me, please help me. Please help our little girl." When she had the baby zipped into her snowsuit, she walked her around the loft until she saw the flashing red lights appear outside.

Lucas had come in hot, and she'd never been more relieved in her life.

She quickly strapped Savannah into her car seat and was halfway down the stairs to the driveway when Lucas brought the fire department SUV to a skidding stop in the driveway and jumped out to take the baby from her.

They didn't say a word to each other as they worked together to get her strapped into the backseat.

"Sit in back with her." He sounded as tense as Dani felt. That didn't do much to calm the panic that had her chest feeling tighter by the minute. She forced herself to breathe, not wanting to become a patient herself when her daughter needed her to keep it together.

He drove fast but not recklessly, the red light on top of the car flashing the entire way as other cars got the hell out of their way.

"Thank you," she whispered between the baby's frantic cries.

He reached back for her hand and held on tight the rest of the way through the dark night. His calm, steady presence was the only thing that kept the panic from taking over.

CHAPTER 17

"A good father will leave his imprint on his daughter
for the rest of her life."
—Dr. James Dobson

Lucas drove much faster than he should have, but with the baby crying uncontrollably the entire way, his nerves were stretched to the limit. From the second Landon had told him Dani was on the phone for him, he'd known something must be wrong for her to call him at work. And the sound of Savvy's crying in the background had put him on high alert. It didn't sound right to him either.

While holding Dani's hand, he kept a firm grip on the wheel with his other hand, determined to get them safely to St. Johnsbury.

"How much longer?" Dani asked.

"Ten minutes. Almost there."

Ten minutes felt like forever to him, and probably to her, too. Thankfully, other cars got out of their way when they saw the flashing lights.

The fire department radio in his vehicle crackled to life with a call about a senior citizen in distress in the neighborhood near where Gavin's parents lived. Landon and the other firefighter on duty would take the call, but Lucas felt bad about leaving them shorthanded. But when Dani had called and he'd heard the way Savvy was crying, he'd bolted out of the firehouse to get home to them as fast as he could.

A tense ten minutes later, he brought the SUV to a stop in front of the ER doors and jumped out to help Dani get the car seat out.

They rushed inside together, and Lucas breathed a sigh of relief when he saw the waiting room was deserted and he recognized the nurse working the desk. He'd known her for years from bringing victims in for treatment.

"Hey, Luc," she said with a warm smile.

"Tracy, this is my friend Dani and her daughter, Savannah. The baby is running a high fever and has been crying this way for more than an hour."

"Bring her back."

Tracy led the way through double doors to the cubicle area.

Savannah screamed even louder when the bright lights hit her eyes.

As Tracy showed them into a curtained room, Lucas noticed how freaked out Dani looked.

So he put the car seat on the examination bed and moved quickly to get Savannah out of the seat and out of the snowsuit. He was alarmed to realize just how hot her body was. Her face was bright red and her eyes swollen from endless tears.

"Poor baby." He held her close to him, hoping he would have the usual effect on her, but not even he could calm her tonight.

After typing the info Dani gave her into a computer, Tracy ran a thermometer over the baby's forehead, her brows furrowing at the reading. "One-oh-three."

"That's up from when I took it at home an hour ago," Dani said.

"Were you able to get any medicine into her?"

"I tried, but she threw it all up."

"I'll get the doctor."

Lucas walked Savannah around the small space, trying all the tricks that usually worked, but she wasn't having it.

The doctor came in a few minutes later, a dark-haired guy Lucas didn't recognize. He looked so young, Lucas wondered if he'd graduated from high school, let alone med school.

"Let's put her on the exam bed, please," the doctor said.

Despite his youthful appearance, the doctor was calm and competent as he examined Savannah, who continued to scream.

Lucas put his arm around Dani and discovered she was frantically trembling. The poor thing had been through enough. Why was this happening on top of everything else? He kissed the top of her head and ran his hand up and down her arm, hoping to offer a small bit of comfort and wishing there was more he could do.

"I think she has a double ear infection, and one eardrum looks perforated," the doctor said. "That hurts and could explain her unhappiness. She also seems a little dehydrated, so we'll get her on some fluids and antibiotics that should make her feel much better."

"She's had a couple of lesser fevers in the last few days that I assumed were from teething," Dani said, her voice wavering.

"Could be that, or it could've been the ear infection coming on," the doctor said. "She'll be fine in a couple of hours. I'll send the nurse in to get an IV started."

While Lucas was filled with relief, he realized Dani's body had gone tight with tension.

She placed her hand over her chest.

Lucas moved so he was in front of her, squatted so his eyes were level with hers. "Breathe, Dani."

Her terrified gaze met his.

"Breathe. Savvy is going to be fine. *Breathe.*" He gave her a little shake to jar her and wanted to weep with relief when she took a big gulping breath. "Again."

As tears slid down her cheeks, Dani drew in a shaky deep breath.

Lucas wiped away the tears that broke his heart, knowing how desperately she wanted to be strong for her daughter. "One more."

She took another breath.

The entire episode took a matter of seconds, but it felt like longer, especially with Savannah continuing to cry without letting up.

He gathered Dani closer to him and held on tight with one arm while placing his free hand on Savannah's heaving chest. "Shhh, my ladies. Everything will be okay." At some point, they had become his ladies, and he would do anything to bring them both comfort, safety, security and anything else they needed.

Dani gave him a gentle nudge, and he released her so she could pick up Savannah and try to comfort her until the nurse returned.

Lucas hugged them both, and after a few minutes, Savannah finally stopped crying and fell asleep. He was afraid to breathe and possibly wake her. The baby's tiny body hiccupped with sobs, even in her sleep.

That's where Landon found them when he came in, wearing the same uniform Lucas had on and carrying his own portable radio. "How is she?" he whispered.

Lucas released Dani and turned to his brother. "Double ear infection with perforation."

"Ouch."

Dani glanced at Landon and gasped. "Holy crap. There really are two of you."

Lucas smiled. "Dani, meet my brother Landon. Landon, this is Dani and Savannah."

"Great to meet you," Landon said.

"You, too. Is it okay if I stare for a second?"

Landon stuck out his jaw dramatically. "Stare all you want. I'm used to it."

Lucas gave him a shove. "Go away."

"I'm so misunderstood," Landon said.

"You're perfectly understood, which is why you need to go away."

"A guy tries to show some concern, and this is the thanks he gets."

Lucas actually was thankful to Landon and the bit of badly needed levity he'd brought to the situation. "How's your patient?"

"Recovering from pneumonia and took a fall at home," Landon said. "Poor guy."

"That's terrible," Dani said as she rubbed the baby's back.

"He'll be okay. I've got to get back to work. Safe to say you're done for the night?" he asked Lucas.

"Yeah, can you call in coverage?"

"I've got people on standby in case we need someone."

"Thanks for covering for me."

"Anytime. Nice to meet you, Dani. I hope Savannah feels better soon."

"Thanks. Nice to meet you, too. Sorry about the staring."

Landon laughed. "It's okay. We're used to it. Catch you later, bro."

"See you."

After Landon walked away, Dani looked up at Lucas. "Holy. *Crap.*"

"I told you we were identical."

"You can't ever shave your beard. You have to promise."

Lucas smiled, relieved to see some color back in her cheeks and that her eyes were once again full of life rather than panic. "I'll make sure you know how to tell us apart. Don't worry about that."

"I'd be so afraid to make a mistake. The beard stays."

"Whatever you say, sweetheart." He'd give her anything she wanted if it meant he got to keep her and Savannah in his life.

Another nurse, whose name was Annie, came rushing in a few minutes later. "So sorry to keep you waiting. We had two more patients arrive in the last ten minutes. That's how it goes—no one and then everyone. Let's get Miss Savannah started on some meds so she can feel better."

Dani laid the baby on the bed.

Lucas could sense her reluctance to put her down and hated to think of her being disturbed, which she would be when the IV went in.

But Annie was good—really good. She did it so quickly and efficiently that Savannah barely stirred.

"Poor thing has worn herself out." Annie hung the bag of medicine on the hook next to the bed. "Mom and Dad should get some sleep, too, while you can. The IV will take a couple of hours."

Lucas startled at being referred to as Savannah's dad. "Oh, I'm not—"

"Thank you," Dani said. "We will."

"I'll check on you in a bit." Annie closed the curtain around the cubicle.

"Sorry," Lucas said, not sure why he felt the need to apologize.

"For what?"

"It was just… Being referred to as her dad…" His heart swelled almost painfully in his chest, full of emotions he'd never experienced before.

"I should apologize to you. After you had the decency to rescue us, you've been completely sucked into our dramas. I was a fool to think I could handle things on my own. I would've frozen to death without you the first night we met, and then tonight, I couldn't get through one night with you at work. I should go back to Kentucky. My parents were right. I can't do this."

"Stop." With his fingers on her chin, he compelled her to look at him. "You're in a new place and had an emergency. I'm the guy people call in an emergency. You did the right thing by calling me. I got you here twice as fast as you could've done on your own without knowing where you were going in the dark. Could you have done it yourself? I have no doubt, but you got Savvy the help she needed as fast as you could. To me, that makes you the best possible mom she could ever have."

Lucas wasn't sure where those words had come from. Perhaps years of listening to his father and grandfather spout wisdom had given him some when he needed it. He could only hope they were the right words at the right time.

"I want to be the best mom to her."

"You *are*. She couldn't ask for better." He put his arms around her and hugged her tight to his chest. "She's going to be okay, and so will you. All you need to do right now is breathe. Everything is fine. I promise. Hold on to me. I've got you."

As she relaxed into his embrace, he wallowed in the fragrant scent of her hair and the feel of her soft curves pressed against him. He gave thanks for whatever higher power had put her car in front of his on that snowy night in Stowe. It occurred to him, standing in that sterile cubicle in the middle of the night, that he was falling in love with her and her daughter, and that falling had never felt so damned good.

After being released from the ER before dawn, they went home and crashed. Lucas had wanted to stay close to them in case he was needed, so he was asleep on the other side of the bed. Dani opened her eyes, checked to make sure Savannah was okay, and then let her gaze wander to the handsome face on the next pillow.

He was sexy even when sound asleep.

His own personal superpower was sexiness, along with kindness, competence, compassion and humor.

And she really, really liked him. And she needed to stop staring at him. She had things to do today, including an appointment with Hannah to talk about her watching Savannah and a date to meet Ella at her former apartment to see if it would work for her and Savannah. She ought to get up, take a shower and get ready for the day while the baby was still sleeping, but she couldn't bring herself to leave the warmth of the cozy bed.

A few more minutes wouldn't hurt anyone.

The next time she awakened, she was alone in bed. She shot up, pushed the wild nest of hair back from her face and jumped out of bed to go find her daughter. In the living room, she found Lucas on the sofa, stocking feet on the coffee table and Savannah asleep in his arms while he watched ESPN.

The clock on the cable box read eleven fifteen. "Oh my God! It's after eleven!"

"You were up all night."

"So were you!"

"I'm used to it. I work a lot of nights."

"She wasn't hungry when she woke up?"

"Nope. She got a good belly full of fluids last night."

"And no fever?"

"She's cool as a cucumber, as my Gramps would say." He glanced up at her, his golden eyes full of warmth and affection. "Everything's fine, Mom. Keep breathing."

"I, um, I should at least brush my teeth."

"We're fine. Do what you need to do."

Unnerved by the effortless way he cared for her daughter as much as how he looked at her, Dani went to the bathroom to brush her teeth. She decided to shower as long as Savannah was settled with Lucas.

Lucas.

How had he become the center of their world in a matter of a few days? It was like they'd always known him, and in many ways, that reminded her of how it had been when she first met Jack. Their bond had been immediate, intense and deep. Not that different, really, from what she felt happening with Lucas.

Her stomach took a little dip at the idea that she could be falling for him the same way she once fell for Jack, thinking that was forever. She'd learned that forever was much shorter than it was supposed to have been.

Grasping the sink, she dropped her head and rolled the tension from between her shoulder blades. Was she ready to be feeling this way about someone new? Would she ever be ready? Probably not but what choice did she have? Her life had gone on, whether she'd wanted it to or not. For a time, she hadn't wanted to go on without him, but Savannah had arrived and given her a reason to keep moving forward.

Her eyes filled with tears.

Dani worried that she'd forget things about him, such as the deep timbre of his voice, the dimple on his right cheek or the way he always smelled like fresh air because he was outside more than he was inside. Maybe she should write down everything she remembered so she could share their story with Savannah someday. She liked that idea.

In the meantime, she wiped the tears from her face and pulled herself together the way she'd done every day since Savannah was born. Her daughter needed her to keep putting one foot in front of the other, and that's what she would do.

Dressed in a black turtleneck sweater and faded jeans, she made her way to the living room, where Lucas and Savannah were where she'd left them.

His gaze took a hungry perusal of her, leaving her feeling overly warm and *seen*. "You look beautiful for someone who was up all night."

"That's because I have a really good friend who made sure I got some sleep."

Lucas gazed down at Savannah, his adoration for her as obvious as the nose on his face. "I love the way she holds on to me when she's asleep, as if she's afraid I'll get away if she lets go. Someone needs to let her know she's stuck with me."

Dani took a seat in the chair closest to where he was on the sofa. "What would you be doing right now if we weren't here?"

"Same thing. After a while, I'd get myself motivated to go work in town for a couple of hours before my shift at the firehouse."

"Don't let us stop you from doing your thing. You've been so great about letting us disrupt your whole life."

He gave her a steady, unblinking look. "Is there anything I can do to make you believe that I'm happy to have you both here?"

"Everything you do makes me believe that, but still…"

"I would think that after yesterday, you'd know just how much I want you here."

The reminder of their passionate kisses made her feel hot and tingly in places that hadn't tingled in a very long time.

"In fact…" Tightening his hold on Savannah, he stood. "Don't move." He went into the bedroom Dani was using and came back a minute later by himself. "Come here," he said after returning to his previous spot on the sofa.

"Oh, um, like… now?"

"Right now." Looking her dead in the eye, he held out his hand to her.

As if operating outside herself, her hand rose to take his, and she let him gently tug her toward him until she was arranged on his lap, his arms around her and his lips hovering a fraction of an inch from hers.

He smoothed strands of hair back from her face. "Hi there."

"Hi." Her voice sounded high and squeaky.

Lucas smiled and cupped her cheek, his thumb tracing the outline of her mouth. "Do I make you nervous?"

She nodded.

"Why?"

"I, um… Well…"

His low chuckle rumbled through his chest.

"Are you laughing at me?"

"Would I do that?"

"Yes, I think you would."

"I think you're magnificent." And then he was kissing her, and Dani didn't have the brain cells to be nervous, because he fried them all with the sexy, almost dirty way he kissed her, as if he'd been craving her and now that he had her, he wanted to gorge. Before she could catch up, he'd shifted them so she was on her back and he was above her, looking down at her with fierce sexiness that made the blood run hot through her veins.

"Is this okay?"

She nodded and reached for him, wanting more of the way she felt when he kissed her. All thoughts of whether it was too soon or if Jack would approve or anything that didn't involve Lucas and his soft lips and persuasive tongue were pushed aside as irrelevant.

Holy God, the man can kiss.

And then he was gone, leaving her panting for more. Confused, she opened her eyes and found him staring at her, looking as stunned as she felt. "What's wrong?"

"Nothing. I... I didn't want to... If you're not ready." He shook his head. "You're turning me into a stuttering idiot."

For some reason, it pleased her to know she wasn't the only one who'd been rendered stupid by a few heated kisses. "You're doing the same thing to me."

"I don't want to rush you."

"I'm okay."

"Are you sure?"

Nodding, she curled her hand around his neck and brought him back to her for more kissing. She wanted all the kisses.

He groaned and gave her what she wanted.

This kiss quickly escalated into pure desperation.

Her legs parted and wrapped around his hips.

His hand slid under her sweater, branding her with the heat of his skin against hers, and when he pressed the hard length of his shaft against her core—

Savannah woke up crying.

Lucas pulled away, and Dani whimpered from the shock of his withdrawal. "Baby is awake," he said gruffly.

Dani blinked him into focus, shocked that she'd been so far gone with him that she hadn't immediately reacted to hearing Savannah.

He sat back, ran his fingers through his hair, his breathing rapid and ragged.

Dani got up on shaky legs, straightened her sweater and went into the bedroom to get the baby while trying to ignore the desire that pounded through her like a separate heartbeat. Lucas had awakened parts of her that had lain dormant since Jack died.

Savannah was all gummy smiles and wiggles when Dani picked her up out of her little nest in the center of the bed.

"Is someone feeling so much better?"

She let out a happy squeal that made Dani laugh.

"I'm so happy to hear that!"

"How is she?" Lucas asked.

Dani turned to find him standing in the doorway, arms propped on the doorframe over his head, looking impossibly sexy. She licked lips that had gone dry and watched his gaze zero in on her tongue. "She's much better. Smiley and squeaky again."

"Just how we like her."

She nodded.

"You want to go see Hannah?"

"We should let her know Savannah was in the ER last night with an ear infection. Even though they aren't contagious usually, we should give her an out."

"I'll call her."

While he did that, she changed Savannah's diaper, washed her up and put her in a clean outfit and got comfortable on the bed to feed her, tossing a receiving blanket over the baby in case Lucas came back.

"Are you girls decent in there?" he asked a few minutes later.

"Yep, come on in."

He came to the door. "Hannah says no worries and to come over whenever. They're home all day."

"Sounds good."

"I'm gonna hit the shower."

"Okay." Dani told herself it was inappropriate to think of him naked and wet in the shower while she was feeding her child. Appropriate or not, the vivid images her brain conjured up had her feeling warm again. She focused on Savannah while trying to keep her mind from going there… But it wasn't easy.

Lucas Abbott and his sexy kisses had woken up parts of her she hadn't heard from since she lost Jack.

But was she ready for the significance of what this could be with Lucas?

She still didn't know.

CHAPTER 18

"A true friend is someone who lets you have total freedom to be yourself—and especially to feel. Or, not feel. Whatever you happen to be feeling at the moment is fine with them. That's what real love amounts to—letting a person be what he really is."
—Jim Morrison

They drove into town in his truck an hour later. He'd offered to go with her to Hannah's, because her house was hard to find and because he had stuff to do in town. But really he just wanted to be with them. He liked how he felt with Dani in the passenger seat and Savvy chattering away in the back.

She'd bounced right back from the drama of the night before, but it would take him—and her mother—a while to get past the fear of seeing her so sick.

"You're going to have to let me start driving myself, you know," Dani said. "Contrary to first impressions, I don't often drive off the road."

"With the GPS being all but useless in the mountains, it's better for me to show you around first, and then you can drive yourself. For example, you need to know that this corner always freezes before anywhere else around here, which is why you have to slow way down so you don't end up down there."

Dani looked to where he pointed. "Oh, um, yeah. That's good to know. How far of a drop is that?"

"Like forty feet? We rescue people there every year, at least three or four times."

"Have I thanked you for driving me?"

Lucas laughed. "No problem. Once you've successfully completed my course called Butler and Outskirts 101, you'll be set to drive yourself. In addition to watching out for black ice, another thing you have to remember is that there're moose everywhere here. I always slow down around these curves, because you never know where you're going to encounter them. Up here a ways is where Cameron ran into Fred on her first trip to Butler. She nearly totaled her car, and he was completely fine. She had two black eyes from the airbag when we met her. At work, we see a lot of moose accidents. When people hit moose, it's not usually the moose that get hurt."

"I'm starting to wonder if I should have my head examined for moving to Vermont."

"Nah, Vermont is awesome. You just have to know the drill."

"If you say so."

He reached across the center console for her hand. "You'll be fine. And if you're not, I'll come rescue you."

A minute later, he gave her hand a gentle squeeze. "Pay attention to this part so you'll know how to find Hannah." Lucas signaled to take a left turn and headed up a winding road. "You have to be careful coming back down this road when it's super cold."

"How many years will I live here before it becomes second nature?"

"You'll have it down in no time. And then we'll have to do

Mud Season 101. That's a whole *other* course."

Dani laughed. "No one told me that Vermont was like moving to a different universe."

"It's mountain life, babe. You'll get used to it."

Savannah's baby chatter suddenly got much louder.

"See? She agrees with me. She likes it here."

"Figures she'd take your side. You're her favorite."

Lucas beamed with pleasure at hearing that. He was head over heels in love with that little girl and the way she clung to him whether she was awake or asleep. "I like being her favorite." He took another turn. "This is where it gets tricky." They drove along for another mile before he slowed in front of a mailbox in the shape of a classic car. "This is their driveway. Nolan is a car freak. Look for the car mailbox."

"Got it."

"You see why I wanted to bring you?"

"Yep. They would've found our frozen bodies a week from now if I'd tried to do this on my own."

"Nah," he said, laughing. "I would've come looking for you much sooner than that." Lucas pulled up to Hannah's house and brought the truck to a stop next to the pen where Hannah's adopted baby moose, Dexter, lived.

"Dani, meet Dexter, the newest member of the family."

"She really does have a baby moose."

"Yes, she does. She's loco over that baby moose." Lucas freed Savannah from her car seat and held her up so she could see the moose.

Dexter looked at them but didn't get up from his napping spot. Upon a quick glance, Lucas noticed his water and feed bowls were full, and he had a thick blanket as well as several stuffed toys in the spacious pen. Typical Hannah to go all out to make him comfortable.

"When we were kids, she used to make my dad rush baby bunnies to the emergency vet after our dogs got ahold of them."

"That's so horrifying and sweet at the same time. The poor baby bunnies!"

"My dad couldn't bear to see her cry over them."

Hannah came to the door with Callie in her arms, smiling widely as she welcomed them. "Come in." She held the door for them.

He kissed her cheek and Callie's. "Hey."

"Hey, yourself."

"Dexter looks pretty well set up in his penthouse apartment out there."

"Nolan won't let me have him inside. He's so mean."

"He's the voice of reason," Lucas said.

"You're either on his side or mine. You can't be both."

"I'm firmly on his side," Lucas said.

"Figures that you guys would stick together."

Dani laughed at their bickering. "I'm on your side, Hannah. He could sleep in a bed in front of the fire."

"That's what I'm saying!"

Lucas raised a brow in Hannah's direction. "And when he's a full-grown moose and thinking he still belongs on a bed by the fire?"

"That's so far away," Hannah said dismissively. "He's a baby now. But enough of this. Let's put these little girl babies down to play." She sat on the floor in front of a blanket full of baby toys.

"Would you mind if I left you ladies for a bit to run a couple of errands?"

"Fine by us," Hannah said for herself and Callie, who was

positioned on Hannah's lap.

Dani took Savannah from him and sat across from Hannah.

Savannah let out a wail of protest.

Lucas squatted so she could see him. "I'll be back very soon, little lady."

"Somewhere in the course of the last few days, Lucas has become her favorite person in the whole world," Dani said.

"He has that effect on women," Hannah said dryly.

"So I've heard," Dani said.

Lucas scowled. "I'm outta here. And don't talk about me while I'm gone."

"You wish," his sister said. "Take your time. Dani and I have *lots* to talk about."

"Why do I feel like I'm going to regret this?"

"Because you will?"

Dani laughed helplessly, and even though it was at his expense, Lucas was thrilled to see her laughing and having fun. If she fell in love with Butler and made new friends like Hannah, maybe she'd want to stay forever.

"When was Savannah born?" Hannah asked after Lucas left.

"November twenty-fifth, same day as Caden."

"That's awesome! So she's a month older than Callie." She resituated Callie to allow her to reach her toys. "I was so happy to hear you got the job at the store."

"Me, too. It's such a huge relief. Your dad is so nice. I'm really looking forward to it."

"He's great, and the company itself is very family-oriented. Not just our family either. We have lots of employees who are also the third or fourth generation in their families to work there."

"I read about that on the website, and it was part of what

drew me to apply. It seemed like the right sort of environment for a single mom. After college, I was an assistant manager of a big department store at home, and it was an all-consuming job. I can't do that anymore with Savannah to think about."

"I think our company will be a great fit for you. Savannah will end up with a bunch of extra grandmothers." She pointed to the tiny lilac-colored sweater that Callie had on. "This was made by Mildred Olsen, who is the longest-standing employee in the company. She works in bookkeeping with my brother Hunter, who is the CFO, and she's in her nineties!"

"That's amazing."

"It's a great group of people. You'll fit right in."

"I hope so. I really love it here and want to make it work."

"Ella said you're going to look at her former apartment?"

"Yes, I'm meeting her there later on."

"You can leave Savannah with me to nap if you'd like to."

"Oh, I wouldn't want to impose."

"It's no problem. Two to four is nap time around here. That's when I work on my jewelry projects."

"I saw your stuff in the store. You do beautiful work."

"Aw, thanks. I enjoy it."

As the babies played with the toys and mostly ignored each other, Dani and Hannah talked about pediatricians, breastfeeding, diaper rash, sleeping habits and teething, and Dani shared the story of their late-night run to the hospital.

"Lucas was a rock. I'm so thankful he was there, even if I tried to tell him not to come home."

"It's obvious to all of us that he's quite smitten with you and Savvy."

Dani wasn't sure how she should feel about that. "It

is? Really?"

"Yep, and we've never seen that before from him."

"I really like him, and Savannah is wild about him."

"And her dad is… not in the picture?"

"He died in an accident almost a year ago."

"Oh my God! I'm so sorry, Dani. I didn't know."

"It's okay. How would you have known?"

"I lost my first husband, Caleb, in Iraq."

"Lucas told me. I'm so sorry."

"Thanks. It was a long time ago, but you never really get over it. You just try to find the best way forward after."

"That's what I'm trying to do, and it never occurred to me that I'd meet someone else and feel… *something* for him. Not yet anyway."

Hannah smiled. "Funny how that happens, right? Nolan was right under my nose for years, wanting to spend time with me, and I knew it, but I wasn't there yet. And then Caleb's old dog Homer died, and Nolan was there for me through it all, and suddenly, I couldn't imagine him anywhere but with me."

"I'm so sorry about Homer, but the way Nolan stepped up for you is such a great story."

"That's life for you. Just when you think you've got it figured out, it throws you a ringer."

"For sure. I thought I'd be with Jack for the rest of my life, and now… Lucas is in the picture, and I like him so much. He's been so great to me and Savannah, and he's so…"

"Don't say anything I can't unhear."

Dani laughed. "He's very sweet."

"My brother? *Sweet?*"

"Very."

"Ah, if you say so. He's definitely a good guy to have around in a crisis."

"I've seen that several times now."

"All kidding aside—and if you ever tell anyone I said this, we can't be friends…"

"My lips are sealed. I promise."

"All my brothers are good guys. They'd do anything for anyone, and I wouldn't hesitate to encourage any friend of mine to date any of them. It might seem like I'm biased because, duh, they're my brothers and I adore them all, but I'd never tell you, especially after what you've been through, that Lucas was a good guy if he wasn't going to be good for you, you know?"

"I do, and I appreciate what you're saying."

"He can be a complete idiot at times, but when it matters, he's someone you can count on."

"I've already experienced that side of him. I haven't seen much of the idiot side, but he's mentioned it exists."

"Oh my God. It totally exists. Especially when he and Landon get going together."

"I met him last night. I knew that Lucas had an identical twin, but it was still a shock to see just *how* identical."

"So many people can't tell them apart."

"That's what he said, and I can see why. I asked him if he would please do me a favor and keep the beard indefinitely."

Hannah lost it laughing. "You wouldn't want to cozy up to the wrong brother."

"I'd like to think I could tell them apart."

Hannah's pretty dark brown eyes danced with amusement. "But it's better to not take chances with these things."

"Right."

"I know you're looking for someone to take care of Savannah

while you're working, and I'd be happy to have her. She'd be good company for Callie. I've worried about how she'll make friends when we're out here in the woods with no neighbors close by and years to go until she can start preschool."

"You're sure it wouldn't be too much for you?"

"Nolan and I talked about it last night, and I'll get a double stroller so I can take them places, because getting out of the house is critical to my sanity."

"I'd want to chip in on that if you're getting it so you can take care of my daughter."

Hannah waved that off. "We're hoping to have another baby as soon as we can, so we'll need it anyway."

Would three babies be too much for the life-force that was Hannah? Possibly, but in the meantime, the arrangement would be perfect for Dani and Savannah.

"I'd insist on paying you the going rate for daycare."

"That's up to you, but you should know I'd do it for nothing so Callie can have a friend to play with. And because I like you."

"No way. I'm paying, and that's the end of it."

Callie began fussing and tugging against her mother's tight hold.

"We can fight about that another time. How about some lunch?"

"You don't have to feed me."

"I need to feed *me*, and I've got plenty of everything. And in case you haven't noticed, I'm enjoying my daughter's playdate very much."

Hannah plopped Callie into a high chair with toys on the tray and made them turkey sandwiches and poured tall glasses of iced tea.

Dani held Savannah with her left arm as she ate and fended

off little hands wanting to grab handfuls of hair. "Why are they such hair pullers?"

"Ha! That's why mine is up all the time."

"Mine usually is, too, but we ended up leaving before I could put it up."

"You need an elastic? I have tons of them."

"Sure, thanks."

"Coming right up. Watch my girl."

"I've got her."

Hannah went into the other room and returned with a black elastic that she handed over to Dani. "I'll take her for you."

Dani passed Savannah to Hannah.

"Hi there, little one," Hannah said. "Are we going to be best friends?"

Dani stepped away from the table to put her hair up while watching Hannah float around the kitchen, bouncing Savannah on her hip. She held the baby's rapt attention and that of Callie, who watched her mother's every move. This would be a good place for Savannah to be while Dani was at work. She had no doubt about that.

"So I want to say something," Hannah began hesitantly, "and I'm not sure I should… That happens to me a lot. I have these thoughts that I want to share in the hope that they'll be helpful, but it might look like I'm not minding my own business. My siblings tell me I'm a terrible busybody, but it's only because I care so much."

Dani smiled. "You can say whatever you'd like to me. You are older and wiser and have walked the journey I'm on, so you get it."

"Yes, I do, and that's what I want to say. I do get it. I know how hard it is to move on from the person you thought you were going to spend your life with. I've been there, and it took me years to get to where I am now. And that's the thing… I wish I'd gotten here sooner. I spent a lot of years wallowing in my grief. It was the most important thing in my life. Until I had Nolan to show me there was still so much more living left to do, and now I have my sweet Callie, too. If I had it to do over again, I would've said yes to Nolan years before I did. For all the time I spent mourning Caleb, he's still gone forever, you know?"

Dani dabbed at her eyes, which were suddenly full of tears. "I do know, and I appreciate your insight. I haven't had anyone to talk to about losing Jack who truly understands what it was like."

"I wouldn't wish it on anyone." She reached across the counter to grasp Dani's hand. "I'm here for you anytime you need to talk to someone who gets it."

"That means the world to me. Thank you."

"You're welcome. And just so you know—I'm not saying any of this because I like you for my brother."

Dani laughed and wiped away new tears before taking Savannah back from Hannah. "That's good to know, and it's nice to hear that you like me for him."

"I really do. I think you could be good for each other."

"We already have been."

"That's an awesome place to start."

"Yes, it is."

"I guess what I'm saying is that it's okay to give yourself permission to do whatever it takes to find happiness again. A lot of people said that to me before I finally heard it and got the message. All that time, I knew Caleb would be so mad at me for wallowing in my grief. He wasn't one to wallow."

"I'm sure he would've wallowed if he'd lost you."

"I'd like to think so!"

They shared a laugh that made their daughters laugh, too.

By the time Lucas returned an hour later, Dani felt like she'd made an important new friend—and found someone she trusted completely to care for Savannah while she was at work. They had put both babies down for naps in the beautiful nursery Hannah and Nolan had created for Callie.

"You ready to go see the apartment with Ella?" he asked.

"Ready when you are."

"We'll be back as soon as we can," she told Hannah.

"Take your time. They're out cold, and I'm going to get some work done and spend a little time with my other baby, Dexter."

"Enjoy that. We'll be back."

"I'll be here."

When they went out to Lucas's truck, Dexter was standing up in his spacious penthouse.

"Can I pet him?" Dani asked.

"I'm not sure if he bites."

"You go first and find out for me."

Laughing, Lucas put his arm around her and directed her toward the truck. "I'm not looking to lose any fingers today." He held the passenger door and waited for her to get settled. "Did you have fun with Hannah?"

"We had the best time. She's incredible."

"She is, but don't tell her I said that. She'd use it against me forever."

"I won't tell."

"The way she's gone on after losing Caleb has been inspirational, to say the least. Losing him totally crushed me. I couldn't begin to know what it was like for her."

Dani raised her hand to his face and, without taking the time to think about what she was doing, leaned forward and kissed him. And when she pulled back, she loved the stunned expression on his handsome face. "You're very sweet to care so much about your sister."

"If I tell you I respect her more than just about anyone in the world, will you kiss me again?"

"I might."

"I respect the hell out of Hannah, more than anyone—"

She kissed him again.

He whimpered, which made her laugh.

"Don't laugh. Kiss." Wrapping his arms around her, he leaned into the kiss, which went from nothing to *something* in the span of seconds. He ended up partially reclined on her as their kisses became frantic and desperate. "What're you doing to me?" he asked when they came up for air several minutes later.

"Same thing you're doing to me. But we need to go. I can't keep Ella waiting."

"Oh. Right. Ella. Apartment." He shook his head and released his hold on her, stepping back to close the door.

In the time it took for him to walk around the truck, she tried to get her breathing to return to normal. The heady, giddy feelings he inspired in her reminded her of the early days with Jack, when he'd had her so dazzled, she could barely function as she counted down the hours until she could be with him again. Everything had suffered—her grades, her friendships and her relationship with her parents, who'd tried, unsuccessfully, to cool things off between her and Jack.

It'd taken time for them to come around to love him like a son, but those early days had been crazy in every possible way—and in the best possible way.

"What're you thinking about over there?" Lucas asked as he drove them down the winding road.

"I was actually thinking about when I was first with Jack and how this, with you, reminds me of that."

"How so?"

"It was the same feeling of excitement and anticipation."

He drew in a deep breath and let it out. "For what it's worth, I share your excitement and anticipation. In fact, if I were any *more* excited…"

Dani covered her ears and laughed. "Stop!"

All the way to town, he kept trying to get her to allow him to discuss his excitement. "Come on, let me tell you."

"No."

"Please?"

"No!"

"You're absolutely no fun."

"I'll show you fun."

"Really? When? Can you give me a time and date so I can get *really* excited?"

"*Stop*," she said, laughing helplessly. It was, she realized, the first time she'd laughed in quite that way since she lost Jack.

They pulled up to the house where Ella was meeting them, and Lucas killed the engine. "I hope you know… All of this… Anything that happens… It's on your timetable. Not mine."

"It's on *our* timetable. It's not just about me."

"No, it really is *all* about you and Savvy. At least for me."

Their gazes were still locked when Ella pulled into the driveway, tooting her horn to get their attention.

Dani looked away, but her heart pounded, and she felt light-headed from the desire he aroused in her. Her body was coming back to life after a long, dark time of despair, and it was all thanks to the handsome, sexy man who'd rescued her.

CHAPTER 19

Being deeply loved by someone gives you strength, while loving someone deeply gives you courage."
—Lao Tzu

Lucas was dying a slow, pleasurable death caused by an overabundance of desire, longing and yearning. Dani had been through so much. He had to take it slow with her and let her set the pace no matter how much he ached from wanting her.

This whole thing had been insane from the get-go. The way they'd clicked from the first minutes they spent together to everything that'd happened since then. He'd never experienced anything like the way he felt when she was around, and all he could seem to think about was doing whatever it took to keep her—and Savannah—in his life.

So what were they doing sitting in front of a potential apartment that would take them away from him? "You don't have to do this, you know."

"Do what?"

"Rent a place. You're more than welcome to stay with me."

"It's very nice of you to say so, but we've been enough of an imposition on you."

"No, you haven't."

Before they could continue the conversation, Ella knocked on the driver's side window. "You coming?" she asked, loud enough for them to hear her.

They got out of the truck.

"Sorry," Lucas said to his sister.

"No problem." To Dani, she said, "Grayson lived here for a short time after I moved out, but he got a bigger place with Emma and Simone. Mrs. Abernathy is thrilled that someone else might want it, and you're lucky it's available. Good apartments are hard to come by around here."

With his hand on her lower back, Lucas encouraged Dani to follow Ella inside, even as he wanted to shout his many objections to this plan. They went up two flights of stairs to the cozy apartment where Ella had lived until she moved in with Gavin. Every step they took made Lucas more out of sorts than he was before.

"This is so cute!" Dani said when Ella had thrown open the doors to the top-floor apartment.

"It's small," Lucas said.

"It'd be perfect for us. We don't need much."

"It's got a working wood fireplace," Ella said, "which was one of my favorite things about living here."

"And how is Dani supposed to lug wood up two flights of stairs with a baby in her arms? And what if she falls asleep before the fire is out?" He leaned into the fireplace and took a look up the chimney. "I bet this thing hasn't been serviced in ten years. If you knew how many fires we get called to for malfunctioning chimneys…" Withdrawing from the fireplace, he turned to find both women watching him—Dani with amusement and Ella with confusion.

"Mrs. Abernathy takes good care of the place," Ella said. For Dani's benefit, she added, "We all had her for math in school."

"I didn't," Lucas said. "She retired before I got there."

"Well, the rest of us had her," Ella said with a questioning look for her brother. "She's a lovely lady and a wonderful landlord. You'd be very safe and happy here, Dani."

"That's good to know."

Lucas propped his hands on his hips, eyeing a spot on the ceiling that might've been water damage. "How will you get groceries up two flights when you have an infant?"

"I've got a baby sling that I can use. It keeps my hands free. I'll make it work. What's the rent?"

"Six hundred, and utilities are included."

"That's a steal."

"I know! It's such a good deal, and she hasn't raised it in years."

"You can tell her I'll take it."

"She'll be delighted. She said to tell you if you're interested that she needs about two weeks to get it painted, and she wants to do the floors, too. They really need it, so you'll want to let her do them."

Dani chewed on her thumbnail as she thought about that. "Hopefully, a room at the inn will open up in the meantime."

"You don't need a room at the goddamned inn!"

"What in the hell is wrong with you, Lucas?" Ella asked.

"She doesn't need a room at the inn." He made an effort not to yell this time. "She doesn't need this apartment. She has a place to stay with me."

"Lucas... You're very sweet to want to keep us, but I moved here to stand on my own two feet, and ever since I arrived, I've been standing on *your* two feet. I need to do this. I need to prove to myself and everyone else that I can take care of Savannah on my own."

"*Why* do you need to prove that? Who cares what anyone else thinks? Of course you could take care of her on your own, but you don't *have* to."

"Yes, I really do," she said softly.

Ella's gaze darted between them. "I, um, I'll leave you guys to work this out, but I'll let Mrs. A know you're interested?"

"Yes," Dani said, keeping her gaze on Lucas, "please."

"Will do. I'll have her call you at Lucas's with the details."

"That'd be great, Ella. Thank you again."

"Happy to help. I'll see you at Sunday dinner, Luc?"

"Yeah, I'll be there."

"Great, see you then."

After Ella left, Lucas and Dani continued to stare each other down until he finally blinked and glanced at the floor, more miserable than he could recall being in a very long time. This was way worse than realizing that Amanda liked Landon more than him. In retrospect, that barely made a blip compared to how he felt about losing Dani and Savvy from his daily life. Sure, he would still see them. At least he hoped he would. But it wouldn't be the same.

"I'm sorry you're upset," Dani said.

"I'm being a jerk."

"No, you're not."

"Yes, I really am, but I don't want you guys to leave."

"It's very sweet of you to want to take care of us."

"I do want to, and I've never wanted that before. Ever." Filled with frustration and confusion, he ran his fingers through his hair. "I don't even know what to do with myself around you. I want to give you space and time and everything you need, but I just want to…"

She stepped toward him, closing the small distance between them. "What do you want?"

"You," he said gruffly. "I want you and Savvy, and I want… I want you."

Placing her hands on his hips, she drew him into her embrace. "We want you, too."

"Then why are you leaving?"

"Because I need to be on my own for a little while."

"*Why?*" He felt like he was fighting for his life, or something equally dramatic, fearing that if they left, they'd never come back.

"Let's go pick up Savannah and go back to your house. We'll talk there."

Lucas wanted to talk now, but he told himself to be patient, to continue following her lead. After all, she'd done this relationship thing before. It was all new to him, and he had no idea what the hell he was doing. He followed her down the stairs and out to the truck, where he again held the door for her.

"You don't have to do that, you know."

"Yes, I do." He closed the door and walked around to the driver's side, taking a series of deep breaths to settle his wild emotions. What the hell was happening? His emotions were never wild. Not like this anyway.

They drove to Hannah's in an uneasy silence that set his nerves further on edge. This was the most important thing ever, and he was fucking it up royally because he had no idea how to behave when it mattered this much. He respected what she'd been through losing her fiancé and trying to build a new life for herself and her daughter, but with every minute he spent with both of them, he was getting deeper into something that had the power to change him forever.

That was terrifying.

"I don't want you to be upset," she said softly. "You've been so good to me. It would hurt me if I hurt you."

"I'm trying not to be upset. After all, I have no right to be."

"Yes, you do. I know you've gotten attached to Savannah and vice versa."

"Not just to her. To both of you."

"I'm not saying I don't want this, between us, to continue. I do want it and you."

Those words felt like a lifeline he badly needed. "You do?"

"Of course I do. Savannah would never forgive me if I didn't keep you in our lives."

Her assurances helped to calm him somewhat, but not completely. He still felt panic-stricken at the thought of losing them now that he'd found them, and why was that, exactly? He hadn't known they existed a week ago, and now... Now, he felt like he'd die if he lost them. How could that be possible?

Tightening his grip on the wheel, he tried to stay focused on the winding bends that led to Hannah's. His heart gave a happy little jolt at the thought of seeing Savvy—and Callie, whom he adored. And then, just as quickly, his heart fell when he thought about not being able to see Savvy first thing in the morning, in the middle of the night or any other time that she was sad or hungry or cranky.

"There are things..." Dani said haltingly. "Things I should tell you. So you'll understand."

"What things?"

"We'll talk. I promise."

Frustration and fear pulsed through him like separate, competing heartbeats. On the way up to Hannah's, Lucas was forced to stop short when Fred ambled out of the woods inches away from the front of the truck.

"*Holy crap!*" Dani cried, gasping at the size of him.

"Dani, meet Fred."

"H-holy crap," she said again, more softly this time. "Is he, can he…"

Lucas reached for her hand, thankful to Fred for breaking the tension between them. "Don't worry. He won't hurt us."

"I-if you say so."

"Keep breathing."

Fortunately, Fred was not in the mood to linger and moved across the road into the woods, disappearing from view after a minute.

"You okay?" he asked Dani.

"I will be when my heart starts beating normally again."

"That's why you have to be careful driving around here."

"I'll drive so slow people will think I'm ninety."

Lucas laughed and continued up the hill to Hannah's. When they arrived, Dexter raised his head to check out the newcomers.

Hannah met them at the door. "You just missed it! Fred was here to see Dex, and they were playing in the yard. It was so cute! And then when Fred was getting ready to leave, he tried to talk Dex into going with him, but Dex went right back to his little wire condo. It was like he was telling Fred he's happy here. Isn't that so amazing?"

She had actual tears in her eyes, and old Lucas might've teased her about weeping over a moose, but new Lucas gave his sister a hug and told her he was happy for her. "We saw Fred on our way up. He nearly gave Dani a coronary."

"He'd never hurt you." Hannah wiped the tears from her eyes. "I know it sounds so silly, but I *love* that Dex is happy here."

"Why wouldn't he be?" Lucas asked. "Three hots and a cot are any man's dream come true."

"Stop," Hannah said, laughing through her tears as she gave him a teasing shove. "He also gets lots of love and attention."

"No doubt that's what is keeping him here," Dani said. "He's a very lucky baby moose."

"I'm the lucky one. I adore him."

In the bedroom, Savannah let out a cry that was followed by one from Callie. He loved that he could so easily recognize Savannah. He would know the sound of her anywhere. "Want me to get them?"

"We'll help," Hannah said. "They'll need to be changed."

Lucas led the way with Dani and Hannah following. The babies were in Callie's crib, where Hannah had put a rolled blanket to separate them. They had reached across the barrier and were tugging on each other.

"Are they playing or fighting?" Lucas asked.

"Playing," Hannah said. "I think."

"Definitely playing," Dani said.

Savannah let out a happy squeal at the sight of her mother and then had one for him, too.

Her reaction hit him like an arrow to the heart. And in that moment, he understood that he loved her. That's why his emotions were so out of control. He loved her and was falling for her mother, too.

Lucas tried to swallow the lump that lodged in his throat, but it only got bigger when Dani lifted Savannah and she reached for him.

Laughing, Dani handed her over to him.

Savannah immediately grabbed fistfuls of his shirt the way she always did.

"Does someone have a crush on my brother?" Hannah asked.

"A huge crush, which is totally not fair to the person who carried her for nine months and hasn't slept since she arrived."

"Preach it, sister. Callie is all about her daddy. He comes home, and it's like Mommy doesn't exist."

Lucas looked down at Savvy's little face gazing up at him and knew there was nothing in the world he wouldn't do for her, nothing she could want that he wouldn't find a way to get her, nothing he wouldn't do to keep her safe, healthy and happy. If she continued to look at him the way she was now, that would be all he'd need in return.

Holy crap, he was going to cry if he didn't get this emotional shit under control. Taking her with him, he went out to the living room, needing a second to get himself together.

Dani followed him. "I should change her diaper."

Lucas turned to hand the baby over to her, and his gaze connected with hers. The turmoil he saw in her pretty eyes went a long way toward calming him. Whatever was happening to him was also happening to her, and as long as they were both feeling this way, he had hope they could figure something out.

Because not having them in his life simply wasn't an option.

He'd been upset when they left the apartment. Dani had seen that as plainly as the beard on his face, and it was her fault. As soon as they got back to his place, she would try to explain to him why it was so important to her to be independent, even if she appreciated that he wanted to take care of her and Savannah.

She changed the baby and took the time to feed her before they set out from Hannah's to head home to Lucas's.

Savannah was fussy, so Dani sat in the back with her, trying to keep the baby entertained while her mind spun with thoughts about her new job, new apartment and the new friend who'd become so much more.

They arrived at Lucas's with some time before he had to be at work. She hoped it would be enough time.

"Do you mind taking her? I want to grab something from my car."

"I don't mind." He took the car seat from her and went inside.

Dani retrieved the baby gym her aunt and cousins had given her as a shower gift and brought it inside. The car was packed full of baby equipment that she hadn't taken the time to unpack, since their time at Lucas's was temporary. His question about lugging things up two flights of stairs when she was alone with a baby had her wondering if she should've looked for something better suited to their needs. But Ella had said good apartments were hard to come by in Butler, and the space was cozy and clean. She would make it work.

Besides, Savannah wouldn't be an infant forever.

Dani brought the baby gym into Lucas's living room and set it up in a corner.

"Where'd that come from?"

"My car. It's full of baby stuff."

"You could've brought in whatever you wanted or needed. I hope you know that."

"I do. Thank you."

"Let's check this out," he said to Savannah, settling her under the arch that had a variety of toys hanging from it.

Savannah batted at the toys with intense concentration, arms and legs on the move.

Lucas laughed. "She likes it."

"Yes, she does." He returned his attention to the baby. "Lucas... Can we talk?"

"Sure."

Situating himself so he was sitting against the sofa where he could tend to Savannah if need be but still see Dani, he looked up at her, giving her the floor.

"I told you I was with Jack since high school, right?"

He nodded.

"We moved in together three years ago. My parents weren't thrilled about that. They wanted us to get married, but we weren't ready even though we'd been together for years by then. I was focused on my career and had a demanding job that became more so as the retail sector transformed practically overnight from brick-and-mortar stores to online. It was a stressful time. All my work friends... We were constantly afraid of losing our jobs and not being able to get another one because there were so few good jobs in retail anymore. Jack was in no rush to get married either. He was in construction, and the company he worked for was booming. Things were good, and we felt like we had plenty of time to get married and have a family."

Lucas listened attentively, but she sensed tension coming from him.

"He surprised me when he proposed. I was totally shocked because we hadn't talked about it at all, but he'd asked my parents for permission and bought a beautiful ring. It was very sweet and romantic. He told me he couldn't imagine his life without me, and he wanted to have babies with me and grow old with me."

Dani wiped away tears that infuriated her. You'd think she'd be able to talk about him after all this time without coming apart. "Of course I said yes. He said it didn't need to change anything, but it changed everything. We started planning the wedding and decided to try for a baby sooner rather than later, so we could be young parents. I think I got pregnant the first second I was off birth control," she said with a laugh. "I'd expected it to take a while, so once again, we were changing our plans. We moved up the wedding, and it was a month away when he was killed in the ATV accident."

Lucas moved to sit next to her and put an arm around her. "You don't have to talk about it if it's too painful."

"I do need to talk about it. You deserve to understand what you're getting yourself into."

"There's nothing you could tell me that would make me not want to be with you."

"It's very sweet of you to say so, but there are things…"

"Tell me, and then we can put it behind us and figure out what's next."

"He was with his friends doing what they'd done a hundred times before. Jack… He cut through a shallow pond, and his vehicle flipped over, pinning him under it."

Lucas winced. "Ah, damn."

"They tried to get him out, but it was too late. They think maybe he died quickly because his neck was broken, but I had nightmares for months about how maybe it wasn't instant."

Lucas held her close to him. "It was probably quick if his neck was broken."

"That's what they said. Anyway, the next few months were a bit of a blur. My mom and dad took over. They moved me out of the apartment, brought me home to the house where I'd grown up and did everything that needed to be done. They made sure I ate and slept and continued to breathe. They made sure I saw the doctor regularly and took care of getting what I needed for the baby. Savannah was born, and they just kept doing everything, and I let them because I didn't have the strength to argue. I didn't care enough to argue.

"Don't get me wrong—I'm so grateful for everything they did for me and Savannah, but then my childhood friend Tom moved back home for a few months after he split with his wife. His mom and my mom apparently got the big idea that Tom and I would be perfect for each other…"

"Oh jeez."

"Yeah, it just made everything worse. When I felt them pushing me hard in his direction… That was when I started to wake up to the fact that I'd ceded control of my life. Then he told me he'd always pictured us ending up together, but then I met Jack, and he'd been so heartbroken. He said now there was a chance for us, except I have *never* thought of him as anything other than a good friend. Something snapped after he said that stuff to me. I couldn't handle being around well-meaning people who would always know about my terrible tragedy and would do whatever it took to make it better for me. I just couldn't do it anymore, you know?"

He nodded. "I get it. We did the same for Hannah after Caleb died, until she begged us to back off and leave her alone."

"People want to help. It's human nature to want to do what you can to make someone you care about feel better. All I know is that I felt better the minute I left my old life behind. That made me feel better, even if it hurt people I care about."

"There's nothing wrong with doing what you need to in order to survive."

"No, there isn't, and eventually, I hope my parents will understand what I did and why I did it. But for now, what I think is best is that Savannah and I make a fresh start on our own."

"Haven't you already done that? You're the one who made the move to leave, who drove the two of you to Vermont."

"And then promptly into a ditch that you rescued us from."

"You know what really bums me out?"

"What?"

"That you don't see the courage it took to get yourself as far as you did all by yourself. If I hadn't come along, you would've been fine because you're strong and capable and you'd never let that little girl want for anything. If only you saw yourself the way I do, maybe you wouldn't feel the need to prove anything to anyone." He kissed her forehead and released her. "I've got to go to work."

Lucas got up and went into his room to change, but he'd left her with a lot to think about.

His words about her strength and courage meant a lot to her. *He* meant a lot to her. Hopefully, she could continue to show him that even after they moved out.

CHAPTER 20

"My father didn't tell me how to live.
He lived, and let me watch him do it."
—Clarence Budington Kelland

Two months later…

Hey Les,

So sorry it's taken me this long to respond to your email. I'm having an exciting Saturday night at home, and Savannah is asleep, so I finally have enough time to write back. Living without cell service has taken some getting used to. Sometimes I feel like I moved to an alternate universe—I feel so cut off without my phone. At first, I wondered how people could live without cell phones, but I'm getting used to it. Sorta! So much to tell you! First of all, my mom gave you my new address, right? Savannah and I are enjoying our new apartment, but my friend Lucas was right about the two flights of stairs being a pain in the *** with a baby. (He's right about most things, but don't ever tell him I said that!) I've gotten good at strapping her into the baby sling and running up and down the stairs, but she's getting so big!

Soon she'll bust out of the baby sling. I can't believe how much she's changing and growing. I enclosed some recent pics below.

Thanks for sending me pics of Jessie. I hope she doesn't forget her Aunt Dani, and YES, I do want you guys to come visit this summer! There's a super cute inn right in town where you could stay, or there're short-term rentals all over our part of Vermont. I'll take time off when you come. Just give me a month or so heads-up so I can put in for the time. I can't WAIT to show you the store and the warehouse. I think you'll love the store—everyone does! I'll use my company discount to send you home with a year's supply of cheddar cheese and maple syrup. Jessie will LOVE the toy department. They have so many cool things—most of which have never seen a battery. I'm glad to hear that the jackass at your office quit. It must be so much nicer to go to work now that he's gone!

I did have a good visit with my parents. Thanks for asking about that. They were happy to see me settled into my new routine and enjoying life in Vermont. I'm really thankful that they seem to have forgiven me for moving away. At least they pretended like they have, so that's all that matters! Aunt Ellen told me that my mom is volunteering at an after-school program that caters to kids who've suffered trauma. She will be sooooo good at that. She has so much love to give, and I think that's a great place for her to be. Those kids are lucky to have her. She hasn't told me about it yet. I'm waiting for her to tell me before I say anything. I'm sure she doesn't want me to think she's moved on from being my mom or some such thing! As if she could ever move on from being my mom! We try to FaceTime on the computer once a week so they can see Savannah, and they got to meet my friend Lucas while they were here. They really liked him, but that wasn't surprising. Everyone likes him, especially my daughter!

And yes, I LOVE my new job! It's so much fun, and the people I work with are like a big family. Everyone is so nice and helpful and excited to launch the catalog in the fall so it'll be in time for the holidays. My job is to make sure the warehouse is ready to fulfill the orders when they start rolling in. Lucas's family has run this business for seventy years, and do you know that they have been collecting customer addresses for *twenty-five years* in anticipation of someday having a catalog?!? We expect it to be a big hit. I just hope we're ready! GULP! You know what they think will be the most popular? The new line of sex toys. No, I'm not joking! We expect them to be the top-selling item in the catalog. I can't make this up! LOL! I love working for the Abbott family. They are so much fun to be around—and they say if I survived the end of the winter AND mud season, I'm almost a true Vermonter. I just have to get through leaf-peeping season to get my final status. From what I'm told, that's the craziest time of year around here, even worse than ski season.

So you asked about Lucas, and yes, we still see each other almost every day. When he works the day shift at the firehouse, he brings dinner over or I cook for him, and he helps with bath and bedtime for Savannah and then heads home. When he works nights, he comes over to see her in the morning and sometimes even takes her to his sister's house for me to save me time (it's in the opposite direction from work for me). Did I tell you he also does incredible woodworking that he sells in the store? He made the *most beautiful crib* for Savannah. I cried when he brought it over and set it up for me. His woodworking skills are incredible, and my daughter is completely in love with him. She can't say anything except for "Lu, Lu, Lu" whenever he is around. No Mama from my child. Just Lu, Lu, Lu. He loves it, of course. Whenever we both have the day off, we try to get out and do something fun, like a hike or picnic. He took me up to see his brother's maple syrup production facility during the heart of the sugaring season, and it was so interesting to see how they boil the sap and make the syrup. It's all very scientific, but his brother Colton is the master.

I've been to Sunday dinner at his parents' house a couple of times, and that's quite something with his nine siblings, their significant others, various cousins, his grandfather, etc. It's wild, but so much fun—and I always hurt from laughing after. They are so FUNNY! I LOVE his mom! She is AMAZEBALLS. The woman never breaks a sweat making dinner for like thirty people and is right in her element with kids and dogs and grandkids underfoot. I have a massive girl crush on the woman! Can you imagine having TEN CHILDREN?!?!?! I can barely handle ONE! She even gave me her number so I can call her anytime I have a baby question or need something. How nice is that!?! Lucas's sister Hannah, who watches Savannah for me while I'm at work, has been such a great friend to me, and her daughter, Callie, has become Savannah's BFF. They are so cute together. They still want to nap in the same crib, even though they're getting too big for that. They cry when Hannah separates them. And did I tell you Hannah is also raising a baby moose named Dexter?!? Only in Vermont, right? I think she might be pregnant again, but she hasn't confirmed it. She's been a little green in the mornings lately, and her face has filled out a bit. I have my fingers crossed for her and Nolan because they want another baby ASAP. She's thirty-seven, so she doesn't want to wait much longer to have No. 2. I've also gotten to know Lucas's sisters Ella (I'm living in her former apartment) and Charley through work, and they're great, too.

So, back to Lucas... He's been so great about giving me the space I asked for when I moved into my apartment, except I wish he'd give me a little LESS space, if you know what I mean... Before I moved out of his place, we'd kissed a few times and it was really nice (and HOT!), but since I left—NADA. He's extremely respectful and keeps his distance, giving most of his attention to Savannah. I've actually begun to wonder if he's lost interest in me that way... I wouldn't blame him after I asked for space and all. On the one-year anniversary of Jack's death, he brought me flowers and said he just wanted me to know he was thinking of me that day. It was so sweet, and he made me cry. I'm not going to lie—that was a rough day. Sometimes it's still so hard to believe that it actually happened, and he's gone forever. I debated taking the day off, but I'm glad I didn't. It helped to go to work and be busy so I wouldn't sit around and cry all day. Anyway... Lucas invited me to go to one brother's wedding in May and another brother's wedding in Boston in June, and I'm looking forward to both of them, but I'm not really sure where things stand between *us*. In other news, I ordered a sexy dress online for the June wedding, which is more formal, and I'm hoping it fits. I'm almost back to my pre-prego weight, but I'm a little curvier than I used to be.

I hope you don't think I'm a jerk for talking about another guy like this. I think about Jack every day. I talked to his mom last week, and his parents are going to come visit us soon. I will tell Savannah all about him when the time comes, but I think I might be ready to see what this could be with Lucas—and only because it's him. I wouldn't want to date anyone else. Anyway, now I'm just rambling and it's getting late. Savannah will be up with the chickens, so I ought to go to bed. Thanks for checking on me and for keeping tabs on my parents. I know it means a lot to them when you and Jessie visit, especially since I took off with their only grandchild, so thanks for that. I can't wait to meet your new little one in the fall! We will definitely come home for a weekend to visit after he or she arrives. I promise to write more soon!!!

xoxo

Love you! Miss you!

Dani

After typing the manifesto email and attaching some new pictures of Savannah, Dani sent it. She stood and stretched and went to pour herself a half glass of wine. Another exciting Saturday night, but after the frenetic pace of her work weeks, she was thankful for the downtime on the weekends.

Her laptop chimed with a new instant message, and she smiled, knowing for certain that it would be Les replying to the email.

Have you tried jumping him?????

Dani laughed out loud. Leave it to Les to put it right out there! *Haven't tried that.*

Why not? Give it a whirl. What've you got to lose?

Other than my best friend in Vermont?

You won't lose him. He's bonkers for your kid. He's not going anywhere. He's been waiting for you to let him know you're ready.

How do you know that?

Obv I don't, but that's my theory…

It's not a BAD theory.

Do it. And then do it again. You don't want to get cobwebs in the hallway.

STOP! OMG! Dani included the laughing emoji.

All kidding aside, I know how awful the last year has been for you. And I absolutely know that Jack would want you to do whatever it took to be happy. If Lucas makes you happy, be HAPPY with Lucas. I give you permission.

Gee, thanks, pal. Appreciate that. I'll think about it.

Don't think—JUMP. Just go for it. He'll catch you. I have a good feeling about him.

I do too.

Keep me posted!

I will!

PS: You sound really happy there, and my goddaughter is GORGEOUS. I'm so glad it's working out so well, even if I miss you girls like crazy.

I am happy. We miss you too. Will check in soon!

You'd better! Smooches to my baby girl.

She'd told Les the truth, Dani thought as she finished her wine and went to brush her teeth before bed. She was happy in Vermont. This new life suited her, and Savannah was thriving. Dani was getting used to being a single parent and settling into a routine that worked for them both. Stepping into the tiny bedroom where Savannah slept, she hovered over the gorgeous mahogany crib Lucas had surprised her with and adjusted the baby's blanket. She kicked it off every night, and Dani replaced it at least three times per night.

That crib had been such a special gift, and she'd been teary-eyed from the moment she'd realized what he'd done through the whole time it took him to put it together. "Only the best for my Savvy," he'd said when he was finished.

It'd been all she could do that day to resist the urge to throw her arms around him and beg him to stay forever. But she couldn't do that when she was the one who'd asked for some time to figure things out. It wouldn't be fair to him.

Savannah was now regularly sleeping through to the morning, and inevitably, Dani woke in a panic when she realized she hadn't heard from the baby during the night.

Looking down at her beautiful little girl, she knew it had been the right thing to move away from home and the memories she'd left behind there. She missed Jack all the time and had begun to accept that she always would. But the pervasive, bone-deep sadness that had made it nearly impossible to do anything other than breathe for months had lifted at some point, and she felt a little better than she had for most of the last year. Not back to normal, by any means, because normal had been permanently redefined, but most days, she felt hopeful, which was a vast improvement over the months of darkness that had followed Jack's accident.

Now she found herself peeking out from behind the curtain into the light to see what else might be waiting for her.

Was Lucas waiting for her? Was that why he'd kept their relationship entirely platonic and mostly focused on Savannah since she'd moved out of his place? What did she need to do to let him know she was ready for whatever might come next? Jumping him seemed a bit extreme, but the thought of him catching her made all her girl parts tingle with excitement.

He was away for the weekend with his father, grandfather and brothers on an annual spring camping trip that he'd been looking forward to for weeks. While the days had gotten warmer, the nights were still cold. She couldn't understand the appeal of freezing one's ass off in a tent and had told him so, only to be treated to a diatribe on the fine art of cold-weather camping.

No, thanks.

He was due home tomorrow afternoon, and they had plans to go to Sunday dinner at his parents' home. Maybe after that, she'd see how she felt about jumping him.

She giggled as she considered the many ways that could go wrong. But when she thought of all the ways it could go so very right, she wasn't laughing anymore.

Lucas was indeed freezing his ass off and loving every minute of the time with his favorite men. But he missed Dani and Savannah so much, he wondered how he'd make it until he got home tomorrow afternoon. He'd have to shower before he saw them, because he stank of woodsmoke and sweat and fish guts and other nasty things. But the second he was clean, he would be on his way over there like the proverbial sucker for punishment he'd become since he met them.

"You've been quiet today, son," Lincoln said when they were the only two left at the campfire on their last night away. "And you are *not* known for being quiet." Linc popped the top off a bottle of beer, handed it to Lucas and then opened one for himself. "What's up with you lately? Everyone has noticed the change in you. Of course, I have my suspicions…"

"Oh yeah?" Lucas asked, amused. "What would they be?"

"I think it might have something to do with our fantastic new warehouse manager and her adorable little girl. Am I warm?"

"Very. I'm in love with them both."

"Aha! I knew it. Your grandfather and I had a wager, and you just won me twenty bucks."

"Did he bet against me?" Lucas asked, delighted as always by his grandfather.

"Not *against* you, per se, but he wasn't as convinced as I am that things are as far along as they are."

"They're not that far along, so he's right about that."

"I'm not following. Didn't you just say you're in love with them both?"

"Uh-huh, but there's nothing happening between me and Dani beyond friendship."

"But you want something to happen?"

"I absolutely do, but not until she wants it, too. And she's not there yet. So I'm waiting."

"Are you now?"

"Yep. She lost her fiancé in a tragic accident last year while she was expecting Savvy, and she's been through a lot. She needs time to get her head on straight, and when she gets there, I'll be waiting for her."

"And in the meantime, you're not seeing anyone else?"

"Nope. I have no interest in anyone but her."

"Hot damn. Never thought I'd see the day for you or Landon."

"Even nitwits grow up eventually, Dad."

"Yes, I suppose they do, not that I've ever thought of you as a nitwit."

"Really?" Lucas asked in his driest tone. "Not ever?"

"Well, maybe once in a while."

Lucas laughed. "It's a well-earned title, but I'd like to think it won't define the rest of my life."

"Certainly not. I may not say it often enough, but I'm damned proud of the work you and Landon do on behalf of the community. You may act like nitwits sometimes, but you're highly trained, competent first responders, and I, for one, respect the hell out of you two."

"That's awfully nice of you to say, Dad. Thank you."

"Not just saying it. It's the truth, and I think Dani would be lucky to have you in her life and her daughter's life."

"I hope she comes around to realizing they're stuck with me. That little girl could ask me to walk barefoot through a snowstorm, and I'd do it for her."

"Oh boy, she's got you wrapped pretty hard, does she?"

"You have no idea. I look at her, and I just melt. That gummy smile and the two little teeth and the drool. I love it all."

"Aww, look at you. My little boy is in love."

"Not so little," Lucas said, pretending to scowl at his father.

"You'll always be my little boy. That's just how it works. Just like your Savvy will always be your little girl."

"She's not really mine, though."

"Isn't she?"

"She had a father who loved her very much. It's important to me to be respectful of him and his memory."

"Of course you should respect him, Luc. I'd never suggest otherwise. But the fact is that you're here, and sadly, he's not. I think it takes a special kind of guy to love another man's child like his own, and I'm sure her mother sees how lucky they both are to have you in their lives."

"I hope she does, but I'm not really sure what she's thinking. Everything is up in the air right now."

"Why is that, exactly?"

Lucas sighed. "When Dani moved into her apartment, she asked for some space. So I gave it to her. And now, I'm not sure how to go about closing the gap and getting back to where we were before she left."

"Seems like you spend a lot of time together."

"We do, but just as friends."

"Nothing wrong with that. Friendship forms a great foundation to build upon."

"That sounds like something Gramps would say."

"I get much of my wisdom from him, but don't ever tell him I said that."

Lucas laughed. "He is nothing if not full of wisdom."

"Indeed. You're not asking for my advice, but if you were, I'd encourage you to talk to Dani about how you're feeling. Maybe you could let her know that you heard her when she asked for space, but you're standing by ready if she ever decides she might be ready for more than friendship."

"I'd like to think she knows that."

"Don't take anything for granted. Clue her in on how you feel so she'll know. Tell her there's no pressure or time limit. That'll matter to her, son."

"I'll talk to her when we get back tomorrow." He wondered how he'd be able to wait that long. Hours after he and his dad went to bed, Lucas lay awake thinking about Dani and Savannah and imagining a life that included them. He wanted to do what Wade was doing—buy a junk of a house, renovate it and make it theirs—and then fill it with kids.

He hardly slept, but woke raring to get home to see Dani and Savvy and tell her how he felt. His brothers were pissed with his impatience by the time they loaded the last of their camping equipment into the trucks and headed for home.

"What the hell crawled up your ass overnight?" Landon asked as the two of them rode in Landon's truck.

Lucas wished he was driving so they could go faster. "Nothing. I'm just ready to go home."

"Yeah, we got that message. The question is, what's the rush?"

"I got stuff to do." His father's advice to air it out with Dani was the only thing he'd thought about since last night.

"You're such a weirdo lately."

"Thanks."

"That wasn't a compliment," Landon said, huffing out a laugh. "Although you would take it as one in your current state of mind. What is *with* you anyway?"

"Nothing."

"Something. I hardly ever see you anymore."

"That's not true. You see me every day."

"At work, but when was the last time we hung out away from work?"

It'd been a while. Lucas couldn't deny that. His every spare minute was spent with Dani and Savannah lately. "We just spent a whole weekend together." Longest weekend of his life. He'd been counting the hours until he could get home to them.

"That's not what I mean, and you know it."

"Look, I'm sorry, okay? I've just been really busy."

"Can you at least be honest? You got a girlfriend and turned into the kind of guy we used to make fun of who forgot he had a life before he got shackled to a woman."

"A, I don't have a girlfriend. B, I'm not shackled to anyone. C, I haven't forgotten about my life."

"I call bullshit."

"She's really not my girlfriend. We're just good friends."

"No one spends as much time with a woman as you do with her if they're not interested in something more."

"I didn't say I was uninterested. I said she's not my girlfriend."

"Now you're splitting hairs."

"I don't mean to, but that's the truth. Yeah, we hang out all the time, but I'm not 'seeing' her that way."

"And you want to be?"

"Hell yes, I do, but it's complicated."

"Because of the baby."

"Because of her and her father, who was killed in an accident before she was born. Dani's had a lot to deal with."

"That's rough."

"It has been, but she's worked hard to get her life back on track and to start over. I've tried to be a good friend to her when she needed one."

"So now you're stuck firmly in the friend zone?"

"I'm not sure."

"You need to find out."

"Believe me, I'm aware of that. I'm going to talk to her when we get home."

"Thus the haste to break camp. I get it now."

Lucas couldn't deny it, so he didn't try. "Aren't you ready to get back to Amanda?"

"Eh, that's not really happening either."

Surprised to hear that, Lucas glanced at his brother. "No?"

"I don't think so. I can't get a read on her. One minute, she's in, the next, she's not. I'm getting whiplash from trying to keep up."

"That sucks."

"It is what it is. I'm taking a step back. Who needs the drama? This is why it's better to just stay single and unencumbered."

"Forever?"

"For now anyway."

A couple of months ago, Lucas would've agreed with him. Girlfriends were a lot of work. Staying single was easier. But his thinking on the matter had changed since he met Dani, and now he wanted to do the work, put in the time and be whatever she needed him to be. Talk about a change in direction...

"Am I dropping you at home or her place?" Landon asked as they got closer to Butler.

"Home. I need to shower first."

"Probably not a bad idea," Landon said, laughing. "We stink."

"You stink. I'm just dirty."

"Whatever you say."

Landon pulled into the driveway at the Christmas tree farm and stopped at the barn. "Home sweet home."

"Thanks for the lift."

"No prob." Landon put the truck in Park and got out to help Lucas with his stuff. "So you have a plan for this convo you're going to have with her?"

Lucas had had hours during the night to go over it from every angle. "In fact, I do."

Landon leaned against the truck, giving Lucas his full attention. "Let's hear it."

"Oh, um, well… I'm going to tell her that I know she's been through a lot, and I respect that she's still putting her life back together, but I'm here, and I'm not going anywhere. If it takes a week, a month, a year, two years, whatever, I'm all in with her and Savvy."

A long silence followed the statement, during which Lucas had no idea what his twin was thinking. And usually, he knew exactly what Landon was thinking.

"That's really beautiful, bro."

Lucas eyed him skeptically. "Are you busting my balls?"

Landon laughed. "For once, I'm not. If you say that to her with the same feeling you had saying it to me, you'll be all set."

"You think so?"

"I really do. Get going. Like you said, you've got stuff to do today."

"Hey, Landon?"

"Yeah?"

"Sorry if I was a dick about everything with Amanda. It certainly wasn't your fault that she decided she'd rather be with you."

"I'm still not convinced she's decided that, but thanks for what you said. I can't stand when things are weird with you."

"Same goes. Let's make sure that doesn't happen again, okay?"

Landon nodded. "Good luck, Luc. I hope you get everything you want."

"Thanks. Me, too."

Chapter 21

*"You know you're in love when you don't want to fall asleep
because reality is finally better than your dreams."*
—Dr. Seuss

Lucas grabbed his backpack, tent and sleeping bag and went inside, tossing the tent and sleeping bag into the garage to be dealt with later. He took the stairs two at a time and headed straight for the bathroom, pulling off clothes as he went. He dropped his filthy clothes into the washer, along with the contents of his backpack, dumped in detergent and started the machine before heading to the shower.

Fifteen minutes later, he was on his way into town. Was the florist open on Sundays? He didn't think so, and besides, he didn't want to tip his hand by showing up with flowers. He didn't want her to think this visit was different from all the others until he got a sense as to whether the words he wanted to say would be welcome today.

By the time he reached her street, he was a bundle of nerves, which was funny in light of the fact that he'd had women practically throwing themselves at him since he was old enough to understand the basic laws of attraction. He'd never been nervous around a woman until now, when it mattered more than it ever had before.

Stopping outside her house, he noticed her car was gone.

His heart fell and sucked all the adrenaline from his system on a great big whoosh of disappointment.

He put the truck in Park and shut off the engine, prepared to wait as long as it took. Glancing at the clock, he saw that it was almost two. She wouldn't be gone much longer with Savvy's nap between two and two thirty, and yes, he knew what time she napped, because he paid attention to everything having to do with both of them. Which was why he also knew that Dani grocery shopped on Sundays, and that was probably where they were.

Sure enough, she pulled into the driveway a few minutes later, smiling when she saw him there waiting for her.

Lucas got out of the truck as Dani alighted from her car. He was pleased that she was still smiling.

"You're back."

"I'm back. Did you ladies miss me?"

"We did. It was quiet without you around." She opened the back door, and when Savvy saw him, she let out what he called her happy screech.

"Lu, Lu, Lu."

His heart melted when she called him that. "May I?" he asked, gesturing to the baby.

"Please do, or she's apt to bust through the straps trying to get to you."

Like the expert he was by now, he released her from the next-stage car seat she'd moved into a month ago and swung her up and over his head, delighting in the happy noises she made at the sight of him. And then he held her close, breathing in the scent of her baby shampoo and sweetness, his every emotion hovering at the surface, threatening to spill over at any second.

"Lu, Lu, Lu."

"That's her favorite word."

"Still no mama?"

"Not yet."

"Any day now." He gazed down at Dani, taking in the reddish-blonde hair gilded by the sun, the face that had become so familiar and necessary to him, the eyes that looked at him with such affection and the lips he was dying to kiss again. Would he ever get to? The not-knowing was killing him. "You got groceries?"

"Yep."

"You take her. I'll get them."

"You don't have to."

"I know I don't." He handed Savvy over to her mother, and the baby protested the entire transaction.

She fussed as he followed them up the stairs with cloth grocery bags hanging from both arms and didn't let up until he put down the bags and took her back from Dani. The minute she was back in his arms, she settled into the little coos that were among the sweetest sounds he'd ever heard.

"*Someone* is getting spoiled rotten by someone else around here," Dani said as she stashed food in the fridge and freezer.

"She's not rotten," he said, feigning offense on Savvy's behalf. "She's perfect." He held her until she started fussing again.

"Time for a snack and a nap." Dani took her from Lucas, and Savvy was so busy yawning that she didn't protest. "Make yourself comfortable. I'll be quick."

Since he had time, he put away the rest of the groceries and then folded the bags into a neat pile. He washed the few dishes that were in the sink and wiped down the countertops.

"Are you *cleaning* my kitchen?"

"Blame my mother. I see dishes and I have to do them, or she'll know. I'm scared of her."

"You are not, but thank you. You didn't have to do that."

"I didn't mind."

"So you missed me, huh?"

"Did you have a good time?"

They both spoke at once, and Dani let out a nervous laugh. "Yes, I missed you."

"No, I didn't have a good time."

"You didn't?"

He shook his head and took a step closer to her, until only a foot separated them.

"How come?"

"I was so busy thinking about you and your daughter that I apparently wasn't very good company on the trip."

"Oh."

"Which is a long way of saying I missed you, too."

"It was only two days."

"I missed you. I missed Savvy. I missed being with you guys and seeing her in the morning and tucking her in at night and talking to you. I missed you."

"Could I ask you something?"

"Anything you want." His heart slowed to a crawl, and if you'd asked him if it was possible for the world to stop turning, he would've said it did in the seconds it took for her to ask her question.

"Do you still want to be more than friends with me?"

"Dani," he gasped, shocked that she had to ask. "I want to be *everything* with you."

He wasn't sure who moved first, but what did it matter when the end result was her in his arms and his lips devouring hers? God, it felt like forever had happened since the last time he'd tasted her sweetness or felt the unmistakable rightness that came over him when he held her. If he had his way, he'd never stop kissing her. He'd carry her into the bedroom and take this sexy encounter to the logical next level. But in the back of his mind was the niggling reminder of why she'd asked for space in the first place and the possibility that she might not be ready for the next level.

Though it pained him, he slowly disengaged from the kiss until his lips were barely touching hers.

"What's wrong?" she asked, tightening her grasp on his shirt.

Like daughter, like mother.

"If we keep this up, things will happen, and I'm not sure that's what you want."

"It is."

"Dani…"

She took his hand and turned toward the bedroom, tugging him along behind her.

Holy shit, this is actually going to happen. A surge of excitement, of raw need the likes of which he'd never felt before, took his breath away, leaving him trembling and hopeful that he could get through this most important of moments without embarrassing himself.

She shocked the shit out of him when she turned to face him and whipped off her sweater, revealing a lacy, sexy bra and full, lush breasts.

He was so blown away by her that he was afraid to touch her.

"Lucas?"

"I'm not going to wake up to find that I'm dreaming this, am I?"

Smiling, she shook her head.

"Because I've dreamed about this before, about you and what it might be like to be able to hold you and touch you and kiss you." He rested his hands on her shoulders and slid them down her arms, watching as goose bumps dotted her sensitive skin. "I dreamed about what it might be like if you and Savvy were mine."

"We *are* yours, Lucas. We have been since the night you rescued us and took us home with you. And you're ours."

There was almost nothing she could've said that would've meant more to him than that did. Empowered by her declaration, he raised his arms when she slid the sweater up and over his head. Though it pained him, he stood perfectly still while she explored the hills and valleys of his chest and abdomen.

"You have muscles on top of muscles," she said reverently, and when she leaned in to kiss his chest, he buried his hands in her hair to keep her there, the pleasure of her touch so intense, it made him dizzy.

"I feel like I've never done this before," he said.

"From what I've heard, you're an old pro."

Though he knew she was teasing, he had to set her straight and compelled her to look at him. "I've never done anything remotely like this."

"What's different about it?"

"Everything. It's you. And you're… Everything." He just kept coming back to that word, which summed it up for him.

She smiled up at him, seeming pleased with what he'd said.

He hoped she was pleased, because he meant it. At some point, he'd need to tell her that no one had ever been everything to him before.

But then she tugged on the button to his jeans, and his mind again went blank as the majority of the blood in his body headed south on an express train straight to his cock. He'd never been harder in his life than he was for her, hadn't known he could want like this or that it could make him feel lightheaded, elated and dizzy all at the same time.

"Your hands are shaking." Her husky voice interrupted his spinning thoughts, forcing him to return his focus completely to her, where it belonged.

"Are they?"

She nodded.

"I'm nervous."

"Why?" She looked up at him with the big, trusting eyes that slayed him.

"I waited forever for you. I want it to be good for you."

"Lucas," she said, laughing, "do you have any idea what you do to me?"

He shook his head. "Tell me."

"All you have to do is look at me, and I'm right there…"

"Where?"

She pressed her body against his. "*There.*"

"That's all it takes?"

"That's all it takes."

"God, Dani, I'm not going to survive you."

"Yes, you will." She reached for him and lured him into another tongue-curling kiss that ended when the need for air beat out his need for her. Lucas buried his face in her neck and breathed in the distinctive scent of her skin. It reminded him of sugar cookies right out of the oven, and sugar cookies were among his favorite things.

And now, she was, too.

She unzipped his jeans, carefully.

He was so hard, he ached, and even the light pressure of the zipper was almost too much to handle. "Let me." Lucas finished unzipping and kicked off his jeans, leaving him only in formfitting boxer briefs that left nothing to the imagination.

She took a long look at him and then licked her lips.

Gas, meet fire.

Lucas kissed her, wrapped his arms around her and moved them as one to the bed, where he came down on top of her, all without missing a beat in the most passionate kiss of his life. He could kiss her forever and never get enough of her sweetness. Still, he wondered if this was real, if she was real. After so many days and nights of wondering if he'd ever have this with her, he almost couldn't believe it was actually happening.

He kissed a path from her neck to the plump tops of her breasts, contained by the sexiest bra he'd ever seen—or maybe it was her that made it the sexiest. It was definitely her. After releasing the front clasp, he pushed aside the cups to reveal full breasts with tips that tightened in the chill of the air.

"God, you're beautiful, Dani." He rested his forehead on her chest and took a deep breath, trying to find the control and patience he needed to make this good for her.

She ran her fingers through his hair, her touch both soothing and arousing.

"We probably shouldn't… I mean, I could get leaky…"

"I don't care."

"I do."

He raised his head to look at her, shook his head and cupped her breasts, running his thumbs back and forth over her tight nipples.

"Lucas…"

"Shhhh." He drew her left nipple into his mouth, running his tongue back and forth over it while pinching the right one lightly between his fingers. "Every part of you is beautiful to me."

Her chest rose and fell in rapid succession as he moved down to rain kisses over her belly before unbuttoning and unzipping her jeans. Dani lifted her hips to help him remove her pants, which he tossed aside as he gazed at her skimpy red underwear.

"Tell me the truth. Did you plan for this, or do you always wear sexy underwear?"

She smiled. "Always."

"It's a good thing I didn't know that all along, or my Dani fantasies would've been even more vivid."

"They were vivid?"

He met her gaze. "*So* vivid. You're all I think about. You and Savvy."

"You're all we think about, too."

"Really?"

She nodded. "Really."

When he tugged on the scrap of red fabric covering her, she again lifted her hips to help him get it off, leaving her bare to his greedy gaze.

She reached for him.

"Hang on. I'm not done looking yet."

Her nervous laughter made him smile as he kissed from the bottom of her foot to her calf to her inner thigh.

"And in case you're wondering, the fantasies didn't begin to do you justice."

"I have stretch marks and leaky boobs and—"

"You're perfect, Dani. I've never wanted anyone the way I want you, so please don't find yourself lacking. You're perfect for me." He settled between her legs and opened her to his tongue.

"Oh God," she whispered, sounding as needy as he felt.

As he slid his fingers into her tight heat, he gritted his teeth against the urgent desire that made him want to rush when he'd much rather savor. They'd never again do this for the first time. It needed to be memorable. Tonguing the tight nub of her clit, he pushed his fingers into her and curled them forward, seeking the elusive spot that would trigger her orgasm.

She gripped a handful of his hair and pulled hard enough to hurt, but the bite of pain only pushed his desire firmly into the red zone.

And then she was coming, crying out as the orgasm seized her, her inner muscles tightening around his fingers. He stayed with her until she calmed, sagging into the mattress as she sucked in deep breaths.

Lucas withdrew from her only long enough to retrieve a condom, roll it on and return to where she waited for him. Wait… Were those tears? "Dani…" Settling on top of her, he made sure to keep most of his weight on his arms as he brushed tears from her face. "What is it?"

"Nothing. I'm just overwhelmed."

"In a good way?"

She nodded. "The best way, but it's, you know… The first time since…"

"I know, sweetheart. We don't have to."

"I want to. I really do." She cradled his face between her hands. "I couldn't imagine this with anyone but you."

"Well, I hope not," he said, hoping to make her smile.

She laughed. "There's no one but you, Lucas Abbott." She drew him into a kiss and moved under him, letting him know what she wanted. "And you know it."

He gave it to her, slowly, carefully, gently, giving her time to adjust and accommodate even as he bit the inside of his cheek in the effort to put his own needs second to hers. Over the last few years, he'd been skeptical, watching his brothers fall one after another for women they couldn't live without. Was it really so different with that special someone? he'd wondered. Well, now he had his answer.

It wasn't different so much as *more*. The emotion and intimacy that came with doing this with someone you truly cared about only made the desire that much sharper. The emotion added another layer to an already magical encounter.

Tears leaked from the corners of her eyes.

He kissed them away as he held still inside her, waiting for her to signal she was ready for more. "Tell me to stop if that's what you need."

"I don't want you to stop."

Lucas tried to remember that while he felt elated to be taking this momentous step with her, it was bittersweet for her as she continued to mourn her first love. "Are you okay?"

She nodded and ran her hands down his back to curve them over his ass.

He shuddered and found himself fighting to hold on to control as her inner muscles tightened around him. "I need to move. Is that okay?"

"It's okay."

Raising himself up on his arms, he kept a careful watch over her as he moved inside her. "Tell me what you need, love."

"Just this." She moved with him, seeming to step out of her memories into the present as the minutes passed. And then she floored him when she reached down to where they were joined to touch herself, triggering an orgasm that finished him off, too.

"That move at the end was hot," he whispered when he could speak again after discovering how very different sex could be when it truly mattered.

"You liked that, huh?"

"Mmm, but I could've done that for you."

"I didn't mind helping out."

Lucas laughed, withdrew from her, disposed of the condom in a tissue, moved to his side and brought her with him. He swept the hair back from her face and wished he knew what she was thinking. "I came in here with a whole speech planned that I never got to give."

"I need to hear it."

"I was going to tell you that I wanted to be more than friends with you, and if you thought you might want that, too, I was willing to wait a week, a month, a year, however long it took until you were ready for more." As he spoke, he continued to run his fingers through her hair. "I was going to tell you that I'm all in with you and Savvy and us."

"You've been so patient with me while I took the time I needed to set up my life here and to be ready for this." Her hand made lazy circles over his chest and belly, which had him thinking about round two. "Thank you for that."

"I didn't do anything, Dani."

"That's not true. You've been an extraordinary friend to me from the first minute we met, and that's meant the world. And even though you wanted this to be more, you took a step back when I asked for space, and you respected my needs. Not to mention, you love my daughter like she's yours, and there's nothing you could give me that would mean more than that."

"I feel like she's mine, but I also feel guilty about that because I'm not her dad. I can never replace him, and I know that."

"You can't replace him, but perhaps you could stand in for him?"

"Yes," he said softly. "I'd be honored to do that. Thank you for allowing me to be part of her life."

Dani laughed. "It's not like it was up to me. She decided that all on her own."

"She digs me."

"From what I've been told, most women dig you. My daughter is no different."

"Your daughter is extraordinary, and so is her mother. I'm completely smitten with you both. I hope you know that."

"You just did a very good job of showing me that."

"Maybe I should show you again, just to make sure you really get the message."

She leaned over to grab the second condom he'd put on the bedside table and handed it to him. "You did leave a few questions unanswered..."

Tightening his hold on her, he rolled onto his back, positioning her on top of him. "We can't have that."

CHAPTER 22

"The water shines only by the sun.
And it is you who are my sun."
—Charles de Leusse

Later that afternoon, they went to dinner at his parents' house, and Dani wondered if everyone could tell they'd spent the afternoon in bed. She might as well have worn a sign on her head that said *I slept with your son/grandson/brother/brother-in-law, and it was incredible.* Surely they could tell just by looking at her that everything had changed, couldn't they?

God, she hoped it wasn't that obvious.

"How you doing?"

She glanced toward the male voice and startled at the sight of Lucas's twin. Like Lucas, Landon was wearing a navy blue Henley, and if it hadn't been for Lucas's beard, she might not have been entirely sure. Then she realized she was staring at him and blinked. "Good. You?"

"It's okay," he said, laughing. "We're used to the staring."

"I'm sorry. I've just never known identical twins before."

He stuck out his jaw. "Admit it. I'm much better looking than he is. You can tell me. He's not listening."

"He is too listening." Lucas came from the living room with Savannah in his arms.

Dani took one look at him holding her child and swooned on the inside. Yes, she would definitely be able to distinguish him from his twin, even without the beard.

"Tell him the truth, Dani," Lucas said, grinning at her. He looked as happy as she felt.

"Sorry, Landon, but I'm rather partial to this one."

Landon rolled his eyes. "I suppose someone's gotta be."

"I've got two ladies who are partial to me," Lucas said, kissing Savannah's head and giving his twin a *take that* smirk. "You gotta come see this, Dani."

"See what?"

"Follow me."

She gave Landon a perplexed look and then followed Lucas into the living room, where Wade, Mia, Colton, Lucy and Elmer were watching the Bruins game.

Lucas sat on the rug next to one of the family's yellow Labs. She wasn't sure if it was George or Ringo, but she loved that they were both girls who'd been named after members of Lincoln's favorite band.

"Wait until you see this, Dani," Mia said.

With Savannah on his lap, Lucas took the dog's tail and dusted the baby's face with it.

Savannah let out a belly laugh that had Dani staring at the two of them.

Lucas did it again.

Savannah laughed. She laughed every time he did it as Dani looked on with tears in her eyes as she realized how much Savannah loved Lucas.

Lucy stood and withdrew a cell phone from her pocket and began recording it.

"Thank you," Dani said to her.

"You have to have this on video. I'll email it to you."

Her parents would be delighted to receive that video and to see Savannah so happy. Her gaze met Lucas's, and they shared a smile full of parental pride in their girl. *Oh God*, she thought. *I'm thinking of him as Savannah's father, and I have no idea if that's what he's signed on for.* He loved the baby. He'd said earlier that he'd be honored to stand in for Jack, but for how long?

Parenthood was a lifetime role, and that was a lot to ask of anyone.

When she glanced at Lucas, his brows were knitted with what looked like concern. "What's wrong?"

"Nothing," she said, her voice high and squeaky, which gave away the lie.

"Breathe."

She held his gaze as she drew in a deep breath and released it slowly.

"Again."

She did it again.

"Better?"

"Yes."

"Whatever it is, we'll figure it out."

"Let's eat," Molly called from the dining room.

Lucas got up with Savannah, and as Dani followed him, Lucy came up next to her.

"Not sure what that was just now, but you two are adorable together," she whispered.

"That was him being amazing."

"I know how that goes. His brother has pretty good game, too."

"You talking about me, babe?" Colton asked as he slid an arm around Lucy.

"Of course I am. You're my favorite thing to talk about."

"See how she objectifies me?" Colton said to Dani.

"He loves when I objectify him."

Colton stuck his tongue out and panted like a dog as he nodded.

Dani cracked up laughing. She did a lot of that around these people.

When everyone was seated around the massive dining room table, Colton stood and cleared his throat. "A reminder that everyone is invited to our mountain next Saturday at noon for a shotgun wedding."

"Colton!"

He grinned at his fiancée. "Are you or are you not knocked up?"

"I'm going to kill you."

"Not before you marry me. Anyone who wants to camp on the mountain, let me know. We've got plenty of room as you know, and well, I'm gonna be a husband—and a dad." His voice broke on that last word, and Dani blinked back tears of her own.

Everyone broke into cheers and congratulations and condolences for Lucy, who, if you listened to Colton's siblings, needed all the sympathy she could get for taking on their mountain man.

"Have I mentioned that he was my twelve-pound baby?" Molly asked as she took a bite of the most delicious lasagna Dani had ever tasted.

Lucy choked on a sip of water.

Colton patted her back. "Too late to turn back now. My devil spawn is already in there."

"I'm sorry," Lincoln said to Lucy. "We did what we could with him."

"*You had a twelve-pound baby?*" Cameron asked, her face pale and her eyes huge.

"And two elevens," Molly said. "Will and Ella."

"I want to know who I can sue." Cameron slapped her hand on the table. "This is information we should've had before we procreated with your children. Don't you agree, Luce?"

Lucy, who'd also gone pale, nodded. "Most definitely. I'm calling my lawyer in the morning."

"Let's make it a class-action," Megan said to hysterical laughter.

"Now, ladies," Hunter said, "let's not be hasty about this."

"You be quiet," Megan said to her husband. "Unless you're staring down the possibility of giving birth to a *twelve-pound baby*, you have no oar in this race."

"Yes, dear."

His brothers howled with laughter.

Dani took it all in, her head spinning as she tried to keep up with the jokes, the conversation, the laughter. Family dinner at the Abbotts' barn was better than any reality TV show she'd ever watched.

"They're lunatics," Lincoln said to her during a rare quiet second. "I apologize for subjecting you to my crazy family."

"I love your family. Sunday dinner has become my favorite part of the week."

Lincoln smiled. "That's nice to hear. By all accounts, you've got our warehouse whipped into shape, and we'll be ready in plenty of time for the catalog to drop."

While chaos swirled around them, she and Lincoln engaged in their own private conversation that no one else could hear due to the noise. "We're getting there."

"I am very pleased with what a great job you're doing, Dani."

"Thank you. That means a lot to me."

"I'm also pleased to see my son smiling all the time. He sure does love your little girl."

"She adores him, and he's made us both very happy. He's a good man."

"Yes, he is. I may be partial, but I'm very proud of the seven good men Molly and I raised."

"By all accounts, you have every reason to be proud of them."

"Raising your children to be good people—it's the only thing in this life that matters if you're a parent. Success and money and all the trappings don't matter if your kids grow up to be entitled jerks, you know?"

"I've certainly known a few people like that in my life, and I agree. When I think about being Savannah's mom, that's my most important job. To make sure she's a good person who cares about others and gives back."

"Your little girl is very lucky to have you."

"I'm lucky to have her. When I lost her dad, I didn't think I could go on without him, but knowing I had to be there for her kept me going through the worst of times."

"I'm sorry for your loss."

"Thank you. You would've liked him."

"I have no doubt."

"I want you to know… I care a lot about Lucas, and I'm sure you must be concerned about him getting involved with me because I have a child and…"

Lincoln shook his head. "I'm not one bit concerned. I've never seen my son as captivated by anything as he is by your daughter—and you, if I'm not mistaken."

Dani's face heated with embarrassment. "You're not mistaken, and the feeling is entirely mutual."

"That's wonderful. I'm happy for both of you."

"I'm rather happy myself these days. I love my new life in Butler."

"It's a great place to live and raise kids."

Lucas, who was still holding Savannah, turned toward her and his father. "What're you saying to her, Dad?"

"I'm telling her to watch out for you and that she can do better."

"Very funny."

"No, it's true," Linc said, deadpan. "I warned her off."

"Dad!"

Dani dissolved into laughter. "That's not at all what he said."

Lucas scowled at his father, who lost it laughing.

She could see where Lucas came by his quick wit.

Savannah started getting fussy right after dinner, so they packed her up to head back to Dani's place. Lucas carried the baby up the stairs and removed her coat. While the frigid winter had departed, spring in Vermont was still cold and raw. Lucas had told her it took until mid-June to really warm up, which was a far cry from spring in Kentucky.

She had bathed Savannah after her nap, so she settled with her on the bed to breastfeed her as she did mostly in the morning and at night these days. In between, she had baby food and cereal.

Lucas stood in the doorway, hands propped over his head on the doorframe. "You need anything?"

She patted the bed. "Just you."

He stretched out next to her and linked his fingers with hers. "I'm here."

"Can you stay?"

"Do you want me to?"

She nodded.

"I'd love to."

For a long time, they existed in peaceful silence, the only sound coming from Savannah. After a while, the sounds stopped and her breathing deepened.

"Is she out?" Lucas asked.

"I think so."

"I'll put her down."

Dani handed her over to him, loving the way he always wanted to be part of whatever was going on with the baby.

She could hear him on the monitor, the rustling of the baby's blanket and the sound of him kissing her.

Dani's heart expanded to the point of bursting. After losing Jack, she'd never imagined finding someone who would love their daughter as much as he would have. She couldn't have dreamed of Lucas.

He returned to her room, unbuttoning his shirt as he came toward her.

"Thank you," Dani said, gazing up at him, drinking in every detail.

"For what?"

"For loving my little girl."

He lay down next to her and put his arm around her. "You don't have to thank me for that. Loving her is the easiest thing I've ever done."

"It takes a special kind of guy to love a child that isn't his, and you, my friend, are a special kind of guy."

"I'm glad you think so."

"It's a lot to ask you to take on."

"Is that what you were having a silent freak out about at my parents' house earlier?"

She nodded.

"You didn't ask me. I'm here for one reason and one reason only."

"What's that?" she asked, breathless in anticipation of his reply.

"Because I don't want to be anywhere but where you two are."

She placed her hand on his face and ran her fingers over the rough outline of his beard. "Sometimes I can't believe you're real."

"I'm real. This is real." He kissed her softly, tenderly and with so much emotion. They came together like they'd been doing this forever. His arms encircled her, her leg slid between his, their bodies aligned, and the kiss became the focus of her existence.

She could kiss him for hours and never get enough.

"Let's get comfortable." He unbuttoned the lightweight flannel she'd bought at the store and helped her out of her clothes.

Under the covers, they came together in a burst of hungry desire as the kiss picked up where it had left off, only with increased urgency. His hands were everywhere, his touch ramping up the need to desperate levels.

"Are you sore from earlier?" he asked as he kissed her neck.

"A little maybe."

"Let me kiss it better." He waggled his brows as he moved down her body until he had her legs propped on his shoulders and his tongue soothing the parts of her that ached.

God, the man had his talents, and this was definitely one of them. He had her almost immediately on the verge of orgasm, and he'd barely touched her. Seeming to realize she was close, he slowed down, dragged out the pleasure and had her trying not to scream from the powerful release he coaxed from her.

He brought her down slowly, until she sagged into the mattress, exhausted and sated and happy.

Being with him made her happy. For a time, she'd thought she might never feel that way again, but he'd shown her that there was life after crushing loss, that she could feel for another man what she had for Jack, but not just any man. Only this one.

"All better?" he asked, his grin smug.

"You're looking rather pleased with yourself, but then again, you have reason to be."

His smile spread, encompassing his lovely eyes.

"It occurs to me that I owe you some of what you just gave me."

Dropping his head, he kissed her belly. "You owe me nothing."

"What if I want to?"

"Oh, um, well... That's a different story."

Laughing, she pushed him onto his back and leaned over him, taking a long look at his gorgeous body.

He wrapped strands of her hair around his fingers. "Go easy on me, killer."

"Why should I?"

He moaned as she licked the outline of his abdominal muscles and whimpered when she moved down to let her hair slide over his hard cock.

She kissed him everywhere but where he wanted her most, doing her best to make him crazy before she took the wide head of his cock into her mouth and sucked gently.

His entire body went taut with tension, and the sound that came from him was a cross between a groan and a plea for mercy.

She slid her lips down his shaft, stroked him with her tongue and wrapped her hand around the base. Remembering the first time she'd done this with Jack had her blinking back tears that came from nowhere. They'd learned about giving and receiving pleasure together.

Dani pushed every other thought from her mind and gave Lucas her full attention, using her lips, tongue and hand to bring him pleasure.

"Dani," he said, his voice harsher than she'd ever heard it.

Keeping his cock in her mouth, she looked up at him.

"Stop."

She released him.

With his hands under her arms, he urged her up until her breasts were snug against his cock. He pressed hard and came between her breasts, groaning and gasping.

And then he released a long breath and wrapped his arms around her.

She could hear his heart hammering under the rapid rise and fall of his chest. "Was that okay?"

His low chuckle rumbled under her ear. "It was fucking awesome. You had me on the edge of losing it from the second your hair touched me." He scooped her hair into a ponytail and then twirled it around his fingers. "Let me up so I can get a towel. I made a mess of you."

When he released her hair, she moved to her back and waited for him to return with a hand towel that he used to wipe her chest and breasts. "You're so very pretty, Danielle. I could look at you forever and never get tired of the view." He placed a kiss between her breasts.

Dani cradled his head to her chest as a startling realization came over her. She loved him. She had fallen completely in love with him over the last few months. Just when she'd thought she'd never love again, Lucas had come storming into her life and given her hope for a future that could be as bright and wonderful as the past with Jack had been.

But was she ready for that?

She still didn't know for sure, and that was the only thing keeping her from complete contentment.

CHAPTER 23

"I love you not because of who you are, but because
of who I am when I am with you."
—Roy Croft

Having Dani's warm naked body pressed against him was like heaven, Lucas decided long after she'd fallen asleep. He'd be reliving the exquisite pleasure of her warm mouth on his cock for the foreseeable future. He was beginning to understand why his brothers had been so eager to settle down with one woman.

In the past, Lucas had been about *all* the women.

Now Dani was the only one he wanted. He couldn't imagine wanting anyone but her ever again, for that matter. During the endless weeks when he'd given her the space she'd requested, he'd dreamed about what might be waiting for them when she was ready for something more. But his dreams couldn't begin to touch the reality of holding her, kissing her, making love to her and sleeping naked with her.

He'd fallen so hard for her and her little girl. The only question he had now was how soon could he ask her to marry him so they could become an official family. If Dani thought it was appropriate, he would happily adopt Savannah and raise her as his own while doing his best to honor the memory of the man who'd fathered her.

Dani turned over and snuggled into his chest. "Why're you still awake?"

"How did you know I was?"

"I don't know. I can just tell."

"I feel like I waited forever to be with you this way," he said, gathering her in close to him, "and now that we're doing this, I don't want to miss a second of it."

"I'm not going anywhere."

"I know."

"Go to sleep."

"Don't wanna."

"What do you want to do?"

"I want to give you a present."

"Now?"

"If that's okay."

"Um, sure."

He disentangled himself from her. "Don't move." Lucas got up, found his jeans on the floor and pulled them on.

"You need pants to give me a present?"

"It's in my truck, and I'd assume you'd rather I didn't run into Mrs. Abernathy bare-ass naked."

"That'd probably be for the best," Dani said, giggling. "Ella told me some stories about how she came knocking on the door when she heard noises coming from the apartment when Ella and Gavin were first together."

Lucas stared at her, appalled. "If you care about me at all, do *not* share the details of the stories Ella told you about her having sex with her boyfriend."

Dani covered her mouth to smother another giggle.

He loved her this way—relaxed, happy, laughing. Hell, he loved her every way, even when she was stressed or in the midst of a panic attack or worried about Savvy.

"What?"

Her question made him realize he was staring at her. Blinking, he shook his head and pushed his feet into his boots. "Nothing. I'll be right back."

He grabbed his coat and went down the two flights of stairs and outside to his truck, where he'd stashed the box for her in the backseat next to the car seat he'd bought so he could drop Savvy at Hannah's or pick her up if Dani was running late.

Toting the box, he went up the stairs and back to her apartment, closing and locking the door behind him. He kicked off the boots he hadn't bothered to tie, dropped his coat over a chair and returned to her room, where Dani was sitting up in bed with the light on.

She gasped at the sight of the large box. "What've you done?"

"I had a couple of months stuck firmly in the friend zone, during which I had a lot of time to think about what I would do if I ever got the chance to be more than friends with you."

"Lucas."

"Do not cry."

"I can't help it! You're so sweet."

"You haven't even opened it yet," he said, both amused by her reaction and dismayed by the possibility of tears. Knowing what was in the box, he suspected there might be actual tears coming.

She reached for the flannel shirt he'd discarded earlier and put it on, buttoning it once under her breasts.

Sexiest fucking thing he'd ever seen was her barely wearing his shirt.

And then she smelled it. "Sawdust, linseed oil, woodsmoke, fresh air. That's what you smell like."

"Clearly, I need to invest in some cologne."

"Don't you dare. I love the way you smell."

Sometimes, the emotion she invoked in him could hit him like an arrow straight to the heart that had him better understanding the whole Cupid thing in a way he never had before. "Open your present."

She went up on her knees to open the flaps of the box and pulled out the first level of tissue paper to discover a dozen paperback romance novels.

"Oh my God..." The look she gave him was full of all the things he felt for her coming back to him tenfold. "Lucas..."

"I'm hoping that maybe you're starting to believe in happily ever after again, and if so, you might be ready to resume one of your favorite guilty pleasures."

She dropped the books to the bed, scooted around the box and threw her arms around him. "Thank you."

"I'll watch Savvy for you so you can read. Anytime you want."

She kissed him full on the mouth as he cupped her ass. "Best gift ever."

"There's more."

"You shouldn't have."

"Too late. I already did. Keep going."

The next thing in the box was a stuffed elephant he'd found in the hospital gift shop when he'd been there on a recent call.

"I wanted to get the elephant off your chest and into your arms. Hopefully, you'll be more comfortable with him there."

She covered her mouth as a sob hiccupped through her.

"No tears," he said sternly.

Tears slid down her cheeks as she shook her head.

"Talk to me."

"I love it," she whispered. "It's the most thoughtful gift I've ever gotten from anyone."

That meant the world to him. He could never be the first man she loved, and he was okay with that, but he wanted to be the last one she ever loved. "There's more."

"This is too much!"

"It's your fault. You needed 'time,' and I had too much of it on my hands."

The exasperated look she gave him was one that wives and girlfriends have been giving the men in their lives since the dawn of time. He loved being on the receiving end of it from her. Under the last layer of tissue paper was a supply of sandpaper in a variety of grades, cans of paint stripper and stain, sponge brushes and a small black box containing a key.

"That's the only other key to my shop, and there's an entire corner there that's all yours. It's set up for when you find a project you want to work on, and you should feel free to come and go there anytime you want."

As tears continued to slide down her cheeks, she studied the key from every angle. "That's the place you go to be alone with your art."

With his fingers on her chin, he compelled her to look at him. "If I have a choice of being there alone or being there with you, I pick you. Every time."

She threw herself at him, sending the box flying and landing on the floor with a loud *thunk* that was sure to get Mrs. Abernathy's attention downstairs.

He couldn't have cared less about her nosy landlord. Not when he had the woman of his dreams in his arms and kissing his face and every other part of him she could reach.

"Best gifts you ever could've given me."

"I'm glad you like them."

"I love them. Almost as much as I love you."

There'd been a time—not that long ago, in fact—when hearing those words from a woman would've had him running to get as far away from the implications that came with them as he could get.

Those days were over.

These days were the best of his life because they included her and Savvy. He tightened his arms around her. "I love you, too, but you have to stop crying."

"Can't. You're so very sweet, and I'm so lucky to have driven my car into a ditch."

Smiling, he said, "And I'm so lucky to have been the one to have found you in a ditch."

Laughing even as she continued to sob, she smacked his shoulder. "You can't say it that way when you tell this story to people."

"I can't tell people that I found the woman of my dreams and the little girl of my heart in a ditch?"

"I suppose if you say it like that, I can't possibly object."

Dani had forgotten what it felt like to be truly happy. Having Savannah had made her happy by giving her someone new to focus on. However, the worries that came with motherhood—and single motherhood, in particular—along with the pervasive sadness that Jack would never know his daughter had tempered some of the elation of having her first child. Making the decision to set out on her own had solved a problem that had become untenable. Both these things were positive steps forward from the darkness that had followed Jack's death.

But until she met Lucas and allowed herself to have genuine feelings for him, she hadn't realized how lonely she'd been or how hopeless she'd felt about ever again feeling the way she did now.

Maybe it was still too soon, but ever since the night he'd given her the box of gifts and they'd expressed their love for each other, everything was different.

It was more. So much more, and she couldn't get enough of the way he loved her and Savannah.

Today, they were up on Colton's mountain to watch his brother marry his beloved Lucy. Even in late May, a chill remained in the air, and snow flurries were predicted for later, but Colton and Lucy had gotten a perfect sunny day to exchange their vows.

Lucy's friend Troy Kennedy had come from New York, and Cameron's dad, Patrick, had flown in from Europe with his fiancée, Mary, to see his daughter's best friend get married. A few of their Coleman cousins had come from Boston, but otherwise, everyone else was local.

They'd put up a small tent with tables and chairs, a caterer from town was doing a barbecue and a longtime friend of the Abbott family played the guitar. Everyone was in tears as Lucy walked toward Colton on the arm of her father, Ray. Her sister, Emma, best friend, Cameron, and niece, Simone, preceded her up the aisle between the rows of chairs that faced the peak of Butler Mountain. It was a breathtaking spot for a wedding.

Wearing black pants, a white shirt with the sleeves rolled up and a black vest with a white flower attached to it, Colton stood waiting for his bride with his six brothers by his side. According to Lucas, Colton couldn't bear to choose just one of them, and because "who gave a flying fuck if he had them all," he'd had them all.

Colton, she had learned, had a way with words.

But as he gazed into the radiant face of the woman he loved, all the words left him as tears flooded his eyes.

Lucy leaned in to whisper something to him.

He nodded and leaned his forehead against hers in a moment of sweet intimacy that had Dani seeking out the gaze of the man she loved.

Sure enough, he was watching her and sent her a small smile and a wink that made her feel special and cherished. He, who could have any woman in the world—and she saw the hungry way other women stared at him when they thought no one was looking—had chosen her and her daughter. And for that, she would be forever thankful. He didn't notice when others looked at him, but she did.

However, today wasn't the day to think about the other women who would never get anywhere near the man who had professed his love for her—and only her. In the dark of last night, he'd said it over and over again as he made love to her, whispering that he'd never said those words to anyone else or felt for anyone what he did for her.

Her heart ached with love for him and gratitude for her renewed belief in happy endings.

She tuned in to the words Lucy was saying to Colton. "You once asked me when I knew for sure that I loved you. It was after you found me passed out on the floor of my bathroom in the midst of a dreadful food poisoning episode. I'd blown you off at the airport, left you to fend for yourself the first time you were in New York City, and you still came and found me and took care of me even when I told you to get out."

"I've never been one to do what I was told. Just ask my mom."

"He's absolutely right," Molly said as everyone laughed. "And I tried to warn you, Luce."

"I know, Molly," Lucy said without ever taking her gaze off Colton. "And somehow I love him anyway."

"Someone's gotta," Will said under his breath but loud enough to take down the entire gathering once again.

These Abbotts were so damned funny.

Elmer, who was presiding over the vows, cleared his throat and cast a stern glance at Will, who didn't seem the slightest bit sorry for his comment.

"Colton, my mountain man, my love, my everything, I give you all of me because I know I'll always be safe and loved and amused and aggravated as long as you're in my life."

"I am nothing if not aggravating," he said gravely.

"And I love you because you know it. I take you to be my husband. I take your mountain to be my home. I take your dogs and your moose and your taps and your hoses and your sugar house. I take all of it."

"She takes your hose, bro," Landon said.

Lucas elbowed his twin hard in the gut.

Landon expelled a gasp of air that only added to the helpless laughter that was turning this wedding into a comedy show.

Dani suspected this family wouldn't have it any other way.

"I apologize for my idiot brother," Colton said. "Now, where were we?"

"We were at the part where I point out that you were probably thinking exactly what Landon said."

Colton shifted from one foot to the other. "I was not!"

Lucy gave him a calculating look. "Do not lie to me on our wedding day, Colton Abbott."

"Well, I maybe had a *passing* thought about you pledging to take my hose, but it was only a nanosecond, and then I recovered my composure. And bit my tongue. Hard."

Lucy laughed even as she shook her head. "I knew it."

Colton hooked an arm around her waist and pulled her in close to him, dropping a sweet kiss on her lips. "You knew it because you know *me* like no one else ever has, like no one else ever will. You get me, Luce, and you have no idea what a gift that is to a guy like me who used to think he was better off alone with two dogs than he'd ever be with a girlfriend. Then I met my Lucy in the sky with diamonds, and I found out how much better everything is when the person you love the most in the whole world is there to share everything except cold-weather camping with you. I thank God every day that there's an internet connection on my mountain, because I know that's the only other thing besides me and our dogs that you need to be happy."

Laughing as she blinked back tears, Lucy said, "Very true."

They gazed into each other's eyes for a long moment before they kissed again.

"And PS, you can have my hose anytime you want it."

"*Colton!*"

Smiling, he kissed the outrage right off her lips.

Elmer cleared his throat and shook his head, his eyes full of amusement. "Almost there, children. First, let's make it legal. Colton, repeat after me. I, Colton, take you, Lucy, to be my wife. To have and to hold from this day forward, forsaking all others, to love, honor and cherish all the days of my life."

Colton never blinked as he stared at Lucy and repeated the words

"Lucy? Your turn. Repeat after me."

Lucy said the words back to Colton, and then they exchanged rings that Hunter produced and dropped into Colton's hand.

"By the power vested in me by the State of Vermont, I pronounce Colton and Lucy husband and wife. *Now* you may kiss your bride, son."

While the rest of the group applauded wildly, Colton kissed his wife just as wildly, their joy infectious when he picked her up and swung her around and gave a wild whoop of happiness.

Dani hadn't realized tears were running down her face until Savannah placed her hand on her cheek and smoothed the moisture over her skin. She smiled down at the little face that had become the center of her universe, wanting to reassure her daughter that she was happy, not sad. How anyone could watch two people completely meant for each other exchange vows and not feel irrationally elated was beyond Dani.

CHAPTER 24

"It takes courage to love, but pain through love is the purifying fire which those who love generously know."
—Eleanor Roosevelt

Lucas slid his arm around her from behind and peeked over her shoulder at Savannah, who screamed with laughter at the face he made at her.

Dani worried all the time that Lucas was going to spoil her rotten, but she never doubted for a minute that he loved her daughter fiercely.

"Sorry about the crap show that is my family." They were trying to be more careful about their language in front of the baby.

"Please do not apologize. That was the best wedding ceremony I've ever attended. Tell me there're all this good."

"Most of them are pretty entertaining. At Will and Cameron's, Fred showed up to crash the reception. Marched right through the tent like he'd been sent an engraved invite. At Hunter and Megan's, Cameron fainted, and that's how we found out she was pregnant. Oh, and Max's baby mama showed up to tell him she was giving up custody. That wasn't funny."

They wandered into the tent and ended up at a table with his parents, sisters and their significant others. While Lucas went to pose for pictures with the wedding party, Dani tried to keep up with the rapid-fire conversation, the inside jokes and the general tomfoolery that went on in the Abbott family.

"We're a lot, aren't we?" Molly said quietly, speaking only to Dani.

"No, not at all."

Molly laughed. "Please, if there's one thing I know for sure, it's that my family is overwhelming, especially to new people."

"They're also entertaining, hilarious, kind and gorgeous. How did you manage to have ten stunningly beautiful children?"

"Aw, you're very sweet to say so." Molly leaned in closer. "Secretly, I agree with you, but a mother isn't supposed to say such things about her own children."

"Well, I'll say it for you. They're beautiful. Every one of them."

"One more than the others, perhaps?"

Dani smiled. "Perhaps."

"His father and I are delighted to see him so smitten with you and your little girl."

"We're rather delighted, too. He's just... He's the best. From the night we met, he's just been so *there* for me in every possible way."

"Sounds like him. He's true blue to the people he cares about."

"Yes, he is. He told me he has a reputation for being immature and silly."

"He does, but he's also known for being a highly trained and competent public safety officer who regularly saves lives. Sometimes I think the foolishness is his way—and Landon's way—of coping with the stuff they experience on the job."

"I hadn't thought of it that way, but you're probably right."

"They don't talk about the job very much, so we don't know what they see, but we know they respond to fatal accidents and fires, and that has to leave a mark."

"Of course it does, and using humor as a release makes sense."

"It doesn't hurt that they're two of the funniest people you'll ever meet."

"He does make me laugh pretty much all the time."

"That's our Lucas—and our Landon."

When Savannah started to fuss after losing interest in the toys Dani had given her, Molly held out her hands. "May I?"

"By all means. I feel like I'm turning her over to an expert."

Molly laughed. "I'm hardly an expert, but I do love babies. And by the way, she's absolutely beautiful."

"I think so, too," Dani replied in the same whisper Molly had used. "She's the image of her father, Jack."

"I'm sorry that you lost him far too soon."

"Thank you. So am I. He would've loved being a dad."

"That's a sadness you'll always feel. I lost my high school boyfriend to cancer my senior year, and I've never forgotten him or stopped being sad for all the things he missed."

"I'm sorry for your loss, too. I'm starting to realize the sadness will always be with me, but that it's still possible to feel joy and hope and happiness again."

"Yes, it is, but it's normal to feel a bit guilty for having those things when he can't."

"That's a big thing to hear from someone who's been through it."

Molly bounced Savannah on her lap, and the baby giggled in response. "Life is so short and so precious, Dani. Do what you need to do to be happy. Your Jack would want that for you."

"Yes, he would."

Savannah's giggles were infectious. "She's delightful," Molly declared. "Lucas tells me she was born the same day as our Caden."

"Yes, she was. Such a coincidence."

"I know! I love the first year of a baby's life. They go from being completely helpless to walking and babbling and eating solid food."

"It's amazing. Just this week, she's suddenly grabbing for everything in reach. Changing her diaper is like a full-on wrestling match."

Molly laughed. "Caden, too. He's a squiggly little worm all of a sudden. I tell Max to enjoy this stage, because he'll be on the move before too long."

"I'm not sure I'm ready for that."

"No one ever is, but it happens fast."

Colton came bursting into the tent with fists full of sparklers that he handed out to guests for when the sun went down.

"Dear God," Molly said. "Now they're going to play with fire."

Dani cracked up laughing at the long-suffering expression on Molly's face.

Lucas returned to the tent and came right over to Dani. "Want to dance?"

The intense way he looked at her sent a shiver down her spine. "Oh, I have Savannah…"

"She is just fine with Grandma Molly. Go ahead, you two."

Hearing Molly refer to herself as "grandma" to Savannah nearly reduced Dani to tears. How lucky her little girl would be to have such an extraordinary woman as an additional grandmother. "Thank you," Dani said to Molly, giving her a look that she hoped conveyed thanks for much more than watching Savannah while she danced with Lucas.

"My pleasure, honey."

Lucas took her hand and led her to the dance floor, where they joined his cousin Grayson and Emma, as well as Ella and Gavin, Will and Cameron and Megan and Hunter.

Colton's friend played "Thinking Out Loud" by Ed Sheeran, and as Dani clung to Lucas and breathed in the distinct aura of sawdust that had become one of her favorite scents, she realized it was the first time they'd ever danced together. She would always remember this special moment with him.

Looking down at her with love and desire and what could only be called happiness, Lucas kissed her right there in front of his entire family. "I couldn't wait for this part of the day."

"This is my favorite part so far. It's even better than Lucy taking Colton's hose."

Lucas snorted with laughter. "That was so awesome—and so *them*."

"I loved it."

"I love having you and Savannah here with my family and how you fit right in with us."

"Do I?"

"You have to ask? Everyone loves you, especially me."

She tightened her arms around him. "I love you, too."

That spring would go down as one of the best times of Dani's life. She watched the natural beauty of Vermont in bloom as her daughter grew and thrived along with her relationship with Lucas, which only got better with every passing day. They fell into a routine of spending every night at her place and spent every free hour they had together.

They worked side by side at the wood barn, where Dani was restoring a dresser she'd found at a yard sale. With the barn doors thrown open to let in the fresh air, Savannah could be there with them in her playpen without fear of her breathing in something dangerous. She was starting to pull herself up, and Molly predicted she'd walk before her first birthday.

On Sundays, they went to dinner at his parents' house, and Dani watched *The Bachelor* or *The Bachelorette* with his sisters on Monday nights while Lucas stayed home with Savannah.

She came home from one of those get-togethers to find Lucas asleep on the sofa with Savannah crashed on his chest.

Dani went to find her phone, which she mostly used as a camera these days, and took a picture of them before she nudged him awake to let him know she was home. "Let me take her."

She lifted Savannah off his chest and successfully transferred her to the crib, tucking her in under the blanket covered with ducks that she wanted to take everywhere with her. Molly had suggested buying a second one so they had a spare for when the first went missing or was in the wash. The idea was brilliant, and Dani had immediately ordered a second one.

Lucas was in the bathroom brushing his teeth when Dani joined him, nudging him out of the way so she could reach her toothbrush.

"Have a good time with the girls?" he asked around a mouthful of toothpaste.

"So much fun. I always laugh so hard with them."

"Any good gossip?"

"Ella was saying they've decided to wait to get married until after the baby comes. With the construction underway to add on to their house, she can't handle any more than what's already on her plate. She also mentioned that the anniversary of Caleb's death is always rough on Gavin, and this year is no different."

Lucas winced. "That poor guy has never gotten over losing his brother. They were best friends."

"It's so sad. Ella seemed a bit stressed about it."

"I'm sure he'll be okay, but it's always a rough couple of weeks for him. He told me once that just seeing the trees in bloom brings it all back."

"I understand that. Jack died on a rainy day, and the smell of rain does that for me."

Lucas turned to face her. "You never told me that."

She shrugged. "It's no big deal."

"It is if you need more on a rainy day than you do on the sunny ones. That's something I should know."

"I can't imagine you giving me more than you already do on any given day."

"There's always more, baby," he said, waggling his brows and flashing the grin that she loved so much.

She went up on tiptoes to kiss him. "Thank you."

"Please don't thank me. You and my sweet Savvy have changed my life in every possible way. There's nothing I wouldn't do for either of you."

"We feel the same way about you."

He surprised her when he lifted her off her feet and carried her to bed.

"Lucas! I didn't wash my face."

"Don't worry about it. It's only going to get dirty again."

The phone woke Lucas much later, dragging him from a sound sleep to reach for the bedside extension. As he took the call, he hoped Dani had told her mom he spent most nights there, just in case it was her.

"Wake up," Landon said, sounding as tense as Lucas had ever heard him. "Three-alarm fire at the inn. Hurry, Luc. It's bad. People still inside, including Amanda."

"Coming."

Lucas shot out of bed and pulled on the first clothes he could find—jeans and a long-sleeved T-shirt.

"What's wrong?" Dani asked, sitting up in bed.

"Fire at the inn."

"Oh no."

He took a second to kiss her. "Go back to sleep."

"Be careful. Please…"

"I'll be fine. Don't worry."

"Lucas!"

"What, honey?"

"I love you."

"I love you, too." He ran back to kiss her one more time before bolting for the door. Five minutes after Landon called, he was pulling up to the inn, which was fully engulfed in flames.

"Jesus," he whispered as he took in the biggest fire he'd seen in years.

Lucas quickly donned his personal protective equipment before joining the other firefighters at the command area they'd established in the middle of Elm Street, the main thoroughfare through Butler.

He recognized firefighters from nearby departments, as well as Richard Smith, the chief of the Butler department, who had taken charge.

"Mrs. Hendricks reported a full house tonight. We've evacuated the entire first floor, and we need more people to check the upper floors—and quickly. Abbott, Abbott, Jenkins, Dicey, Monroe and Grimes—get in there. Pair up and stay together." Another team was assigned to getting water on the fire.

Off to the side, the inn's hysterical owner was being comforted by paramedics, who'd wrapped her in a blanket.

"What about the nearby structures?" Lucas eyed the store and the spray of embers raining down from the inn.

"We're on it, Lieutenant." The chief made eye contact, probably hoping to reassure Lucas that they'd do what they could to save his family's business.

"Let's go," one of the other firefighters shouted as they quickly grabbed self-contained breathing apparatuses and strapped them on.

They headed for the inn's back door, where the flames were less intense. Whatever had sparked the blaze had originated at the front part of the building. Lucas had inspected the inn's fireplaces himself over the summer and found them all to be in good condition. He hoped to God he hadn't missed something.

As they ran toward the rear of the inn, Lucas saw his brother glancing nervously at the store and knew he was thinking the same thing as Lucas. Had anyone thought to notify their dad about the fire?

His stomach hurt at the thought of the store being consumed by fire. They couldn't let that happen, but more important, there might be people still inside the inn, and getting them out had to be their top priority.

It was often said of first responders that they ran in as everyone else ran out, and Lucas thought of that every time he went into a building on fire. The rush of adrenaline and the need to save people drove him and the others who dedicated their lives to the fire service. And yes, you needed to be a tiny bit crazy in the first place to get a charge out of running into a burning building.

Knowing there were innocent people in need of rescue only amped up the stakes.

"Up here!"

He and Landon raced up the back stairs and started working the second floor, going door to door to check each room. The closer they got to the front of the building, the hotter the fire burned. Inside the last door on the right, Lucas found a family of three huddled in the corner. He could barely make them out in the darkness and smoke, but they were backlit by one of the security lights outside.

"Landon!"

His brother followed him into the room.

"We need to get you out of here!"

"My wife is having a panic attack. I can't get her to move." The man's eyes were wild as he held his wife and daughter.

Landon crouched in front of the woman. "Let us get you out. You don't want your daughter to die in here. You're a good mom. You want to save her."

The woman, whose face was streaked with tears, nodded.

Landon scooped her up.

"Follow him," Lucas told the man, who carried his daughter. "Stay low and hurry. Run as fast as you can."

As Landon ran toward the back exit, Lucas kicked in the last door on the left side of the hallway, and a fireball knocked him off his feet and slammed him against the far wall. A cry from inside the room had him collecting himself and crawling toward the woman lying on the floor.

"Can you move?" he asked her, doing a double take when he realized it was Amanda.

"I hurt my ankle."

"Crawl with me. I'll lead the way out of here."

"Lucas, I'm scared."

"I've got you. Come on."

As he waited for her to catch up, he glanced up in time to see the entire ceiling and everything above it coming down on them. He didn't have time to scream as he lunged toward her, hoping to protect her from the worst of the blow. In the second before hell rained down on him, his only thoughts were for Dani and Savvy.

CHAPTER 25

"Love recognizes no barriers. It jumps hurdles, leaps fences,
penetrates walls to arrive at its destination full of hope."
—Maya Angelou

Dani couldn't go back to sleep after Lucas left. In the distance, the sound of sirens had her nerves on full alert to the disaster unfolding across town.

She said a prayer for the people in the inn and the firefighters working to rescue them.

After a while, she got up to make herself a cup of tea, hoping it would calm her enough to get some rest. She'd be a wreck at work tomorrow if she didn't sleep.

While she waited for the water to boil, she went to the windows that faced town and could see the flames and smoke in the distance, which did nothing to help settle her nerves.

Taking her tea to the sofa, she sat with her legs curled up under her and tried not to dwell on how much this night reminded her of the day Jack died. Like now, she'd had a bad feeling about him doing something he did all the time—going out on the trails with his buddies. The whole time he'd been gone, she'd had a sense of foreboding, and when his brother had come to find her, his eyes ravaged and his face covered in tears, Dani had known right away that the worst had happened.

Her screams had brought the neighbors running to see what was wrong.

Allowing her mind to travel back to the worst day of her life, she relived it all, from the minute she'd opened the door to find Braydon on her doorstep, to demanding to see Jack, to being taken to the coroner's office. It'd been a mistake to see him, she now knew, because she would've been better off to remember him only as he'd been in life.

Sitting on the sofa, her tea gone cold, she fell into a rabbit hole of memories—the wake and funeral, the beautiful words his heartbroken friends had shared, the people, the food, the despair and the pervasive fear that she would lose the baby they'd only recently found out they were having.

They hadn't even told their parents about the baby yet.

And then he was just gone.

Forever.

Dani reached for the phone she'd left on the coffee table and opened her photos to scroll back to last year, to the photos she hadn't looked at in weeks now, the last photos there would ever be of him.

His dark blond hair was always standing on end, despite her constant attempts to tame it. He'd had the bluest eyes of anyone she'd ever known, except his daughter, and a dimple in his chin that she'd loved to kiss.

She recalled what Molly had said at the wedding about losing her first love and how you never get over it or stop being sad for all the things they would miss. Dani would never get over losing Jack, and she would make sure his daughter knew him and knew how much he'd loved her.

He'd sung to her belly, talked to the baby, made promises he hadn't gotten to keep. Dani would keep them for him.

She yawned, returned the phone to the coffee table and was on her way back to bed when someone knocked on her door.

Her stomach fell, and she froze, staring at the door, unable to move.

Another knock. "Dani." *Hannah.*

No, please. Not again.

More knocking. "Dani, open up."

"We should've called." Another voice, maybe Ella?

"No, we shouldn't have." More knocking. "Dani, please."

Dani moved to the door, pulling it open to Lucas's sisters, who were there in the middle of the night for only one reason. Something was terribly wrong.

"Is he dead?"

Hannah shook her head. "No, but he's hurt. I'll stay with Savannah. Ella will take you to him."

"I... I don't think... I mean... I can't."

"Yes, you can," Hannah said firmly. "He needs you, Dani. He was there when you needed him, and now he needs you."

Hannah's words snapped her out of the fear and into action. "Let me put some clothes on and check on Savannah."

She ran into her room, grabbed the first clothes she could find and jammed her feet into running shoes. After checking to make sure the baby was still sleeping soundly, she pulled on her coat. "She'll be hungry when she wakes up. There're bottles in the fridge and cereal in the cabinet."

"Go," Hannah said. "We'll be fine."

Dani followed Ella down the stairs and into the car that had been left running outside.

"Tell me the truth," Dani said when they were on their way to the same hospital they'd taken Savannah to for her ear infection. "Is he going to die?"

"I don't know that. My mother called to tell us he'd been hurt and that someone needed to tell you and get you to him."

I can't do this again. I can't. Her chest started to tighten with the telltale signs of panic. She heard Lucas's voice telling her to breathe.

Just breathe.

So she did, forcing air past the panic that wanted to consume her.

Breathe, Dani.

If she closed her eyes, she could picture him with her, as he'd been a few short hours ago, brushing his teeth, picking her up and taking her to bed, where he'd made love to her and then held her while she slept. That couldn't be the end for him or for them. They were just getting started.

Tears rolled down her cheeks as she asked Jack and her late grandmother to watch out for Lucas, to keep him safe.

The entire Abbott family had descended upon the emergency department waiting room. Molly came over to Dani and hugged her.

Dani clung to the woman who'd been so kind and welcoming to her. "Is he… Have you heard…"

"We're waiting to hear more."

"What happened?" Dani asked, pulling back from Molly.

"The ceiling and third floor came down on him," Colton said, his expression grim. "He was trying to get Amanda out of her room and managed to get her under him. He took the full brunt."

Dani's knees turned to water, and the only reason she didn't drop to the floor was because Will reached for her and stopped her fall.

"Easy," he said.

Dani broke down into helpless sobs. The thought of Lucas being badly hurt, or worse, was unbearable.

Landon came rushing through the main doors, his face black, his hair standing on end and his eyes wild. The pervasive stench of smoke came with him. "Is he…"

"We don't know yet, son," Lincoln said as he embraced Landon.

"It was bad," he said softly. "I was sure they both were dead."

"Well, they're not," Molly said with a meaningful glance at Dani. "And we're not going there."

Landon fixed his gaze on Dani before coming to hug her. "I'm sorry. I didn't mean to make it worse."

"It's okay." With Landon's arms around her, Dani wondered how she'd ever thought she might've mistaken him for Lucas. No one could be mistaken for Lucas, not even his identical twin.

"He saved Amanda's life," Landon said, sounding as tearful as Dani felt.

"Yes, he did," Lincoln Abbott said, squeezing Landon's shoulder, "and thank goodness for that."

Hearing he'd saved the life of the woman he'd once wanted only made Dani feel proud of him, having no doubt he'd given Amanda his very best in her time of need. That's who he was.

They waited a long time. She had no idea how long before a doctor came out to talk to them. "Lucas Abbott's family?"

A crowd turned to him.

"Whoa, okay, then. He's stable, and other than a fractured left arm that will require surgery to repair, we're not finding any other serious injuries. He got *really* lucky."

Relief made her lightheaded. Thankfully, Landon kept an arm around her, offering steady, unwavering support that she greatly appreciated.

"He's asking for Dani. Is she here?"

"She's here," Molly said.

"Two at a time, please," the doctor said.

Molly offered her hand to Dani. "Come on, honey. Let's go see him."

Dani didn't want to see him hurt or in pain, but she couldn't bear to stay away either. She took Molly's outstretched hand, and they followed the doctor to the room where Lucas was being tended to by two nurses and another doctor. The first thing she noticed was the same overpowering smell of smoke that had clung to Landon. And like Landon, Lucas's face was filthy. His broken left arm was braced and propped on a pillow.

He raised his uninjured arm to Dani. "Come here," he said, his voice gruff.

She went to him and took his hand, drinking in every detail of his precious face.

"Are you breathing?" he asked.

"Just barely."

"It's safe to breathe. I'm fine."

"You're not fine."

"I *am* fine, and so are you. Let me see you breathe."

Holding his gaze, she took a deep breath and then another. He squeezed her hand. "Sorry to do this to you."

She laughed as euphoria replaced gritty fear, her emotions all over the place. "Don't apologize to me. You saved Amanda's life."

"Maybe so, but all I could think about was you and Savvy."
Tears flooded her eyes.

"Keep breathing."

"Is there something I could use to clean his face?" Dani asked the nurse.

"Of course. Let me get you some wipes."

Lucas turned to his mom, who was on the other side of his bed. "You okay, Mom?"

"I am now." She leaned over to kiss his filthy forehead.

The nurse returned with a pack of wipes that she handed to Dani.

Lucas watched her intently as she wiped the soot and grime from his face.

"There you are," she said when his handsome face had been revealed.

"Much better," Molly said. "I'll go out so the others can come in."

"I will, too," Dani said.

"No." Lucas grasped her hand. "You stay."

"Your family wants to see you, and they only want two of us in here."

"Stay," he said emphatically.

So she stayed while first his father and then Landon came in.

"Jeez, bro," Landon said, visibly emotional to see Lucas awake and alert, "way to take ten years off my life."

"Sorry about that."

"If you wanted to break your arm on the job the way I did, I could've done it for you."

Smiling, Lucas said, "Is Amanda okay?"

Landon nodded. "She's banged up but fine, thanks to you. We got everyone out, thank God."

"And the inn?"

"Almost a total loss, but we got the fire under control, and it was contained to the inn."

"Well, that's a huge relief."

"No shit, right? Before you nearly got yourself killed, all I could think about was the store."

"I know. Me, too."

"Mrs. Hendricks is vowing to rebuild."

"She'd be crazy not to with it being the only inn in town."

"People have taken in all the inn's guests and made them comfortable."

"Any idea what caused the fire?"

"The state fire marshal is on the way, but we think it might've been electrical."

"That's good news. I was hoping it wasn't one of the fireplaces I inspected."

"Nah," Landon said, laughing, "you're all good. And thank goodness for that." He teared up and dropped his head to his brother's chest. "Don't do that to me again, you hear me?"

Lucas wrapped his good arm around his twin. "I hear you."

Watching them and witnessing the bond between them, Dani wiped away more tears. When she thought of how close they'd come to catastrophe, her knees did that liquid thing and her entire body ached the way it had after she lost Jack.

She never wanted to feel that way again. How would she stand watching Lucas run out to fires and other disasters that others were running away from, knowing he could be hurt or worse at any time?

The panic began as it always did, with the elephant squeezing the air from her chest and spots dancing before her eyes.

"Dani!" Lucas's shout cut through the chaos in her brain. "Breathe."

"What's wrong?" Landon asked.

"Panic attack," Lucas said.

"Oh damn."

"Look at me," Lucas said in a tone that others would find harsh, but it was everything she needed. "Breathe, Dani."

She looked into the golden-brown eyes that had held her in their thrall from the very beginning and drew strength from his unwavering devotion to her and her daughter.

"Breathe, damn it!"

"Do I need to get someone?" Landon asked, sounding stressed.

"Breathe, Dani. Please breathe."

His plea cut through the noise and grounded her in the moment. He was here. He was fine. He was going to *be* fine. And as long as he was fine, so was she.

Oxygen flooded her system in one big whoosh of relief.

"That's it, baby. Keep breathing. Just keep breathing." As he spoke, he guided her onto the bed with him, holding her tight against him with his good arm as he whispered words of reassurance and brushed kisses over her hair. "I've got you, and I'm never letting you go."

"Sorry," she said when she could speak again. "Didn't mean to make it about me."

"Of course it's about you. It's about both of us, and I knew this would hit you so hard after everything you've been through. I don't want you to worry about something happening to me."

"Too late," she said with a tearful laugh.

"Most of the time, being a member of Butler's fire service is very rewarding but also extremely unexciting. When I promise you that you don't need to worry about me, I mean it. The chances of something like this ever happening again are slim to none."

With every reassuring word he said, he brought her further back from the edge she'd been hovering on, making her believe that it was okay to have faith that this time, she'd actually get her happily ever after.

She realized Landon had left the room, and no one from the family had taken his place.

"Better?" he asked after a long silence.

She nodded.

"I'm sorry to have frightened you so badly."

"It's not your fault. I'm proud of you for rescuing Amanda. Everyone said she probably would've been killed without you there to protect her."

"I just did my job."

"You did much more than that."

"Where's my little girl?"

"At home with Hannah."

"Good," he said, his eyes closing. "Everything is all right, Dani. I love you and I love her, and we're going to have a long and happy life together."

"I hope so."

"I know so. Now tell me how you really feel about six—or seven—kids."

"Um, well, I'm a little concerned about the twelve-pound-baby situation."

"I was only six pounds."

"Because you were a twin!"

Lucas laughed. "It'll be fine. I promise. You know I'll be there for you and Savvy and the baseball team we'll have together no matter what happens."

As far as assurances went, Dani decided, they didn't get much better than that.

Epilogue

Elmer got to the diner before Linc and ordered coffee from Megan, his granddaughter-in-law. He absolutely loved the girl who'd made his Hunter so happy. And now the two of them were expecting his great-grandchild, and Megan fairly glowed as she went from table to table, talking and laughing with customers and refilling coffee cups.

Gone was the angry, bitter young woman she'd once been after losing her parents and nursing an unrequited crush on his grandson Will. She'd set her sights on the wrong Abbott brother, and once she tuned in to Hunter's affection for her, things had worked out just the way they were meant to.

With her other customers settled, Megan slid into the booth across from Elmer. "Phew. Feels good to get off my feet. My ankles are huge."

Elmer's brows furrowed with concern. "You just say the word, and you're on leave. We'll get someone to cover for you." Technically, he owned the place, but he was smart enough to leave the running of it in her capable hands.

"Not yet. I'd go mad sitting around at home for months with nothing to do."

"You tell me when, and don't you dare wait until the day before that baby shows up. Your life won't be your own for the next thirty years. Take some time off before he or she arrives and enjoy the peace and quiet before it's gone forever."

"Thirty years? I signed on for eighteen."

Elmer released a deep guffaw. "Rookie. You'll find out soon enough that parenthood is a forever proposition." He leaned in. "Enjoy the first eighteen years. That's when they *have* to mind you. After that, it's like the Wild West of them telling you they can do what they want because they're 'adults' now. My Sarah and I used to refer to our girls as 'a-dolts' during the young adult years."

Megan grimaced as she laughed. "Good to know."

"Don't worry. I'll be around to guide you through it."

They shared a warm smile. "I'm counting on that."

Lincoln arrived, and Megan stood to let her father-in-law sit.

"Morning," Linc said, sliding in to make room for Megan.

"Morning." Megan poured coffee into the mug she'd put on the table for him.

"Thank you, honey. How're you feeling?"

"We were just talking about that," Elmer said with a stern look for Megan. "Her ankles are swollen, and she's going to take some time off before the baby arrives."

"He's the boss of me," Megan said, grinning.

Elmer laughed. "That's right, and don't you forget it." He loved her like one of his own and enjoyed the friendly sparring they engaged in every day.

"You'd never let me forget it." Megan hauled herself up. "Back to the salt mines. My grandfather-in-law is a ruthless taskmaster."

Elmer grinned widely, pleased with the title she'd given him. "Take it easy. That's an order."

She saluted him and went to switch out the coffeepot for a fresh one.

"We need to keep an eye on her," Elmer said to Linc when Megan was out of earshot.

"I believe," Linc said, "her husband is keeping a close eye on her." He nodded to Hunter, who came through the door to the diner and went straight to his wife behind the counter, rubbing her back and studying her intently.

"Does my heart good to see those two together with a little one on the way."

"Mine, too. We did good work there."

"*I* did good work there."

Linc rolled his eyes at the predictable reply. "Whatever you say. I suppose you're going to find a way to take credit for Lucas and Dani, too."

"Well, I did give him some rather necessary advice when he was on the verge of messing things up with her."

"So did I!"

"I bet mine was better," Elmer said gleefully. Needling his son-in-law was one of his favorite pastimes. He loved the heck out of Linc, despite the fact that he'd had *ten* children with Elmer's precious daughter Molly. The two of them were the happiest couple in town, despite their ten children. And because Linc knew Elmer loved him like a son, he got away with pushing Linc's buttons.

"Whatever. We need to call this one a draw and move on to our next victims."

"And who will that be?" Elmer asked, stirring cream into his coffee.

"Landon and Amanda. The poor girl is a wreck since the fire, and he's been running himself ragged taking care of her at his place."

"Is that right? I wondered where she was staying since the inn burned."

"Yep, he took her home with him that night, and they've been together ever since. But word is she's not coping well with her near-death experience. We've had to postpone the staff training on the new intimate line again, until she's back on her feet. We already postponed the rollout once to coincide with the catalog, but now we're waiting on her to feel better to proceed."

"I can't even imagine what a shit show that training will be."

"Speaking of shit shows, we've also got the photo shoot coming up for the catalog."

"Not to mention the society wedding for Wade and Mia in Boston and Will and Cameron's baby due soon."

"It's going to be a busy spring and summer in Butler," Linc said. "And I have the perfect plan in mind to help Landon move things along with Amanda."

"And what's that?"

Lincoln released a huff of indignation. "You think I'm telling you my strategy? Think again."

Elmer eyed his son-in-law with newfound respect and a healthy dose of amusement. As their "game" had progressed, Linc had become a worthy adversary—not that there were any true adversaries when the end result was his beloved grandchildren finding their true loves.

"Game on, my friend," Elmer said, relishing the challenge of another couple to "encourage" along the road to true love. "Game on."

***

Thank you for reading Lucas and Dani's story. I so enjoyed spending this time with them and watching Lucas become a full-grown adult man with a woman and child to call his own. I'm sorry it took me eighteen months to get this next book the Vermont series to you. As many of you already know, I lost my dad unexpectedly last summer and that threw my entire life and my writing schedule into an uproar I'm still recovering from nearly a year later. I was supposed to have been writing this book last summer, and it got pushed back due to contractual obligations.

I promise you won't have to wait that long for the next one, which will feature Landon Abbott. After that, we will see what's up with Max Abbott. I know many of you want to see some of the Coleman cousins get their turn, too, and we'll see what happens. I'll keep you posted about series news in the Green Mountain Reader Group at facebook.com/groups/GreenMountainSeries. Make sure you join the Till There Was You Reader Group at facebook.com/groups/TillThereWasYou4/ to chat about Lucas and Dani's story with spoilers allowed and encouraged.

If you're not on my newsletter mailing list, make sure you join at marieforce.com to be notified when new books are available and to receive news of sales and events in your area.

A lot of people make it possible for me to write books all day, including my husband, Dan, and the HTJB team: Julie Cupp, Lisa Cafferty, Holly Sullivan, Isabel Sullivan and Nikki Colquhoun. Thanks go to my awesome editors, Linda Ingmanson and Joyce Lamb, as well as my stellar publicist Jessica Estep and my primo beta readers Anne Woodall and Kara Conrad. Thank you to my new Green Mountain beta team, including Isabel, Katy, Jennifer, Alice, Nancy, Betty, Marchia, Jessica and Deb. Thank you to my friend Paul Ripa for helping me with some of the firefighter details in this book.

Thank you most of all to the readers who wait patiently (and sometimes impatiently) for each new book. I appreciate you all more than you'll ever know!

Much love,
Marie

OTHER TITLES BY MARIE FORCE

Book 4: Falling for Love *(Grant & Stephanie)*
Book 5: Hoping for Love *(Evan & Grace)*
Book 6: Season for Love *(Owen & Laura)*
Book 7: Longing for Love *(Blaine & Tiffany)*
Book 8: Waiting for Love *(Adam & Abby)*
Book 9: Time for Love *(David & Daisy)*
Book 10: Meant for Love *(Jenny & Alex)*
Book 10.5: Chance for Love, *A Gansett Island Novella (Jared & Lizzie)*
Book 11: Gansett After Dark *(Owen & Laura)*
Book 12: Kisses After Dark *(Shane & Katie)*
Book 13: Love After Dark *(Paul & Hope)*
Book 14: Celebration After Dark *(Big Mac & Linda)*
Book 15: Desire After Dark *(Slim & Erin)*
Book 16: Light After Dark *(Mallory & Quinn)*
Book 17: Victoria & Shannon (Episode 1)
Book 18: Kevin & Chelsea (Episode 2)
A Gansett Island Christmas Novella
Book 19: Mine After Dark *(Riley & Nikki)*
Book 20: Yours After Dark *(Finn & Chloe)*
Book 21: Trouble After Dark *(Deacon & Julia)*

The Treading Water Series
Book 1: Treading Water *(Jack & Andi)*
Book 2: Marking Time *(Clare & Aidan)*
Book 3: Starting Over *(Brandon & Daphne)*
Book 4: Coming Home *(Reid & Kate)*

Single Titles
Five Years Gone
One Year Home

Sex Machine

Sex God

Georgia on My Mind

True North

The Fall

Everyone Loves a Hero

Love at First Flight

Line of Scrimmage

Historical Romances
The Gilded Series
Book 1: Duchess by Deception
Book 2: Deceived by Desire

Erotic Romance
The Erotic Quantum Series
Book 1: Virtuous *(Flynn & Natalie)*
Book 2: Valorous *(Flynn & Natalie)*
Book 3: Victorious *(Flynn & Natalie)*
Book 4: Rapturous *(Addie & Hayden)*
Book 5: Ravenous *(Jasper & Ellie)*
Book 6: Delirious *(Kristian & Aileen)*
Book 7: Outrageous *(Emmett & Leah)*
Book 8: Famous *(Marlowe)*

Romantic Suspense
The Fatal Series
One Night With You, *A Fatal Series Prequel Novella*
Book 1: Fatal Affair
Book 2: Fatal Justice
Book 3: Fatal Consequences

About the Author

Marie Force is the *New York Times* bestselling author of contemporary romance, including the indie-published Gansett Island Series and the Fatal Series from Harlequin Books. In addition, she is the author of the Butler, Vermont Series, the Green Mountain Series and the erotic romance Quantum Series. *Duchess By Deception* is the first in her new historical romance Gilded Series, that will continue with *Deceived By Desire* in September 2019.

Her books have sold 7.5 million copies worldwide, have been translated into more than a dozen languages and have appeared on the *New York Times* bestseller list many times. She is also a *USA Today* and *Wall Street Journal* bestseller, a Speigel bestseller in Germany, a frequent speaker and publishing workshop presenter as well as a publisher through her Jack's House Publishing romance imprint. She is a three-time nominee for the Romance Writers of America's RITA® award for romance fiction.

Her goals in life are simple—to finish raising two happy, healthy, productive young adults, to keep writing books for as long as she possibly can and to never be on a flight that makes the news.

Join Marie's mailing list for news about new books and upcoming appearances in your area. Follow her on Facebook at *https://www.facebook.com/MarieForceAuthor*, Twitter *@marieforce* and on Instagram at *https://instagram.com/marieforceauthor/*. Join one of Marie's many reader groups. Contact Marie at *marie@marieforce.com*.